WHILE MY GUITAR GENTLY WEEPS

WHILE MY GUITAR GENTLY WEEPS

DEBORAH GRABIEN

MINOTAUR BOOKS

A THOMAS DUNNE BOOK
NEW YORK

A THOMAS DUNNE BOOK FOR MINOTAUR BOOKS.
An imprint of St. Martin's Publishing Group.

WHILE MY GUITAR GENTLY WEEPS. Copyright © 2009 by Deborah Grabien. All rights reserved. Printed in the United States of America. For information, address St. Martin's Press, 175 Fifth Avenue, New York, N.Y. 10010.

"I Knew the Bride (When She Used to Rock 'n' Roll)," © Nick Lowe, 1977, Anglo-Rock, Inc. Used by permission.
"Tore Up Over You," © Hank Ballard, 1956, Fort Knox Music, Inc. and Trio Music Company. Used by permission.
"That's What Love Will Make You Do," © Milton Campbell, 2002, Trice Publishing Company (BMI) / administered by Bug Music. Used by permission.

www.thomasdunnebooks.com
www.minotaurbooks.com

Library of Congress Cataloging-in-Publication Data

Grabien, Deborah.
    While my guitar gently weeps : a JP Kinkaid mystery / Deborah Grabien.—1st ed.
        p. cm.
    ISBN 978-0-312-59096-3
    1. Rock musicians—Fiction   2. San Francisco Bay Area (Calif.)—Fiction.   3. Musical fiction.   I. Title.
    PS3557.R1145W46 2009
    813'.54—dc22

                                                        2009012725

First Edition: September 2009

10 9 8 7 6 5 4 3 2 1

This one's for all the sidemen

ACKNOWLEDGMENTS

Where to begin?

Matt Hayden and my astonishing husband, Nicholas, of course, for all the tech stuff about guitar-making and studio equipage that I either forgot about years ago or never knew in the first place.

Ita, for giving me input on how her fictional avatar would handle bodyguarding an oversexed superstar with a social conscience, and what she'd wear while doing it.

Marlene, for the feedback, and because she rocks.

Kate McKean, amazing agent lady.

Bill Nighy, for so brilliantly providing the inspiration for the character of Mac Sharpe.

And then there are all the WIP readers, following John and Bree down the long and winding road that lets us dance through rock and roll.

WHILE MY GUITAR GENTLY WEEPS

PROLOGUE

"On three. JP leads it in. One—two—"

A downbeat, a movement of my right hand, and there it was: a full, rich major seventh. Major sevenths are too cool—lush and evocative, all kinds of stuff left dangling behind it, a promise of something sultry and maybe a bit regretful to come. It's the kind of jazz chord that's best played on a semi-hollow-body guitar—playing one of those, you need to be in a very different head space, or maybe a different soul space, than when you're thrashing away at a Paul or a Strat.

The drums kicked in next, Billy DuMont timing it with the kind of easy touch a drummer gets only from knowing he or she can trust the rest of the band. Billy's one of those rarities, a drummer reliable enough so that any bassist would feel safe turning their back on him. Billy has a nicely pared-down rig for rehearsals: bass drum with pedal, snare, cymbals, a high hat setup. He hit it, caught my eye, grinned at me.

Tony and Kris came in together on the second downbeat. Tony had his favourite pair of portable electronic keyboards side by side, his Kurzweil and his Roland; he'd already added some nice fills to the lead-in. Not surprising, really, how easy with it he was—after all, he'd written this particular song.

And Kris, rock solid, ran his hand up the neck of his funky old P Bass and down again, echoing Tony's new stuff perfectly. They'd probably been working on this one over the weekend—they were completely synched up.

Harmony, synchronicity, waiting for the lyric to—

"Shit!"

The music spiralled, faltered, stopped. Everyone turned to stare. I didn't; I didn't have to.

Of course, the problem was Vinny Fabiano. These days, it always seemed to be Vinny Fabiano. Truth was, he seemed to be more problem than anything else, including musician: a problem with pricey toys and a bad hairpiece and a huge sodding ego. I'm not a member of the Bombardiers—I was just sitting in, as a favour to Tony and Kris—but it seemed to me that things hadn't been right from the moment Vinny'd come on board as the Bombardiers' front man, after Anton Hall had finally drunk himself into a premature grave six months ago.

"I can't get the sound I need from this pile of crap!"

Actually, I thought, Vinny himself was a pile of crap; the stuff in question was really quite nice. I'd had a moment of lusting after the guitar he was currently blaming for his own shortcomings, a Paul Reed Smith Private Stock custom, complete with waterfall inlays. It was absolutely gorgeous, but I own a pair of PRS axes—sent to me in hopes of an endorsement deal—and I always have to remind myself that, as lovely as they are, my hands and the PRS necks don't really mesh well. Still, the idea of any player blaming his instrument for not sounding right was infuriating, especially an instrument as nice as this one.

Tony opened his mouth and shut it again. He caught my eye and rolled his own slightly. The look said, nice and clear, what he wasn't saying out loud: *Here we go again.* The three roadies carefully didn't look at us, or even at each other. It doesn't take much to fuck up the balance or the vibe at a rehearsal, you know? Vinny was proving to be far too good at doing just that.

"What's up?" Damon Gelb had been sitting at the board, adjusting levels, checking the MIDI setup. "Talk to me, Vinny."

"It's this fucking amp!" He looked, for one moment, as if he was seriously considering putting the toe of his flashy cowboy boot through the amp in question. If he had, I might have committed mayhem; the amp was a superb 200-watt Dumble, with a Matchless double stack behind it. It wasn't the amp's fault Vinny hadn't bothered to get familiar with how it worked with the PRS, or with his four separate pedal effects. If Tony was right, Vinny had a habit of doing this: He'd get hot for whatever he thought the trendy bit of gear was at the moment, get his hands on it, and then never actually bother taking the time to learn how to use it properly once he had it.

"Sounds fine over here." Damon was being patient. He pretty much had to be. A sound engineer who gets shirty with the band, no matter how hard the band may have it coming, doesn't last long. "What do you think it's missing?"

"I want some fucking *grit* in there." Vinny's speaking voice was completely different from his singing voice; it was nasal, really irritating. "What's wrong with this piece of shit? Where the hell is Rosario?"

"Right here, man." The tech in question—weird name for a bloke, I thought, but maybe it was a New York thing—hurried over. I wish I could say Rosario wasn't brownnosing Vinny, but the truth is, he never stopped. One of these days I would have to have Kris and Tony over for dinner, get my old lady the chef to lace their food with truth drugs or something, and find out what had been going on in their heads when they asked this loud, swaggering idiot to take over for Anton. I mean, yeah, the bloke could sing. He could even play. But worth the grief? Hell no.

While Rosario fiddled with the setup, I closed my eyes and waited. I had to keep reminding myself that this was my problem for only three songs, because this wasn't my band. The thick-necked little ball of aggro currently whistling through his nose and bullying his guitar tech was not anyone I had to work with on a regular basis, and thank Christ for that. If it had been for anyone other than Tony or Kris, I wouldn't have been here for dust. It was one of the few things I'd disliked about being a sessions bloke, back before I became a full-time member of Blacklight: having to cope with pissy little egos like Vinny's.

My hands and feet had both begun tingling a bit, letting me know that the stress, and maybe sitting with my legs in one position too long, was stirring up my multiple sclerosis. I crossed and uncrossed the legs; Tony gave me a worried look, but I shook my head at him. Fuck it, I could deal. I just felt really damned sorry for the rest of the band, you know?

Finally, they got something Vinny seemed to think he could live with. I couldn't actually hear any difference, and unlike Vinny, I *do* know how the stack works. Behind me, my own 50-watt Marshall half stack was on standby, doing its usual reliable thing. The Bombardiers' roadies, Doug and Mickey, had been helpful, handling all the heavy lifting for me. I used to make it a point of pride to move my own gear, but these days, I wasn't shy about asking for backup, even with Bree helping me. This particular illness has a way of kicking macho to the curb.

We got back to the song eventually, and Vinny was happy

enough with his gear to do it right the first time. I wasn't a fan of his singing voice. Where Anton had been distinctive and clean, Vinny went for the sob-in-the-voice thing, as if he thought he was in some nightclub in an Italian '60s flick, singing "Santa Lucia" or some stupid bit of fake sentiment to Sophia Loren, or some rubbish. All he needed was Michelangelo Antonioni filming him. But he did get quite a lot of feeling out of it, at least when he managed to keep the nasal twang under control.

We got one more of the three songs done before seven o'clock. I'd stopped to take afternoon meds, stretch my legs, insisting that we take the break the rest of the band had forgotten about. It was odd, but Vinny never seemed to give me any grief about anything. I couldn't imagine why he left me alone. I'm not physically imposing, not at all. But he never seemed to want to get into my face.

At seven, the buzzer outside the corrugated loading dock rang, and I got up. Bree would be outside, behind the wheel of the Jag. She was never late.

"Right," I told them. "Here's my ride. That's me out. See you all Saturday, yeah? We can pick it up then."

CHAPTER ONE

No one has any business being chirpy at eight o'clock in the morning. It's a pity no one's ever bothered to tell that to the MRI tech at the San Francisco Magnetic Resonance Imaging Center.

"Morning, Mr. Kinkaid." He said the same thing every time, in the same infuriating happy tone of voice. After eight years, I could have set my watch by it. "Long time, no see."

"Right." *Not long enough, mate.*

Bree'd caught my irritation—I saw her head turn. I kept my voice nice and even; no reason to upset her, yeah? The fact that I was nervous, edgy, that I hated this particular bit of nonsense with a stone passion—she couldn't help me with that. It was out of her control—hell, it was out of my control. The best I could do was to keep it low profile, not make a huge deal about it, grit my teeth and get through it. "So, let's get on with it. Which locker this time?"

They don't let Bree come back with me for the procedure itself, which is just as well. She's as tough as they're made, but she doesn't like needles and she's mildly claustrophobic. She also doesn't deal well with the idea of anything being less than perfect for me, so between the dye injections and watching me disappear headfirst into the bowels of the MRI machine, she'd have completely flipped her shit.

I kissed her, made a face at her to cheer her up, and left her in the waiting room with a cup of coffee she'd empty and refill three times during the next hour and a magazine she wouldn't even pretend to read. Once I'd turned my back to follow Ramon into the back room, I let the mask slip.

I really don't want to slag off on the MRI people. They're competent and pleasant, and good at what they do. It's not their fault that I hate everything they do to me once a year.

That begins with the damned dye they shoot me up with. It's weird, you know? I mean, I used to be a junkie. Okay, right, so I mostly snorted and it wasn't for all that long, but the few times I shot, I had no needle issues. I think it's the idea that they're shooting me up with colour that gets to me. You can't even get high behind it.

Then there's the noise. When you've got what I've got, the MRI is all neck and up; they don't give a shit about what's happening on your kneecaps. They're looking for little white spots on your various bits of brain, a telltale spread of the disease, lesions that tell them whether there's a whole new section of your body that's going to be losing the myelin, the covering on your nerves, the things that keep you functioning.

So your head is stuck inside this tiny coffin thing, you aren't allowed to move for the better part of an hour, if you open your eyes during the process, all you can see is the inside of the machine about an inch from your face, and you've been shot up with something that has its own number on the periodic table.

And then, right around the time you've seriously started wondering if you're trapped in here forever and everyone's gone off and left you alone while they watch a soccer match or go to a baseball game, the machine starts *booming* at you. Every boom is another bit of your brain that's being looked at—they bounce pulses or something off it, to give them a picture. And in between taking these images of various sections of your brain, the tech makes comments at you through a loudspeaker in the machine itself.

The perky male tech I always seem to get saddled with is a bloke called Ramon. Eight in the morning, and the little git's making conversation, actually wanting answers to things, and then, of course, not giving me time to answer him.

"So, how was your tour? Lie down, please." I opened my mouth and he added, all bubble and chirp, "Now, remember— no moving, no talking. Any movement will cause the test to—"

"Bloody hell, Ramon, I've been coming here as long as you've been out of grade school, all right? I know the drill. Let's just get on with it, yeah? And why the hell do you ask me questions if all you're going to do in the next breath is tell me not to talk or move?"

He looked hurt, for about a nanosecond. Of course, it didn't last; it never does. He tucked a sheet up around me, arms flat at my sides, making sure I was warm enough and, of course, completed my bizarre sense that I was playing the corpse in a movie. Then the table I'd been arranged on began the long, smooth slide into the MRI machine itself, and I took a deep breath, trying to prep my head, get into the mental state I need to be in to cope.

Bang, booma-booma-booma, bang.

Every section of brain gets a series of these odd pulses from the MRI, and they're all different. My initial method of dealing with them—trying to write music to the rhythmic patterns— was unrestful enough to make me completely fuck up their tests. One memorable MRI, I found myself muttering out loud, *Bloody hell, mate, will you stop mucking with the beat?* That one got me an interruption of the test, a snap from Ramon, and a do-over, all of which I could have lived without.

I sussed out early on in the course of the disease that the best way to get through this particular form of misery was to concentrate on something, anything at all, that wasn't related to the MRI. This time, the choice was easy. I went with a really nice recent memory: I thought about the previous Sunday, the huge post-tour party we'd thrown for our band, Blacklight, at our Pacific Heights house, and how it had turned into an uproarious engagement party.

The rhythm shifted, stopped, and Ramon's voice crackled into the sudden quiet: "Next test, three minutes forty seconds. You doing okay, Mr. Kinkaid? Don't talk or move."

Boomboom-BAM-boomboom-BAM.

I let my mind go back a bit. I thought about how Bree had proposed, how she'd looked, what she'd said, her white velvet dress, her high heels, her red hair hanging down, and her eyes the colour of the stone in the engagement ring I was planning on ordering for her. I remembered how she'd asked me, remembered pulling her into my arms, how a cheer had gone up, not even remembering, at that moment, that if I'd done this myself years ago, I wouldn't be a new-made widower with a wife who'd committed manslaughter and then suicide.

"Next test, Mr. Kinkaid. Long one—four minutes eight seconds. Don't talk or move."

Boomboomboom-BLIP.

I remembered how I'd felt when Bree had gone, disappeared, and how I'd felt when I thought I might not see her again. I thought about the smell of Afghan food, the taste of stale coffee at four in the morning in a Manhattan police station, the feel of a Les Paul neck in my hands, the fact that I could still play at all.

After that, I turned my mind off completely. I went Zen and was able to drift off for a bit.

Forty minutes, fifty minutes, and the table was moving, and my head was free. Ramon took the bolster out from under my knees. I swung my legs off the table and offered a hand.

"We'll send these to your doctor, Mr. Kinkaid. It should take about ten days. Same time next year?"

Into my locker, out of the hospital gown, wad the miserable rag up and toss it in the dirty-clothes hamper. Back into street clothes, pop the Velcro closing on my black Prada shoes shut, out into the waiting room, wave good-bye at everyone, take a moment to kiss Bree—good and hard, because even though she's always there, and I'm always chuffed to see her, I'm always even more chuffed than usual to come out of an MRI and find her waiting for me—out into the street, into the car, and home.

"John—tell me again why we're going to this thing?"

It was a gorgeous afternoon, just beginning the long slow slide into evening. The Bay Area gets some of its most extreme weather around late summer and into early autumn—we'd got lucky, and the first day of Indian summer hit the Bay. The result was a glorious sunlit dream of a day, mid-seventies, without a touch of fog anywhere.

We were halfway across the Golden Gate Bridge, heading north into Marin County. Sailboats dotted the Bay. Even Alcatraz, which usually gives me the creeps, looked benign.

I've never learned to drive, and Bree, behind the wheel of our Jaguar S-type, loathes driving the bridges. Can't say I blame her, not really. The lanes are narrow and there's nothing but a few plastic orange sticks to separate you from oncoming traffic. Besides, it's a damned long way down. She rarely makes any conversation when she's navigating one of the bridges. Her attention is usually reserved for glaring at other drivers who look to be coming too close to the Jag. So the question was a bit of a surprise.

I twisted round in my seat. "What, going to this party? Because we were invited, love. Why not?"

"Just curious, that's all. I mean, except for Tony and Kris, do we know any of these people? Who else will be there? Whose house are we going to again?"

"A bloke called Paul, Paul—shit, I can't remember his other name. He owns the 707, that club on Francisco Boulevard, up in San Rafael. We went there last year, for that Halloween gig, remember? Paul Morgenstern, that's it. Not sure you actually met him at the Halloween show. Nice bloke."

She was silent. It occurred to me suddenly that, right, she had issues about going to other people's gatherings if it even looks to be part of my professional life. I regarded her profile. "Bree, love, what's up? It's just a party: nosh, liquid, natter. Tony says Paul's got a nice place, wraparound views, sundecks, the whole Sausalito thing. Did you not want to go? Why didn't you say something before? We can turn right round again and go home if you want—although you look brilliant in that dress. Shame to waste it." I wasn't blowing smoke about that, either. She was in dark green jersey, clingy and hot, with some high-wedge sandals.

"No, it's fine. I just didn't know if we knew anyone, and you're not usually into the whole socialising thing after a tour. No big." A BMW cut a bit too close to us, and she shot the driver a look that would have sent Darth Vader wailing for his mum. "How about staying in your own lane, you asshole!"

She merged into the through traffic, took the Jag through the rainbow-painted tunnel at the top of the steep bit of bridge headland called the Waldo Grade, and took us down into the winding, twisty streets of the Sausalito hills.

Of course, there was absolutely no place to put the car.

Tony, who'd rung up to pass on Paul's invite, hadn't mentioned that the house had parking for only six people maybe. And, of course, the street was already parked solid.

Bree pulled over to the curb. She was working herself into a bad mood; I could tell.

"Well, shit. This is going to mean a hike. I'll let you out and find a parking place. I'll be up as soon as I can."

"Sod that. If you suffer, I suffer, or at least give the supporting arm. Let's park and we'll walk up together." She opened her mouth to protest, and I kissed her. "I said no and I meant it. Stop treating me like I was a hundred years old, okay? Or at least pick your spots. Once we're married, I intend to come the full pissy husband over you. We'll hike up the hill together. No arguing, damn it."

We got a break at that point—Paul, our host, came out with Tony's wife, Katia. He stuck his face up near Bree's window.

"Hey, JP! You made it! Excellent! We saved a parking place for you—Tony reminded me you were handicapped, so we kept a space open around the side. Hi, I'm Paul. You must be—Bree, right? Really cool to meet you. Tell you what, why doesn't JP get out first? He can snag you a couple of chairs and some food, and you can follow me back and park. Great car, by the way—I love the new S-types. I was thinking about getting one, but Jag doesn't make an SUV and I need something large enough to haul equipment. . . ."

I climbed out and he climbed in. He was still chattering as Bree pulled out.

The house was as gorgeous as advertised, although what really made it was outside: it had a huge deck, two levels, that curved most of the way round, with views of everything but the side of the hill. It was one of those redwood things, built in the '70s and common in the Marin hills—soaring ceilings and skylights everywhere. You have to walk down to get to the house from the driveway, something else that's common in Marin. Occasionally, after a really wet winter, sinkholes open up on city streets and hillsides give way, and pricey houses with spectacular views fetch up as splintered piles of kindling hundreds of feet below where they'd started, usually with the underinsured owner swearing under his breath.

The entryway into Paul's place was typical, opening out into an enormous room surrounded by glass. The view was outrageous, well beyond spectacular and all the way into *Are you kidding me?* territory. It caught me as I was halfway across the main room, fielding greetings, dodging the occasional question about the weirdness that had been my last tour. I've played for Blacklight for a good long time, but this last tour had seen, among other things, the murder of a would-be biographer and my estranged wife's suicide. I wasn't really happy discussing any of it with relative strangers, so I'd settled on a policy of smiling vaguely and changing the subject, or else just dodging the questioners entirely.

But that view stopped me cold, just gawking. It was so amazing, it actually pulled the eye away from the walls, which were covered with paintings—if you blocked the windows, you'd have thought you were in a gallery or a museum. Personally, I was glad no one had blocked the windows. It would have been a tragedy to miss that view. You could have stuck every painting from the Prado to the National Gallery up on those walls, and the view would have won, no contest.

The glass doors, which ran wall to wall and floor to ceiling, looked southeast, and the entire bay was spread out like some *National Geographic* photographer's wet dream of a magazine cover. The sun was halfway down and everything was crimson. The towers of the Golden Gate Bridge and the top of the Transamerica Pyramid, across the water in San Francisco, looked to be on fire under all that red sun. It was absolutely gorgeous.

Over at the front door, a flutter of green jersey caught my eye: Bree, standing in the doorway, looking around. I waved at her, and she edged her way through the crowd.

"Hey. John, I've just realised—do you have your afternoon meds with you? Because it's after six." She did a double take. "Whoa! Do you believe that view?"

"Gorgeous, isn't it? And yeah, I need to take meds. Tell you what, love, I'll find us a place to perch. Do you want to go cast your professional caterer's eye over the craft services and get us some nosh and water?"

She grinned. "Craft services? Sure. I thought I saw a big tray of rumaki—I bet I know which caterer he used. You go find chairs and get your meds together—I'll be back with water and a couple of plates in a few."

She disappeared into the crowd. I craned my neck, looking between shoulders and floppy hats, until I finally spotted a couple of folding chairs pushed up against a wall in the far corner of the main room. I began picking my way through. The party was jumping.

Halfway there, I got intercepted by Tony and Kris. They each had plates, and Tony was balancing his food in one hand and a beer in the other. They had a bloke in tow, someone I hadn't met before.

"JP! Oh, good, you're here—where's Bree? Hey, I wanted you to meet my friend Bruno Baines. Bruno is an incredible luthier from up the coast, in Mendocino—he did the most amazing guitar for Vinny. Bruno, this is our friend JP Kinkaid. He plays with Blacklight. They just finished up a huge tour for their new CD—"

"I know. I saw the Oakland show, from about the sixteenth row." He was a little bloke, smaller than I was, and young, most likely in his thirties. "Wow, it's really nice to meet you. You're a big fan of traditional Gibsons, aren't you? I counted three onstage. Was that a stock Goldtop Les Paul I saw? Late fifties vintage?"

"Yeah, all of my Gibsons are stock. I'm not fond of noodling with the electronics—I'd much rather play the thing. So if I don't love the sound, I don't buy it in the first place." I offered him a hand. "Always pleased to meet a guitar maker. You made Vinny an axe? I don't think I've seen it. Last I saw, he was playing a very flashy PRS private stock, but he's pretty scattershot about what he likes to use for—"

I broke off suddenly. There was something going on across the room. All the noise, the chatter of conversation suddenly seemed to drop away, and a single voice cut across. It was Bree.

"I don't know who the hell you think you are." Her voice was black ice, and I turned around fast, and so did Tony and Kris. Everyone else was already staring. "But you have precisely five seconds to take your hand off my ass. If the clock hits six seconds and your hand is still there, I take the santoku knife off the sushi platter and I cut your nuts off with it and wear them for earrings. And then I tell everyone who they used to belong to. Back *off*, little man."

"Fuck!" I couldn't quite see what was happening through the crush of people. That's the problem with being not quite five foot eight. I could see Bree's upper half quite easily, but since she was in four-inch wedges and she's five-ten barefoot, no surprise there, you know? And she had her back to me, but even from here, I could see her shoulders, braced and warlike. She hadn't been joking about the santoku. "Tony, *move*, mate. Who the hell—"

"'Little man'?" A voice rang out, nasal, furious, male. I recognised it right off. "Who the fuck do you think you're talking to, bitch? Do you know who I am?"

I was moving, Tony in front of me. The crowd parted for us like the Red Sea.

16

"Yes, as a matter of fact, I do." Bree had turned, and was looking down at him. Never mind the words, just her voice was an insult. "You're Vinny fucking Fabiano. And you're looking older every day."

Shit. Ten feet to go, eight feet, seven . . .

I gave Tony a good hard shove. He stumbled and moved aside, just in time for me to see Vinny Fabiano, both hands balled up into meaty fists, rear back and take a roundhouse swing at Bree.

Of course, I went nuts—completely flipped my shit. I was too far away to do anything, but Bree saw it coming and side-stepped; Vinny, even in his cowboy boots, was still six inches shorter than she was. If he'd connected, he'd have knocked all the air out of her, maybe broken a couple of ribs, and I'd have broken his fucking neck. Just then, I was planning on doing that anyway.

What happened next was so beautiful, I get a lovely inner glow whenever I remember it. Bree—perfectly calm, mind you, not a hair out of place—stepped up and kneed Vinny in the nuts.

She wasn't joking about it, either. She reached down, got him by the shoulders, and jerked him forward, putting the full force of a nice long leg behind it for maximum impact. Perfect. I wondered who'd taught her that, or if women do it by instinct.

And Vinny's face—Gordon bleedin' *Bennett*. Perfect. His eyes popped, he made a little squeaky noise, and all the air went out of him. He went down like—well, like a bloke who'd just been nailed in the groin by a woman with six inches on him and a reason to inflict maximum damage.

There was a moment of silence. Then three people, including Bruno Baines, got hold of Vinny. He was sagging and whimpering and covering his nuts, and trying to get some oxygen back into his lungs, and Bruno and the others were trying to hold him upright. I suppose they thought he might not be too damaged to try for another swing at Bree. God knows, Vinny might just have been that stupid. I didn't know him well enough to guess.

In the meantime, Tony and Kris had got hold of me and were hanging on to both my arms. I couldn't imagine what they thought they were on about, until I heard someone screaming, "You little shit, you tried to hit my old lady, I'm going to fucking cripple you!" and realised it was me, yelling like a nutter, not even knowing I'd opened my mouth. I'd actually thought I was calm. Rage, the genuine article, is really peculiar, you know?

And of course, there were easily sixty people watching all this go down. Right. Lovely, just lovely. The story was going to be all over the music community in Marin County by morning.

The problem is, the music scene in Marin is ridiculously incestuous. Everyone's got their nose dipped into someone else's business. If you ring up a plumber in Mill Valley, a retired sound engineer in Novato will be telling a drummer for his cousin's band in San Anselmo an hour later that you broke your loo flushing a kilo of pot because a roadie from a former band of yours had it on good authority that the feds were at the door. It's all gossip, all rumour, and it's always been that way. I'm glad I live in the City.

Bree saved the situation, or maybe she made it worse. She looked at Vinny—who had gone quiet, except for the whole oxygen-gathering thing, and was looking from her to me and back again—and said, calm and clear, "Paul, thanks for saving us the parking spot, but this really isn't our kind of party. Maybe another time. John? Can we go, please? I want some dinner."

"Right. Bring the car round, love, will you?"

I'd calmed down—Tony and Kris had let go of me, but they were staying close. I shrugged them off. "Tony, ring me, yeah? Unless you want to come out to dinner? I'm thinking Angelino's, if we can get a table. We have a few things to discuss."

CHAPTER TWO

We fetched up down the hill, having dinner at Angelino, a superb Italian place in the heart of Sausalito's main drag, right across from the water.

We were lucky to get a table, actually, since we were quite a crowd. Kris and his wife, Sandra; Tony and his, Katia; and Bruno Baines, the luthier, had all opted out of the weirdness of Paul Morgenstern's little do and followed us down the hill. I thought we might have a long wait, because Saturday night is busy, and the place is deservedly popular. Bree says the pappardelle with mushrooms alone is worth the cost of the bridge toll.

Luckily, they know Bree. We've eaten there before, quite often. Plus, losing the false modesty? Three well-known rock and rollers. That's one benefit of celebrity: If the famous person in question isn't a raging berk or a menace to the health and safety of the other patrons, it's a cachet for the restaurant. I'm not above using whatever fame I've got to get into things without the long wait. And since I'd gone shaky, I wanted food, some water for my meds, and a sit-down.

They gave us the entire rear, a semi-private section; Billy DuMont had caught us up at our car and told us he'd meet us, so we got them to save a small side table as well.

"Wow." Bruno Baines looked around at the snowy table linens, at the gleaming panelling, at the fantastic view of the San Francisco skyline. He had an electric guitar case in one hand. "Nice place."

Bree smiled at him. She seemed preoccupied, and at first I thought she might be reacting to Vinny's bullshit, but no. Of course, it was me she was fussing over. "John, are you okay? I just remembered—I got distracted by that fuckwit trying to feel me up, and I never got you water for your meds. Damn! I ought to go back up there and kick him again."

She caught the busboy's eye and made the classic gesture of pouring and drinking with one hand. Thirty seconds later, there was a carafe of lemon water on the table and glasses for everyone. I swallowed my dose of antispasmodic, the stuff they prescribe to keep muscle spasms in check for people with MS, and patted Bree's hand.

"It's okay, Bree, I'm fine—no need to fuss. The big question is, how are you, love? I only got a side view, so I couldn't tell, and I want a straight answer, no bullshit: Did that little berk connect at all? Because if he did, I'm going back up there, and by the time I'm done with him, that beautiful kick of yours is something he'll dream about with longing. And yeah, I'll get you those bollocks earrings off him as well."

"Wasn't that something?" Katia was grinning like a loon. "God, Bree, that was so damned funny. 'You're looking older every day'—oh, mercy!"

"Ha! I liked the phrase 'little man.' Or, no, I didn't like it. I mean, ouch. If Bree'd used that on me, I might have been tempted to take a swing at someone myself. Unbelievably insulting, especially in that tone of voice." Tony regarded his wife. "Is that envy I'm hearing?"

"If she's not envious, I am." Sandra was frankly blissed. "I've wanted to kick him since the day I met him. Hell, I could kick him for a week, wearing the pointiest-toed shoes I own, and I'd still feel unsatisfied. He's *such* an asshole."

Bruno was nodding at us. "I hope no one minds if I raise my hand and ask to be put on the waiting list for the privilege of kicking Vinny. I've been working on a guitar for him for the past two months, and he's a nightmare to deal with. I mean, I'm glad to get the gig, but Jesus, what a diva!"

That got my attention. "Right, Tony said something about a guitar. What sort? Acoustic?"

"Electric." He nodded at the guitar case he'd been lugging about; he'd slid it behind the chairs and against the wall, out of traffic. "He was supposed to try it out tonight, but I guess he was too busy trying to, um, well, do other things. Kind of a bummer, since he still owes me over nine grand for it, and he was supposed to pay me, and I could use it. The materials on this thing cost almost as much as the deposit. Plus, it was really labour intensive."

Bree looked up from her menu. "Nine thousand dollars? You made Vinny Fabiano a guitar that cost nine thousand dollars? Jesus. That's one expensive instrument."

"Actually, the agreed price was twelve thousand. He paid me a deposit. I'm trying to collect the rest."

The waiter arrived with bread and dipping bowl. We ordered, and I turned to Bruno.

"Twelve grand. That must be one hell of an axe. Is that it, in the case? Can I get a look?"

Tony was grinning. This is all standard, you know? It's how musicians work. Tony isn't a guitarist, he's a keyboard player; he doesn't play guitar and he doesn't own any, either. Kris is a bassist, but he lives and dies by the Fender Precision Bass. He's got no interest at all in fancy custom stuff. He admires the great artisan basses, the Alembic and Tobias exotics; they just don't tempt him. He's all about the P Bass.

But they'd come across this bloke, and they were doing their best to hook him up with potential customers. That meant they thought his stuff deserved the business. Since we live just down the road from luthiers like Alembic, his work had to be really eye-catching. We understood each other perfectly.

Bruno pushed his chair back. Bree, who was between us, vacated. He laid the case across the empty chairs and opened it.

My first thought—after my jaw hit the floor—was that I'd never seen anything so gaudy in my life. My second thought was that this bloke was going to be up to his arse in orders from world-class players. Even before I touched it, I could see the quality of the work.

"Bloody *hell*."

That guitar was so gaudy, it verged on ridiculous. Surreal, you know? The top was red, not basic guitar cherry red, but the precise colour of the tops of the Golden Gate Bridge and the Transamerica Pyramid an hour before, when I'd looked through Paul's windows and thought the Bay was on fire. Bruno had used a really clear red wood for the top of the thing, something exotic, probably padauk, and he'd carved the top out by hand, shaping and curving the silhouette, sinuous and graceful. The damned thing was absolutely gorgeous.

Lovely as the wood and the lines were, it was nearly buried under the inlay work. I'm not a fan of that sort of thing, generally, any more than I'm a fan of guitars shaped like pigeons or swords or busts of Beethoven. I like guitars that look and feel like guitars. Yeah, so, I'm a snob and a purist. It's the way it is.

The inlay work on this monster was completely insane. There's no other word for it. Half the instrument was covered with marquetry, a mixture of different woods, mother-of-pearl, and what looked like gold wire. I've never seen anything quite so over the top. It was a design, abstract, not an actual picture of anything real. There was something about the design that reminded me vaguely of vintage wrought-iron grilles on old-fashioned European lifts, or maybe in hotels in New York in the thirties. Art deco, you know? He'd used solid black pickup covers, so all the art deco stuff twined around them. There was no pickguard.

I lifted an eyebrow at him. "May I?"

"Absolutely." Everyone was looking chuffed at my interest, and Bree was staring at the guitar in fascination. I reached in and lifted Vinny's guitar carefully out of its case.

The weight of the thing nearly bent me backwards. I play vintage Les Pauls from the '50s and '60s. They aren't light guitars, but this outweighed them by three pounds, maybe more. If three pounds doesn't sound like much, think about having to stand in place for two hours, holding that extra weight. Take my word for it: Eleven pounds really is heavier than eight. The older I get, and the more my MS settles in, the more aware of that I seem to get.

I balanced it on one knee and turned it over. The back had a continuation of all that marquetry from the front. The neck was pretty enough, bound in flame maple. All the fittings on the front—bridge, tailpiece, nut, the lot—were solid brass. From the looks of it, they'd been gold-plated, with 24-karat gold.

I settled it, and ran my fingers up the neck, giving it a chance, getting the feel of it. There was a telly, one of those flat-screen affairs, suspended over the bar at the front of the restaurant, but the bartender had turned the volume down. I started playing one of the longer guitar runs from "Long Day in the Hot, Hot Sun," the first single off Blacklight's newest CD.

When I stopped a couple of minutes later, I realised the entire restaurant had stopped as well. Our waiter, standing a few feet away with a cart loaded with our dinner, had his mouth open—he realised it, caught a look from the restaurant manager, and got his face back under control. Everyone in the restaurant had stopped eating, stopped talking, and was staring at us. A few people had put their heads together; there were looks of recognition, and I heard the whispers start up. *"Isn't that— no, it couldn't be—oh my God it is! . . . "*

I handed the guitar back to Bruno. "Ah. You use the PRS neck style. Not my thing, I'm afraid—I've got a pair of them, and they're gathering dust. They never get played. This one's also on the heavy side for my tastes. Gorgeous instrument, though. The quality just sings. Brilliant job, mate. You do really nice work."

"Thanks—that's some high praise." He put the guitar away. "The neck on this one was by Vinny's request—okay, make that demand. He's not big on requesting. I do classic Paul necks, SG necks, 335 necks, Fender necks . . ."

"Right." Everyone in the restaurant was still staring, and I mentally kicked myself. I sometimes forget that people actually recognise the music, you know? Odds were good that our nice peaceful dinner—which I'd hoped would cool everyone down after the incident with Vinny—was going to get disrupted at least once, by an autograph or photo-opportunity request.

I shot Bree an apologetic look. This was supposed to be in aid of getting her a peaceful meal after the scene up at Paul's, and instead, we were bound to have at least one interruption, and possibly more. "So all that fussy inlay and marquetry stuff was also Vinny's idea? Not that it isn't beautifully done, just that it's not my thing."

"Oh, he wanted much more. Believe me, this one is subtle, compared to what he was asking for when he first sketched it out. I actually toned him down—he wanted full-sized mother-of-pearl and sterling-silver dragons fighting each other. You said you like them light? I did a Paul-style a few months ago, a Deluxe that weighed in at just under five pounds."

I watched him put Vinny's flash guitar away, and settled down to my salad. "Are you serious? You did a custom Paul under five pounds? What did you do, chamber it? I mean, a Paul's a solid slab of wood, and as much as I love mine, they're heavy buggers. One's over eight pounds, the other one's over nine."

"Yep. I chambered the hell out of it, as much wood as I could take out and still have a guitar. Basically, the only wood left in there is the core, to hold the electronics. The pegheads, the neck—everything was done with weight minimisation as the goal. Just under five pounds. I could probably even shave a bit more off. . . ." His voice died away as a thirtyish blonde bore down on the table, pen in hand, fluttering her eyelashes.

"Excuse me, I'm *terribly* sorry to interrupt your dinner, but aren't you JP Kinkaid? I'm a *huge* fan of Blacklight, would it be a *terrible* imposition if I asked for your autograph?"

I'd signed three autographs and posed for a picture with a family from Florida—much to the amusement of my mates—before Billy DuMont finally wandered in. Everyone except Bree, who'd gone rather quiet for some reason, immediately pounced on him and demanded information.

"Oh, man, *what* a movie you missed." He was grinning like a madman. "Paul was wringing his hands like a bereaved widow, he was so freaked out. Vinny kept saying, 'That was JP's old lady? That was JP's old lady?' over and over. I think he was drunk before the kick, but after it? Not so much. I'm just surprised he's not still curled up on the floor, sobbing. If you want the truth, I feel kinda sorry for the guy—he's so damned clueless, he just manages to put his foot in it no matter what. Sometimes I wonder if he's addicted to the taste of his own shoe leather."

"What in hell does the fact that I came in with John have to do with anything?" Bree was outraged. "Does he think it's acceptable party behaviour to grope women who *aren't* there with John? Hey, look at my cute party trick: I grab women I don't know by the ass, especially women who aren't with John Kinkaid, and then get pissed off when they call me on it? What kind of bullshit is that? What planet is that guy from?"

"Well, he's terrified of JP. So between you kicking his stones halfway up his intestines and JP screaming that he was going to kill him, he was pretty limp." Billy suddenly grinned. "Oh, man. Poor Paul. What a party killer—except, of course, it didn't. It just changed the course of the conversation."

"You've got to be having me on." I was as gobsmacked as Bree, but for an entirely different reason. "What do you mean, he's terrified of me? He's got thirty pounds on me and he looks like he bench-presses motorcycles for fun as a morning workout. I'm just a skinny old geezer with a degenerative disease and a heart murmur. What in hell are you on about, Billy?"

"It's professional terror, JP, not physical." Tony was looking amused. "Okay, so Vinny's now the front man for an established band. But the Bombardiers aren't Blacklight. We're just the old reliable local standbys. No one's going to call us to headline a stadium show, not in this lifetime. Blacklight? Different class entirely—you're a rock star."

"That's pants." I just sat there, blinking at him. "He's intimidated by my, what? Celebrity? Bollocks to that."

"JP, come on, man, don't be coy. In his head, you're the Big

Red Rooster, king of the heap, that whole barnyard pecking order deal. Before he signed on with us, he was a solo act, doing clubs. Hell, when we first caught his act, he was doing a solo gig up at the 707 and the place was half-empty. Haven't you noticed that he never gives you any shit about anything? How many autographs did you just sign? Come on, JP, you're not dumb."

"No, but I appear to be dim." I shook my head. This was too damned weird. "What a peculiar bloke."

"What I want to know," Bree asked, "is how big a bribe does Mrs. Morgenstern demand, to allow Vinny within fifty miles of one of her parties? Because the guy is a menace. Come to think of it, is there a Mrs. Morgenstern? I don't remember meeting one. Granted, we weren't there long enough for me to actually be introduced to people—John, stop laughing at me!"

"The lady formerly known as Mrs. Morgenstern is named Angie." Sandra signalled the waiter. "Could we get the cheque? Thanks. What was I saying? Oh, yeah, Angie. Angie is a shark. You know the kind I mean, don't you? One of those women with very tight abs and very, very shiny teeth. She is now the former Mrs. Morgenstern, and she's a lot wealthier than she used to be, and so are her lawyers, and I imagine, so are his lawyers. It was a really nasty divorce. No kids, luckily. Some people just shouldn't be allowed to spawn."

As we waited for the valets to bring the cars around, Tony brought up the question on my mind.

"JP, look—about the sessions? I know you probably don't want to be within a mile of Vinny after what he tried on Bree. I get it. I just wanted you to know that, if you just don't want to deal with him, we'll understand. It would suck—you know how cool we all think it is that you're sitting in—but the universe won't be pulled into a black hole if you back out, and we won't be pissed off. It's totally your call. Not going to pressure you. I don't want to add to the stress levels. Hell, you've got a wedding coming up."

"Well, the wedding stuff, that's mostly on Bree's plate. I'm doing sod-all about getting that together—she's in charge." I shook my head. "It's okay, Tony. I'm not backing out. I'm having a very good time, and I love the material. I expect I can find a way of dealing with Vinny that doesn't involve me beating him to death. Of course, if he tries any more shit with Bree, he dies."

The valet drove up with our car. Bree, who'd been having a quiet talk with the two women and Bruno, headed over.

Tony snorted. "I'd say that's the last thing you need to worry about."

"Ooooh, I'm *terribly* sorry to interrupt your dinner, but aren't you JP Kinkaid?"

The lady now fluttering her eyelashes at me was stark naked and pinned firmly in place under me. I'd got a grip on both her wrists, and I was laughing like an idiot, which made hanging on to her that much trickier.

She batted her lashes at me again. "Would it be a *terrible* imposition to ask for your autograph? . . ."

"Knock it off, Bree." I bit her lightly on the earlobe. "I'll tell you what, I think you like it when that happens. I've noticed that every time someone with breasts and too much lipstick asks for my autograph, we get home and I get laid. Turns you on, does it? You little groupie, you."

"But I'm a *huge* Blacklight fan, Mr. Kinkaid! Ooooh, and speaking of *huge*, would it be a *terrible* imposition if I asked you to . . ."

"Right, that's it, you cheeky little bit." I got one leg over her, which got us belly to belly and knee to knee. Then I remembered what one of those knees had been up to earlier in the evening, and thought better of it. She tried to wriggle free, but it was a token attempt; she wasn't serious. Good job, too, because I wasn't letting her go anywhere, not for the next fifteen minutes or so. . . .

"Hello, darling." There's something comforting about ritual; I've used that particular line to Bree so many times after a good rowdy slap and tickle that it's become a sort of coda to the actual sex. "Bree, did I say how sorry I am that you had to deal with Vinny's bullshit? And how proud I was of your right knee? Cheers, love. Brilliant job."

"Mmmmm." Her eyes were half rolled back in their sockets, trying to focus. She was still rippling, still cascading along, still not all the way back from whatever wonderland I'd taken her to. "What? Oh—right. Vinny, knee, nuts. You weren't mad?"

"Bloody hell no! Why? . . ."

"Awkward. I mean, Tony's one of your best friends, Vinny's fronting their band. Mmmmm." She rolled over suddenly and reached for me. "Talk later."

Talk later . . . Right. Another fifteen minutes, this time mostly her fifteen minutes of tripping, with me doing what I really love doing at that point in the evening: navigating her there. It's bloody wondrous, watching this happening, but it's even better knowing what to do along the way. There are times she seems to stop breathing, for minutes at a time, and I know just how to get her back. It makes me feel like that bloke in *My Fair Lady*, you know? Pygmalion? Bringing things to life.

"Hello, darling." I touched my tongue to her cheekbone and tasted a bit of salt. "Enough?"

"Mrmphmrmph. Don't know yet." Her eyes were beginning to clear finally. "Hello back at you, beautiful man. God, I love you. No, don't think about getting up. Did you want water? I'll get it. Are you going to still sit in? Even after the knee?"

"Am I going—? Oh, right, okay, Bombardier sessions. Yeah, I am. I mean, Tony asked me to do it, Bree. And Kris and Billy made it pretty clear they want me in for this. So it's a majority-rule thing, you know? Three to one. Besides, I'm not sure Vinny doesn't want me there, even after tonight. He may be the world's most complete berk, but he's also a musician. Besides, if everyone's sussed him properly, he's digging having a superstar to work with. And no, you're not going to get up and get me water. If I get thirsty, I'll get it. I've got perfectly good feet."

"Okay. John, that thing was amazing. Really shiny." We were facing each other, side by side. There was moonlight slipping down the wall opposite our bed, and outside in the hallway, I heard Bree's Siamese, Farrowen, give that distinctive little *wow-wow* noise Siamese use for complaining. "Shut up, cat!"

"Shiny? Oh, right, Bruno's guitar." Her skin had gone all pearly, damp around the edges; she looked to be mostly made of moonlight herself. "Shiny's not in it, love. That was staggering work. That bloke's not going to have time to sleep, he's going to have so many guitar players queuing up, trying to kick his door down, demanding instruments. I'm not looking at the moment— maybe in a few months. Between the wedding and the Bombardier sessions, I've got too much on my plate right now to think about it. But a five-pound Les Paul, that would make me a happy man. What are you—?" She'd reached a hand out and got hold of me, and was doing some astonishing things. "Jesus, Bree. Come *here*."

Fifteen minutes. This time, afterwards, she lay and watched me trying to get my heart rate back under control. Anyone who thinks long familiarity with each other mucks up the sex is an idiot. "Hello, darling," I told her. "You know, if that offer of a glass of water happened to still be on the table, I wouldn't say no. My legs are going to be useless for a few minutes. You've got a definite talent for turning my knees to water."

"Pitcher and glass, at your service. Here you go." She sat up beside me, cross-legged in a sort of yoga tuck, which is an amazing effect when the woman in question is naked. "Isn't twelve thousand dollars a lot?"

"Isn't—? Oh, the Shiny Guitar. Right. Actually, no. It's a high-end custom axe, and twelve thousand is still a lot less than either of my Pauls are worth." I took a mouthful of water. "Hell, you pay our annual insurance, you tell me. The Deluxe isn't that valuable if you look at it in terms of vintage and availability, but my Goldtop Paul, the '57, ought to be covered to the tune of about thirty thousand, maybe even forty. Isn't it? No, from the way your eyes are bugging, I suppose not."

"I'll call the insurance people tomorrow." She tilted her head. "So the Goldtop is worth up to forty thousand dollars? Is that because it's vintage, or because it's yours? Wouldn't a new one, a copy, be worth a lot less? Or if it belonged to some schmo on Market Street?"

"Yeah, probably. Mine's stock, which adds to the collector value, but the intrinsic value's there, Bree. A collector would dish out forty grand for it without knowing it was mine. Once he found out I'd owned it—or Luke, or Jimi Hendrix, or anyone famous—you could add ten grand to that, at least. There really isn't any limit. Eric Clapton sold his Fender Strat for just under a million dollars at a charity auction a while back."

"A mil—" Her jaw had dropped. "You're joking, right?"

"No joke. It's a historic instrument, and he sold it for a good cause—raising money for his Crossroads Centre, down in Antigua. Since I'm not selling my Pauls, it doesn't matter. Still, a chambered one, half the weight of one of mine? I'd pay ten thousand for one of those without a blink. And if I got to spec it, choose the electronics and the trimmings, I'd probably go higher. Live by the Les Paul, die by the Les Paul. What?" She'd shivered.

"Nothing. Goose walking over my grave." She suddenly slid down beside me. This time, the signals were pretty clear

32

that what she wanted was a good cuddle, not a good orgasm. I obliged, lifting one arm, letting her snuggle up.

"So when do you head back to the Bombardier rehearsals?"

"Monday." I stroked her hair for a moment and then let loose with a cavernous yawn. It had been a very long day. "And if I said I wasn't this side of curious to see how Vinny's going to approach me? I'd be lying."

CHAPTER THREE

"On four. JP leads it in. One—two—three . . ."

The next song on the rehearsal agenda was a rocker, with a standard boogie vamp for the lead-in. I was finger-picking and playing bottleneck on this one. The lead-in really should have come from Vinny, and there was no vocal, not yet; we'd got there early and Vinny was late. Annoying as that was, it meant we could get some work in on the instrumental section of Tony's second song for the new CD. Nice, peaceful concentration on working out the knots in the song. Excellent.

This one was fun to play, with odd rhythmic stops before each chorus. Songs written by piano players, they tend to be dotted with odd random rhythmic stops, trills that go all the way up the keyboard into tinkling tiara runs, in places where a guitar player might write hard chucks instead, to syncopate the rhythm. On this one, I got to play a longish slide break. I love that; I began as a blues player, and at heart, I still am. I don't get to do much of it with Blacklight.

Damon Gelb had two boards running today. At the moment, he was adjusting the various input levels, tapping a foot, looking appreciative, just relaxing and grooving along with the song. It really was nice and peaceful without Vinny.

We'd just finished and were taking a break when he arrived. He was carrying an enormous bouquet of white roses.

Before we'd started up, I had a quiet word with Tony about how I intended to deal with Vinny. I was going with a wait-and-see attitude. I didn't need to prove anything or indulge in some sort of macho display—the bloke had done something offensive, been warned by the object of his action, disregarded the warning, and been publicly and humiliatingly thumped for it. I was playing it by ear, letting him make the first move.

"Hey, guys—sorry I'm late. I had to pick these up on the way, and there's no place to park at the Flower Mart." His eye lit on me. "Oh, man, hey. JP, I'm really glad you're here. I needed to say I was sorry I fucked up, and I didn't know if you were coming back." He grinned, a genuine grin. "They would have crucified me if you didn't. Anyway, I'm really sorry. Of course I wouldn't have grabbed her if I'd known she was yours, man. I don't poach on other people's women. Anyway—these are for your old lady."

Everyone was watching. I could see Damon Gelb, keeping his face carefully blank—he must have heard the story, unless he'd been at the party and I hadn't noticed. Considering how crowded Paul's place had been, it was certainly possible. Tony, behind Vinny, was not quite rolling his eyes. "Right. Basically, you're apologising for trying to handle merchandise that belongs to me? And the roses are for the merchandise?"

"No—shit, man, come on. You know what I mean."

It was unbelievable. He had no clue what I was talking

about. He'd gone out and blown a wad of dosh on roses for Bree, not because he felt he'd done something offensive to her, but because he was afraid he'd upset me. There was no point in being pissy at him; he honestly was trying to do what he thought was the right thing. He seemed to be missing something in his makeup, some basic sense of reality, or maybe balance. In his head, my woman was my property.

"Hey, JP, say something, man, okay?" Vinny was looking puzzled and a bit uneasy. "Doesn't she like roses? Because I can go get something else. Would you give them to her for me?"

I cocked an eyebrow at him. "She loves roses, thanks. But she's not my property, Vinny. She's very much her own property. Thing is, you ought to be apologising to her, not to me. She's the one you tried to damage. So I think I'll let you deliver the roses yourself, when she picks me up later, yeah? With whatever apology to her you think is appropriate. Oh, and by the way? Her name is Bree. *B-r-e-e*. Not a nickname. It's her name. Bree."

"Cute name." He'd been strapping on his guitar. I'd been so distracted that I hadn't noticed just what he'd been pulling out of the case. But I noticed it now, and I nearly choked.

"Bloody *hell*."

It sat there, dangling off the strap, gleaming under the studio overheads. I'd seen it before, or one just like it, and that had belonged to Ron Wood of the Rolling Stones—if I remembered it right, his had been stolen and never seen again. And this one looked just like it.

No damned way—it had to be a copy. I'd have to consider long and hard before I spent the kind of money Vinny had to have spent on that guitar, and I was going to see well over a million dollars from the American leg of this last Blacklight tour.

"Is that—? That's not a Zemaitis you've got, is it?" Now that I looked at it, it wasn't exactly like Ronnie's stolen axe, if I was remembering the top of that one properly. This one seemed to have extra knobs. It had been customised to the nines.

"It sure as hell is. Isn't it cool? Want to check it out? I got it a few weeks ago off some Japanese collector, a guy in Osaka. He was unloading some of his stuff. It cost an arm and a leg, but I'm not sure I love it."

"If you don't, I do." Did he have a clue what he had? I stared at it. The entire front of the guitar was inlaid mother-of-pearl, in the chessboard pattern. A pearl-top Zemaitis? The new ones, reproductions, listed at well over twenty thousand dollars. If it was vintage, one of Tony Zemaitis's original axes . . . "What's the year on that, Vinny?"

"It's a 1982, according to the paperwork. Rosario! Where the hell are my power cords, man? You're supposed to have this shit laid out and ready for me!"

I'm afraid I was distracted for the rest of the rehearsal. I kept taking sideways looks at the Zemaitis and wondering just who in hell Vinny Fabiano actually was, you know? Unless I was losing my mind, that guitar had run him fifty thousand dollars, and probably more. Where in sweet hell had they found this bloke, anyway?

I ran some bottleneck work as Damon tweaked sound levels, and thought back. I remembered the day I'd found out that the Bombardiers were formally asking Vinny to join the band as a replacement for Anton Hall's voice and guitar.

No one had been surprised when Anton died; the real surprise was that he'd lived as long as he had. He'd been a thorough soak for as long as anyone had known him, at least forty years. He hadn't wasted time with the lightweight stuff like beer, either—Anton was a Southern Comfort man, like Janis Joplin before him. They used to get blitzed together, along with a few other local rockers. Anton had been the baby of that group, and he'd been the last one to go. End of an era.

But even though Anton dying was no surprise, it was definitely a problem. The timing of his death put the Bombardiers in a deep hole. They were under contract for a new CD, and it was already late; Anton had got weaker and sicker, and the schedule lapsed badly. Record label suits aren't sentimental as a rule, and they don't really give a damn about anything except the bottom line. All they knew, or cared about, was that the Bombardiers had messed up on their contract obligations. The suits made some pointed comments, which morphed into hints and threats of lawsuits and asset attachments and dropping the band entirely. It was a mess.

So the Bombardiers needed a singer, a front man, and the front man had to be a decent guitarist as well. They'd needed one fast. And somehow or other, they ended up offering the gig to Vinny Fabiano.

I couldn't imagine why. I mean, okay, he was a decent songwriter, a passable but not inspired player, and he had a very distinctive voice. But he was a very different style to what they'd had with Anton, and from what I could see, they'd been trying to adjust to Vinny, rather than having Vinny adjust to them. It didn't make sense. There are any number of decent singers who are also good guitarists in the Bay Area; you can barely turn sideways in any of the clubs without poking one in the ribs. Why had they hired Vinny?

Someone had said something at Angelino, about how they'd first seen him at a solo gig at the 707. Maybe he was a protégé of Paul Morgenstern's—Paul was a decent producer, he knew a lot of people, and he had a reputation for wanting to give unknown musicians a leg up in the industry. Paul was a good bloke. He'd been around since the glory days of Bill Graham, mostly back on the East Coast, and he loved the music. It would be just his thing to have thought, okay, the Bombardiers need a front man, this front man needs a band—not exactly rocket science, get them together. The more I considered that, the more logical it sounded. After all, they were both from New York, and New Yorkers are clannish, especially the musicians.

He had to come from family money, did Vinny. If you added the likely cost of that Zemaitis to the cost of the PRS he'd been playing, and tweaked it with the twelve thousand dollars he'd been willing to shell out to Bruno Baines, we were talking close to a hundred thousand dollars. And Vinny hadn't earned that playing solo gigs at 707, or anywhere else. . . .

We got a lot done that afternoon. Vinny might not have been sure whether he loved the Zemaitis or not, but the rest of us thought it was wonderful. It had a very distinctive sound, and I'd been right about there being some heavy modifications to the electronics package. Maybe it was our enthusiasm or maybe it was the magic of the axe itself, but whatever it was, Vinny was playing well. He even took a suggestion from Damon that he ease back on his vocal punches to give it a more consistent balance with the established Bombardier style, and went with it. The result was a damned good take on the song.

At ten of seven, Damon looked at the oversized clock on the wall behind us. "Hey, guys—that's it for the day, okay? Great stuff. I need to set up for a download and CD burn. I'll have copies for everyone tomorrow."

I got up and stretched. Behind me, Rosario was expertly coiling cables and stowing Vinny's effects, while the Bombardier regulars did the same on their respective piles. The oversized sheaf of roses had been put in water to stop them wilting.

At seven exactly, I heard the triple-tone beep of our Jag's horn. I turned and grinned at Vinny.

"Right," I told him. "Showtime. Give me a minute and let me tell her what's going on."

I headed out the front door. Bree had the Jag in the loading area; she rolled down the window and craned her neck out for a kiss. I obliged her and took a deep breath.

"Look, Bree—a certain bloke whose nuts came out on the losing end of an encounter with your knee wants to apologise. He's also got a prezzie for you. Be warned—he really doesn't speak your language and he's clueless, but it's an apology, and they're very pricey roses. All right? Can you cope?"

She blinked at me. "I suppose. Hell, roses? You never buy me roses. I could use a nice cabana boy, for when you're on the road. Maybe I should bring him home and try to housebreak him? . . ." She ducked back, laughing, as I took a mock swipe at her. "Sure, bring him on, what the hell."

In the end, she shut down the Jag's engine and came inside. She hadn't been indoors at the Bombardiers' rehearsal space since they'd bought it twenty years earlier. She got a nice look around, but what I really wanted was for Vinny to get a good look at who she was, what she was, at the fact that she'd been known, liked, respected by my mates long before he ever got there. And—yeah, okay, right, might as well be truthful about it. I wanted him to get a good long look at what I had, and what he didn't. I like showing Bree off. Barnyard cock crowing, I am.

Bree played it perfectly. She was gracious, cool, elegant; she accepted his apology, made appreciative noises over the roses, exchanged some familiar conversation with the rest of the band, shook Damon's hand, and was nice to the roadies.

"Right," I said. "I'm hungry as a stray cat—it's well past time for my supper. I'll see everyone Wednesday."

One of the cruellest jokes the fates can play has got to be starting something out nice—and then suddenly slamming everyone involved. It's a nightmare thing, you know? If a dream starts off with making love in a green meadow with brilliant music playing somewhere and then turns dark, the horror's that much worse.

Tuesday night, we were having Bree's mum, Miranda, over for dinner. Bree was in a good mood, concentrating on her menu and assembling the ingredients. Her mum spent a lot of money putting her through culinary school, and Bree gets a special kick out of doing a perfect meal whenever Miranda's there to eat it. Besides, Miranda's got an insane schedule, and Bree doesn't trust her to stop for proper food.

I'd been out of the house most of the day, running a little errand of my own. I'd fixed it up ahead of time with Tony: The story, if Bree asked, was that Tony was looking at a new live recording rig, and he wanted my company and my opinion. Of course, she didn't ask, which was just as well. I'm a piss-poor liar.

What was actually going on was, I had a meeting with a jeweller about a ring, across the Bay Bridge, over in Berkeley. He'd been recommended to me through several people; apparently, this bloke did custom rings with precious stones and was the jeweller of choice for the wives of a few notables. I'd rung him up from the rehearsal space, when Bree wasn't around to overhear it, and set up the appointment. Tony offered to provide the wheels for me to get there, since obviously using my usual driver wasn't on for this one.

I already knew what I wanted for her, which helped, and I'd let the jeweller know in advance. A diamond was right out— Bree doesn't like them. She has a thing for emeralds. Actually, she rarely wears jewellery; hell, she doesn't even have pierced ears, but she says something about an emerald sings to her. When I asked her what, she thought for a moment and said, "The colour. Maybe the intensity. Maybe the flaws. Maybe how easily they can be damaged. Maybe everything. I just love them, John. I don't know why."

41

So I wanted an emerald, set into dull gold, with enough room on the band for a particular inscription. The jeweller, who turned out to be a nice old bloke about eighty years old with a very secure office up on the fourth floor of a downtown building, was ready for me. He'd pulled out three locked steel boxes that turned out to be full of envelopes containing loose stones, and set out a selection on little squares of black velvet. Everything, all the stones, had been sorted by size, clarity, flaws, price. It was all very ceremonial, very ritual.

I don't really know what sort of alchemy precious stones have got, but they've definitely got something, because the moment the right stone presented itself, I knew it. I'd picked up and looked at a good dozen other ones, and they were all nice pricey green rocks, but none of them said *Bree's, buy me now* to me. This one did.

It wasn't the biggest one, not by any stretch, just under a carat in weight, as it turned out. It had a visible flaw, a dark strange smudgy particle of carbon trapped inside that looked as if a thundercloud had been frozen in green ice. The flaw was along one facet, not in the middle. The stone was a very deep, weirdly mysterious green.

"That's it." I held out my hand. "That's the one. May I?"

He was smiling at me, and I got the impression I'd done something right, completely by accident. Without a word, he moved the callipers—he'd been holding the stone up to the light when I made my decision—and gently dropped the stone into the palm of my hand. It immediately warmed up my skin. None of the other stones had done that.

"Right," I said. "That's it. This is Bree's stone. Now, let's talk about setting it. . . ."

A damned good afternoon. If it wasn't making love in a green meadow with brilliant music, it came pretty close: I'd found her stone, I'd found the setting, I'd forked out a few thousand dollars, and I'd bought Tony lunch. I'd even been asked for an autograph in the restaurant parking lot.

Tony dropped me off at home a little while before dinnertime. I let myself into the house and stopped in my tracks, getting hit in the face with an incredible smell of cooking. The incredible smell was laced with Bree's voice. She was singing.

I stood there in the hall for a moment, just breathing in and listening, loving it. The smell was gorgeous. I never managed much interest in food before Bree, but I'd developed at least the ability to pick out individual smells over the years. So, I was able to identify a few of the mingled scents: lamb, cinnamon, something that was probably meat stock.

As nice as the smell was, the singing made me happier. Bree has a very distinctive speaking voice, dark and musical. In fact, she's an above-average singer, although not a trained one—a contralto, with a lot of strength behind it. There's smoke in there, and passion. It's not so much that she has a great singing voice as that she can sing—and yeah, trust me, there's a difference. I've come across people with technically perfect voices and four-octave ranges who sounded as sterile as a hospital operating theatre.

She was singing a favourite of mine, a wonderful old Hank Ballard tune, "Tore Up Over You." Our Victorian has fifteen-foot ceilings. The acoustics are tricky, but they're also impressive, and her voice was spiralling along the cornices and window fittings, all the way from the enormous kitchen at the back of the house. She sounded happy, which was an odd contrast, because the lyrics aren't. *"Ever since you've been gone / I just cry all night long. . . ."*

I slipped into the living room, grabbed the Martin acoustic I keep in a stand by my favourite rocking chair, and headed into the kitchen with it. I was tiptoeing, keeping quiet. She was still carolling away: *"Since the day you said good-bye / you hurt me so, no lie, no lie. . . ."*

43

She had her back to me. Whatever the lamb-and-cinnamon thing was, it was already bubbling away in the oven—that's why it smelled so strongly. She was prepping potatoes, peeling them with her favourite chef's knife at a terrifying speed, dropping the peelings into a tin, to be used as garden mulch later on. She had her slicing tool—she calls it a mandoline, but I've never been able to do that without feeling silly because, to a guitar player, a mandolin is something different—out on the work island by the window and was whipping the potatoes into disks so thin, you could see through them. *"Tore up over you and I just can't find my way. . . ."*

I perched quietly on one of the high stools by the door and settled the guitar in my lap. I wasn't about to make any noise while she was cutting, not with the knife, not with the wicked blade on the slicing tool, either. She could lose a finger that way. But the moment she stopped . . .

There was a buttered ceramic dish on the work island, and hot stock bubbling in a saucepan on the big Viking range. The kitchen—that's Bree's work zone, the way the studio or the stage is mine, and she's at home there and so professional, she can scare me. That's not a far-fetched comparison, either, between her cooking and my playing. I don't want to sound like a pompous prat, but music and cookery, they're both art forms. They both take a lot of concentration if you want to do either of them properly.

I saw some tart Granny Smith apples, already sliced as thin as the potatoes and macerating in lemon juice. I love that word, *macerating.* Bree'd told me that's what the lemon juice does, which is to stop things like apples and potatoes from going brown and discoloured in the air. There was also a glass bowl full of grated cheese. Right. Apples, potatoes, cheese—that meant she was making something she calls a *pommes savoyard*: apples, potatoes, stock, cheese, baked together in layers. In the window seat that overlooked our garden, two of our three cats—the two boys, Wolfling and Simon—watched her. Farrowen, sitting in the doorway with her tail curled round her feet, was watching me. Siamese are contrary, even for cats.

Bree began layering the ingredients in the dish. She was still singing: *"You never loved me like you told me so / If you did, how could you go?"*

Right. Safe now. I started playing, letting the guitar slip in under her voice, singing a bit of backup myself: *"It was you, not me, that left / And went away with someone else. . . ."*

She jumped and turned, laughing. "John! You scared the hell out of me—No, keep playing! *Tore up over you, and I just can't find my way. . . ."*

She's normally shy about doing anything musical around me, and that's despite the fact that she can play guitar herself, by ear, and piano as well. But she won't do it. So the times she does, I get a particular kick out that.

We finished the song, me doing a nice solid run with a metal slide in the middle, Bree waiting for the music to come back round to the verse again, layering apples and potatoes and cheese and boiling stock that—if I was smelling it properly—had been beaten with pureed roasted garlic. When the verse came back, I grinned at her, and she turned pale but she sang it, and so did I, backup, because her voice is much stronger than mine: *"Tell me what did I do / To make you go away? / Tell me what can I do / To make you come back to stay? / Tore up over you, and I just can't find my way. . . ."*

I got up, laughing, and snatched a quick kiss. "Hello, love. Let me go put the guitar back, yeah? This house smells absolutely brilliant—your mum's in for a treat. Lamb with something to do with cinnamon? And that pommes thing you make?"

"Lamb shanks braised in quatre épices. *Pommes savoyard*

45

with Gruyère cheese. And a salad, and bakery bread." She kissed me again. "Mmmmm. Hey. Hi."

Miranda showed up around six, straight from hospital; she was on duty that day. I took her coat and her doctor's bag and gave her a quick peck on the cheek.

"Hello, John." She allowed the peck and smiled at me. "Recovering from the tour all right? Not letting the wedding prep drive you too insane?"

"Yes to the recovery, no to the insanity. That's poor Bree's gig, thank goodness." I could hear Bree bustling around back in the kitchen, putting the finishing touches on dinner.

I've never been able to tell what Miranda Godwin was thinking. Bree resembles her mum physically, although Miranda is a Nordic-looking blonde and Bree is a redhead. I had no clue what Bree's dad had looked like—his chopper had been shot down in Vietnam when Bree was a toddler. He'd been an army medic, doing a volunteer tour in the dangerous days of the mid-sixties. Miranda had once let it slip that she'd gone out of her mind with grief and burned every picture she had of him, because she couldn't bear to have any around. That floored me, because she always struck me as having everything under complete control.

I wondered, sometimes, how much of him was there in Bree, reminding Miranda as her daughter grew up. Bree had got her height and long legs and deep-sunk eye sockets from her mum, but not the colouring; that dark auburn hair and the muddy green eyes, those hadn't come from Miranda. And the mobile way Bree's features moved—that wasn't Miranda, either. Dr. Godwin is elegant and unrevealing, pretty much all the time.

She followed me into the kitchen. Bree had just finished setting the table, and I bit back a crack of laughter, because she'd got Vinny's roses in a cut-glass vase, set out in the middle of all the best plates and cutlery and glasses.

"Mom! On call at the hospital today? I hope you're hungry—lamb shanks and a *savoyard*."

"Hello, sweetheart. Yes, I'm ravenous, and of course, you never let me down with food, ever." Miranda hugged her daughter, but it was a light, fast hug. Neither woman is big on that sort of contact. If Bree wants a hug, something serious is going down somewhere. It's just not her thing.

Dinner was as good as I'd expected, as good as Miranda had expected. The cats circled our ankles, were shooed off, and found corners to sulk in; the conversation went from Miranda's new colleague on the Mission Bells Clinic board of directors to the Bombardier rehearsal sessions to Bree's announcement that she was getting really tired of wedding planning, and couldn't find anywhere appropriate to host it, and had trying to plan a simple secular wedding always been this complicated?

From there, we somehow fetched up on the boggy ground of what had happened on the tour I'd just finished with Blacklight. Stone-faced or not, it was obvious that my about-to-be mama-in-law had something on her mind. Bree noticed it as well, because her shoulders had hunched up. Finally, between bites of salad and lamb, I lifted an eyebrow at Miranda.

"Okay," I told her. "You've got that crease between your eyes, and your voice has gone careful. Did you want more about what happened? Perry Dillon's murder? Cilla's suicide? Come on, Miranda, spit it out. Let's get it over, all right?"

She lifted an eyebrow of her own back at me. Between us, Bree had gone very tense. The bruise she'd got trying to control my wife, who'd been deep into heroin withdrawal and thrashing about, hadn't completely faded from her cheekbone yet—it was nearly gone, and she was hiding it under makeup, but it was still there, faintly. If you knew where to look, you could still see an echo of it.

"You're very observant sometimes." Miranda tilted her

head, looking at me, not at Bree. "I do have a question, not about what happened, but on a related issue. This is something you may not have had time to think about yet. It's probably none of my business, though."

"Mom—"

"No, love, it's all right." I held a hand up, and Bree stilled. "I can't imagine you being nosey parker for the fun of it, Miranda. What might I not have had time to think about yet?"

"Well." She buttered a heel of sourdough. "I know—I always knew—that you'd let your wife live in the London house you bought together. That's right, isn't it?"

Bree's hands were balled into tight fists on the table; she keeps her nails short, but I could see skin going white as she dug in. Christ, it was ridiculous. Cilla was dead, done, over, and here was Bree, about to marry me, and she still locked up hard at the mere mention of what had been. How long before she got clear of it? Just how much damage had I done over a quarter century of inertia, not wanting to deal with the expense and unpleasantness of a divorce?

I reached out and lifted one of her hands to my lips, and kissed it. She managed to breathe a bit and pick up her glass, and I nodded at Miranda.

"Yeah, that's right. Cilla had the London house. I had an account set up, to pay monthly costs and make sure she had an income—" My own eyes suddenly went wide as I got to where Miranda'd been leading me. "Bloody hell!"

"Ah." Miranda was smiling. "I thought so. There's an account you need to have a look at, and make arrangements for, because otherwise you're pouring money every month into— what? A home and income for someone who no longer exists?"

She took a sip of water. "Don't look so harrowed, Bree. John really does need to think about this, and so do you, if you're really about to become legally married in the State of California. It becomes your money, not just John's."

"You're right. I'm damned glad you reminded me—I'd forgot all about that, and the money's been piling up in the account." I grinned at Miranda. Tell you the truth, I was just grateful that she'd managed to get Bree to chill after tensing her up in the first place. "Half my worldly goods, and there's quite a lot of worldly goods, there. Bree, love, it's not going to be a big complicated deal, yeah? It's just you and me, now."

"Exactly." Miranda took a bite of her bread. "Much simpler than it would be for a full family. After all, it's not as if there are children getting support. That would have been a very different matter. If you and Cilla had had any children, or if Bree hadn't miscarried, that would have added a lot of financial levels to it. But as it is—"

She stopped dead. My face must have given it away. Maybe Bree's face did as well.

I heard a small harsh rasp of sound as all the air went out of Bree. Her hand opened, and the glass crashed to the flagstone kitchen floor, shattering, spraying bits of crystal. Wolfling and Simon jumped, hissing and spitting, and disappeared through the swinging doors.

Lovemaking, a green meadow, brilliant music playing. And then the dream turns horrid.

I heard my own voice, very quiet, not sounding like me at all. "What? What miscarriage? What the hell are you talking about?"

Bree was on her feet. Without a word, she was gone, fled, out of the kitchen and up the stairs. I heard the distant echo of the bedroom door as it slammed behind her.

"Damn." Miranda's voice shook a bit. "It never occurred to me she hadn't told you. She promised me she would. Dear God.

John, I'm so sorry. I would never have said anything if I'd thought you didn't know. This has to be a horrible shock—"

"When?" I should get up, I thought, go upstairs, make sure she was okay. I couldn't, not yet. My legs were gone, dead, not up to holding me. "When was this?"

"Why are you asking me?" There was trouble in her face. "Bree should be the one to tell you, not me."

"Yeah, she should. But she didn't, did she?" Control, I thought, stop the voice shaking, at least, even if the legs won't cooperate. "And now that you've spilled it, the coy deal won't fly. Damage is done, you know? I want some answers. When?"

"The morning of her eighteenth birthday." Miranda's voice was cold, very remote. It bit, hard and deep. "Seven weeks after she heard you being interviewed on the radio, inviting her to the Candlestick show you played. Do you remember that, John? She didn't come home that night. And your group was touring—I seem to recall you had another six weeks' worth of shows, and then you went home to London, presumably to your wife. It never occurred to me you didn't know. Are you going upstairs? You should."

"She never told me." I was numb, and shivering. "Do you honestly think I wouldn't have come straight back if I'd known? What sort of monster do you take me for? Jesus, Miranda! I may be lazy, but I'm not cruel. You ought to know me better."

I sucked down air; my heart was doing very odd things. I must have given it away somehow, because Miranda was suddenly up, feeling my pulse, feeling my brow. I tried to pull away.

"Stop acting like a melodramatic baby," she snapped at me. "Don't move. You had a heart attack a month ago and you've got multiple sclerosis. You're a very bad colour. My bag's in the hall—I'm getting my scope. I said, don't move! Just take even breaths, not too deep—in, out, easy. Try not to pant. Good. I'll be right back—keep it going."

I closed my eyes. There was a sickness at the pit of my stomach, wondering, how many more things? How many more secrets, lying in wait for us like land mines? Why hadn't she told me?

I felt something cold press against my chest, and my eyes popped open. Miranda listened to my heart for a minute.

"It's slowing down. Good." She put the scope away. "John, talk to her. I'm the one who dropped the brick, true, but you two are the couple. You need to cope. I don't usually give advice, but you have to get it out in the open air. You can't have these big secrets from each other. Go talk to her."

"She won't thank me for talking right now." Was she up there in tears? Was the door locked? My stomach turned over.

"To hell with her thanks. Don't give her a vote." That got my attention; she sounded angry. "John, I'm probably the most hands-off parent on earth, but I'm telling you, get up there, if your legs will hold you up. If they won't, I'll go up there and drag her down if I have to."

She meant it; I could tell. Experimentally, I put some weight on my legs—they shook, talked to me for few seconds, a few more seconds' worth of ataxia, and then I steadied myself and nodded at her. "Right. Okay. I'll go up."

"Go. I'll let myself out." She kissed my cheek lightly, surprising me. "It seems I've been unfair to you, all this time. My mistake. I'm sorry, John. I should have known better. Go talk to Bree. Tell her I said good night, and thank her for dinner."

I took the stairs very slowly. Upstairs, the house was silent. There was no noise at all. I tried the knob on the bedroom door, and it swung open.

Memory, bloody memory. She was sitting in her rocking chair, the mate to mine. Mine's downstairs in the front room, but Bree's lives up here. She'd sat in that same chair, with that same look on her face, hands folded in her lap, eighteen years old, listening to me tell her that my wife was ill and needed me, and that I had to go.

Eighteen years old, a couple of months shy of nineteen. I'd been gone for nearly seven months. I'd missed her nineteenth birthday, just like I'd missed her eighteenth birthday. And apparently, on her eighteenth birthday . . .

I didn't stop to think. It didn't seem a good moment for thinking, you know? I just walked up behind the chair, bent, laid my cheek against her hair, and draped both arms over her shoulders.

"I would have been here." The house was quiet; we seemed cocooned in our own history, like a pair of butterflies. "Please tell me you know that. All you had to do was tell me—I'd have been here."

"I do know." Her hands came up, and covered mine. "I've always known. It just—I can't explain. I thought about telling you, when I found out I was pregnant. But it seemed so—so damned *dishonourable*, somehow. Emotional blackmail, just so manipulative. Hey, Mister Guitar Player Rock Star guy, you bagged yourself a virgin and she got knocked up first time out, forget the tour and the fact that you're married to someone else, just drop everything else and come back and deal with it."

I stayed quiet. She sighed. "My mother talks too much about stuff that doesn't concern her."

"Was it very bad?" Another memory, another moment of horror: my London house, a scream from the kitchen, Cilla lying in a pool of her own blood, Cilla herself writhing in pain . . . "Don't lie to me, love, okay? I wasn't there at the time, but I can carry my share of the memory for you. Pass it along, will you? Please? I'm right here."

"It was pretty grim, yes." The room was darkening around us, twilight becoming night, stars popping up out over the Golden Gate. Bree felt relaxed under my hands, almost limp.

52

"I'd known for about two weeks—I was scared shitless about telling Mom, but of course she guessed. I probably looked different, or smelled different, or something. I ended up telling her, and we had the Talk—you know the one, or no, you probably don't. Anyway, she asked me what I wanted to do, what my choice was. There were pros to keeping it, and cons, and she pointed all that out. I never dreamed of not keeping it. I don't know why—it's not as if I wanted a baby. And I knew that at some point, I'd have to tell you. God, I hated that idea, just hated it."

I was silent, holding her, touching her. She wasn't tense at all; the calm was genuine. The most good I could ever do for this, it seemed, was to shut up and listen, and just be there.

"Mom backed me up, of course. She'd have backed up any choice I made. But she told me I had to tell you, and I said I would. She was on call at the hospital on my birthday—she was still serving her suspension from the Clinic—so she took me out for a movie the night before. We saw *The Elephant Man*. She left for the hospital early, I remember that. School ended early that year, graduation was June tenth, and it was nearly July."

Behind me, the door clicked open; I hadn't closed it properly. Farrowen stalked in and jumped into Bree's lap.

"I'd been trying to figure out how to let you know. I was in bed, sleeping in, just being lazy, and all of a sudden I got this cramp, really sharp." She was stroking Farrowen with one hand, and I heard the Siamese begin to purr, a soothing rattle of sound. "A spasm, like I'd suddenly been jabbed with something, inside the right thigh. I sat up and then everything felt cold and wet and I realised I was sitting in a puddle of liquid, blood, other stuff. It was a mess. I ruined everything, the mattress, sheets, blankets, everything."

She looked at me in the dimness. Her voice was very gentle. "Do you really need to hear this, John?"

"I think I do, yeah." She felt quiescent as a cat herself. I wondered how hard-earned this peace was, if it was even real. "The fact that you'd gone through this whole thing, never said a word, and a year later Cilla demanded that I come back for a similar thing, and I went— No, never mind. Go on, Bree."

"There isn't really much more. I remember I doubled up. It hurt like hell, and I couldn't get much air into my lungs, but I yelled for Mom, but I was alone in the house. I called her at the hospital—it took forever to get downstairs to the phone, I was bleeding in waves and every step felt as if I was being kicked. I was scared half out of my mind and I thought I was dying. It turned out there was some sort of malformation or something on one ovary—they knocked me out and removed it the next day, the ovary I mean, because it had a really high cancer risk. They told me it was unlikely I'd ever be able to carry a baby to term."

I was silent. There really wasn't anything to say, you know? Nothing to be done, either.

Bree leaned her head back against me and sighed, a good deep sigh, enough air to draw a small protest from the Siamese in her lap. "Good thing I never really wanted one, anyway, not after you came back." She sounded genuinely at peace. "Honestly. You're all I've ever needed."

CHAPTER FOUR

"On the downbeat, eight bars. Take four on 'Liplock'—JP and Billy, lead it in. One—two—three—four—"

Four bars of guitar, my Goldtop for this one, hard slamming boogie in a D–A progression, heavily rhythmic, the sort of bite to the music that starts out in the groin and ends there as well. Four bars and there was Billy's drum snapping into it, like towels drying on the line on a windy day, or maybe a pair of hips, either dancing or doing someone, rhythmic and hard. Four more bars and here came the bass and the piano together. It needed a good harmonica, I thought, maybe Jack Carter wailing away as a ramp-up to Vinny's vocal. I made a mental note to bring that up with Tony.

"Mama, pretty mama, honey lock your lips on me." Vinny was in damned good voice today. The lyric was gritty as hell, verging on actually dirty, and he was going with it, not trying for

his usual sob-for-the-drama rubbish. *"Slide 'em down lower, I'll be yellin' like a banshee. . . ."*

I caught Tony's eye. God bless music, man. He'd known something was wrong, something was off—Bree was getting the Jag serviced, and so Tony had picked me up instead. He hadn't asked me any questions. He never did. But he'd known, and we drove over to Freelon Street in complete quiet.

He did ask me if everything was okay, as he was helping me unload, and I nodded. "Just something from a long time ago, that I hadn't heard before," I told him. "Everything's fine."

I hoped that was true. The more I looked at things, the more I realised that the load Bree'd been carrying for me all these years might easily have broken her back.

So I was lying, and he probably knew it. Tony knows me, after all; outside of Luke, he's probably the closest male friend I've got. But once we got into working out the song, and the notes started pumping, and Vinny brought the heat into the vocal, we were all together, you know? It was right there, hot and cold, me teasing little snarling bits of sex into it, Kris catching the smoke in the guitar's contrail and turning the bass line into something that, musically, was just as much about the pump of hips as it was about holding down the bottom.

Bless music, man. It keeps me alive; it keeps me sane. There are days I think it keeps my heart beating.

I caught an edge, something in the progression up the Paul's neck, a sort of musical sidestep, and ran with it, kicking in the stomp box I had in the Paul's setup: an Ibanez Tube Screamer. If you want dark and dirty, the old screamers are perfect toys.

The Paul went gritty, biting deep, and heads turned, Tony grinning like a madman, Vinny smacking some serious rhythm lines—he'd swapped back to his PRS today, and the Zemaitis was nowhere in sight—against a cascading piano run. We hit the chorus, and Vinny came back in: *"Lock 'em on me low, there's a fire down below, lock me down, honey, take it deep, take it slow. . . ."*

We finished the song. This was the fourth take, and honestly, it was going to be tricky matching this one, much less topping it. If we could pull this off during the actual recording sessions, the Bombardiers were going to have a major contender for the suits at their record label.

"Fantastic!" Damon was on his feet, pumping a thumbs-up at us. "Guys, that was really intense. Vinny, perfect vocal—and JP, man, where in hell did that line come from? That was, like, total sex. So hot, dude. It kicked some serious, serious ass."

"It really did cook, didn't it? I wonder if getting Jack in, laying down mouth harp, might really kick it over the top. Just something to think about. And Vinny, might be interesting to give the Zemaitis a listen on this one, yeah?" I stretched and looked over at Damon. "I need to take pills. Break, all right? What time is it?"

Kris set the bass in its stand and stretched. "Half past six. Damn, time flies when you're rocking out, doesn't it? Vinny, I'm with JP—I really want to hear what the Zemaitis does on this one. Groin power! I like that mean little rhythm curl you did—you know, when JP did that double back-strum? . . ."

I got up, heading for my jacket. Before I could go anywhere, one of the Bombardier roadies was there with a bottle of cold spring water. "Here you go, JP. And here's your coat."

"Ta." I swallowed my pills, hoping they'd kick in fast. There was a tingle in my right leg, an ominous painful twitch. It brought back the memory of a bad morning in New York a few weeks ago, dragging myself from a bench in Central Park to my hotel on a leg that didn't even want to point the foot in the right direction, an episode of motor control loss that had scared me badly. I turned to Damon.

"Look, it's only half an hour to stopping anyway, and I've

gone achy as hell. I didn't get much sleep last night and the MS is letting me know all about it. Would anyone mind if I bagged it for the night? No, Tony, not to worry, I'll ring Bree—she'll have the Jag back by now. You stow your gear and go take Katia out to dinner or something. I'll pack up my guitars and be ready when Bree gets here."

"Good call." Damon was loading a blank CD into the Korg. "Let me start on the burns—just that last version for now. JP, we'll have copies in fifteen minutes. That work for you?"

"Yeah, sounds good. Cheers, mate." One ring, two, three . . . I rubbed my right leg, felt it wanting to buckle, and swore under my breath. "Come *on*, Bree, answer the phone. . . ."

"Sorry, John." She got it just before the voice mail kicked in. Her voice was breathless, a bit strange. "I was in the bathroom, and the phone wasn't. How was rehearsal? Did you take your meds?"

"Yeah, I took my meds, but we knocked off early. My right leg's gone iffy on me, and I'm not feeling too well, actually. Can you come get me, love? I know Tony was going to do it, but if you don't mind—or I can get a taxi."

"Of course I'll come get you." She sounded distracted. "Give me a few minutes, and I'm on my way."

I put the Paul away and coiled the cables; the effects boxes had already been put away by the roadies. Tony had virtually nothing to do, since the keyboards don't get moved, and Kris and Vinny had left their axes on the stands. There was something solid and comforting about the old P Bass with its worn spots in the finish, but it was pretty drab next to the PRS. The dragon inlays were gleaming under the lights, and the blue glaze on the body looked like water moving. It really was a gorgeous guitar. I found myself wishing Luke could get a butcher's at it—he's a huge fan of PRS axes. It would have been right up his street.

Damon had finished burning the master CD and had begun the duplications for the band. I spared a moment to remember the old days of rehearsal, when recording a session meant a lot more work than it was now, with servers and CD duplicating devices and programmable software options.

Bree arrived about twenty minutes later, just as Damon was handing us copies of the CD. Right—synchronicity. The Jag has a great sound system; I'd pop the CD in on the way home, give it a listen, play it for Bree, see if it sounded as good as I thought it did.

"Right," I said, "here's my ride. See everyone—when? Saturday, is it? Okay. Night, all."

Bree loved the song. We played it on the way home, and then, once we'd got home and pulled the Jag into the garage, we turned the car speakers up high and sat in the car, listening to it again. The garage is pretty thoroughly soundproofed; it has to be, because I've got a recording studio in the back half of the basement. In Pacific Heights, there are noise ordinances, and anyway, you don't want to piss off the neighbours.

I was being very careful with my old lady right then. Things were fragile—in fact, Bree was fragile—and I'd never once thought of her that way, not in all our time together. There were some huge gaps in our early days, things I had no clue about. I was beginning to realise that some of those gaps might be wider and deeper than I'd thought.

Finding out about the miscarriage had been a gut punch. But in a way, finding out that Miranda—who'd lost her job for two years because Bree insisted on trying to protect me when I was helpless—had thought I was capable of the cruelty to abandon her pregnant teenage daughter was even worse. I may not have a lot of moral courage, but I've got enough to know she wouldn't have thought me capable of it if I hadn't given her some solid reasons to do just that. It was a shitty feeling. I couldn't help wondering what else had happened while I was on the road, in detox, fighting with Immigration, drinking too much, separating from Cilla and London, bouncing back and forth like a damned refugee. . . .

"John?" Bree was behind me, rubbing my shoulders. "Honey, you should wake up if you plan on getting any sleep later."

I'd taken my aching leg to my favourite chair, and apparently I'd fallen asleep for an hour. She'd been quiet while I dozed, keeping the telly off, letting me rest. She was right, though. If I dozed much longer, I was in for a restless night.

"Do you want tea?" She massaged the base of my neck, finding the knot that always seemed to be there after I'd been playing one of the Pauls these days, teasing it out with her fingertips. "I was thinking about something herbal. I didn't sleep very well last night, and I don't want a repeat."

I knew she'd slept badly. I'd lain awake a long time myself, going over our early days, times together and apart, trying to see where the holes were, what else might be waiting to jump out at us. She fell asleep before me, but she'd been restless, turning, muttering in her sleep.

"Love some tea," I told her. "I'll come keep you company. Have we got any decaf Earl Grey? And maybe heat up some of that lamb from last night? I didn't get dinner—I could eat."

The tea must have been what was needed, because I was out within moments of kissing her good-night. I was still out at ten the next morning, when my cell rang. Bree jumped out of bed and took it out in the hall so that the conversation wouldn't disturb me.

She was gone for only a minute. I heard an exclamation, bitten off; whatever else she said, she kept her voice low. Then she was back, standing next to my side of the bed, her face even paler than usual, her hair wild and messy.

"John." She was controlling her voice, and the green eyes were wide with shock. "John—it's Tony. It's—he says . . ."

Her voice died. She swallowed hard. I sat up fast, reaching for the phone. Good job I got it when I did, because her fingers were too limp to hold it.

"JP? Is that you?" His voice was barely recognisable. "Oh Jesus, thank God."

"Tony? Crikey, mate, what's wrong?"

"Jesus. Oh man. I just got a call from the cops. Damon went down to Freelon Street this morning." He stopped, his breath ragged and uneven. "He walked in and found Vinny. John— he's dead, man. Vinny's dead. Someone bashed his head in with his own guitar."

Not five minutes after I'd swung myself out of bed and into a hot shower, Bree was answering my cell phone again.

I thought Bree had already gone downstairs to get coffee going, when I heard the ringtone on the phone. I was just turning off the water and swearing when I heard the bathroom door open. Bree's voice came through the steam.

"Hello? Patrick! Hey! Good morning, how are you? How's New York treating you—? What?"

That got my attention. The only Patrick we knew in New York was Patrick Ormand, the police lieutenant who'd originally pegged Bree for murdering Blacklight's unofficial biographer during our last American tour. We'd got lucky—he turned out to be a huge fan of the band, and once he'd figured out that Bree hadn't killed the bloke, he decided he liked us, or at least that he liked Bree. The result had been that he'd done his best to keep the signal-to-noise ratio down. We owed him for that; he could have played it for publicity, you know? Controversial victim, world-famous rockers—the case had all the elements of fifteen minutes of fame for him, but he hadn't gone that road. If he had, the media circus would have been ten times as bad as it had been.

Last time we'd seen him, he'd been visiting the Bay Area during the band's tour closer at Oakland. We'd put him on the guest list. So far as I knew, we hadn't heard from him since. I hadn't, anyway.

"But . . ." Bree stopped, listening. "Wow. Just—wow. Look, hang on a minute—John's about to climb out of the shower. I think you'd better talk to him. Hold on."

I climbed out and lifted an eyebrow. She held the phone out to me. She had a really peculiar look on her face.

"It's Patrick Ormand. He wants a word with you."

"Right." I took the phone from her. "Good morning. Look, can you hang on half a minute? I need to pat myself dry."

"Of course."

Two minutes, and I was dressed, if still a bit damp round the edges. "Okay. So, Bree said you wanted a word with me. What's going on, then?"

"Official business, I'm afraid." It was genuinely weird, hearing his voice on the phone again, weird and unsettling. He sounded just the same as he had when he'd been the copper in charge of the Perry Dillon murder: same southern drawl thing going on, same neutrality, not giving anything away. I'll probably never be comfortable with this particular voice at the other end of the line. "I was wondering if I could take up an hour of your time and get some information about the case. I'll probably also need to get a statement signed."

"Information about what?" What in hell was he on about? "I thought the entire episode was over. I mean, you have Cilla's confession on tape, and we've signed all the statements. What else could you possibly need?"

There was something in his voice that I couldn't quite pinpoint. Apology? Amusement? "Not that case. Oh, damn, that's

62

right, I don't think I've spoken to you two in a few weeks. I'm not with NYPD anymore. When you saw me in Oakland, I was out here for an interview with SFPD. I'd been back and forth with them for nearly six months—they finally decided I'd work out. So here I am. I just told Ms. Godwin—didn't she tell you?"

"Gordon *Bennett*! No, she didn't." My jaw had gone slack. "So, what? You've transferred, or whatever the word is?"

"Nah, not a transfer. This is a straight job change. SFPD Homicide likes my particular skill set—even though it took them half a year to decide that. They liked my background, too. They've put me in charge of the Fabiano murder. They seem to think I have easier access to you guys than anyone else on the squad would have, and that I can expect more cooperation. So . . ."

I burst out laughing.

I know, totally inappropriate. Honestly, though, I couldn't help myself. Looking up, I caught Bree's eye; she was grinning and shaking her head. I got some control over it after a minute.

"That's bleedin' amazing. Look, do we need to come down there, wherever there is? Because I took a huge scunner to cop shops back in New York, and if I don't have to go near one, I'm damned if I'm going to. Tell you what, hang on." I covered the phone. "Bree, he's SFPD now, and he's doing Vinny's murder. He has questions. Can we have him over?"

She was reaching for her shoes. "Home court? Hell yes. I was going to suggest it. Ask him if he'd like some lunch. I wonder what homicide cops eat?"

He showed up about an hour later. I don't know that I'd ever really bothered to take a look at the bloke, beyond a pair of very chilly light eyes and teeth that had seemed more suited to the wolf who'd munched up Red Riding Hood's grandmother.

Part of the problem was that whole thing about first impressions being the ones that stick. When we first came across him, he was in pure predator mode, a hyena chasing a gazelle, and the gazelle in question was my old lady. All I saw when I looked at Patrick Ormand was danger. He'd seemed rather more humanised back at Blacklight's Oakland show, in jeans and a T-shirt, but I'd been busy at Oakland, between dodging reporters and Blacklight closing the tour and having Bree ask me to marry her, and hadn't paid him much attention.

When I let him in, he was in the same sort of nondescript suit I'd come to associate with detectives—the kind of gear that makes me think they all must shop at the same chain. And even though he didn't seem nearly so watchful as he'd been back when Bree was a suspect in Perry Dillon's death, I still found myself guarded. There's something about the suit that acted as a kind of camouflage, at least for me—you saw the persona, not the person behind it.

The reality was a good-looking bloke right around Bree's age, compact and a bit fine-boned, brown hair beginning to recede at the temples, and those chilly-dirty eyes. It would have been a help to be able to put a name to the colour, but what colour is winter sidewalk ice?

His first comment, when I opened the door and shook hands with him, might have been designed to ease off the barriers.

"Jesus," he said, and looked around our entry hall. "My entire apartment would fit in your hall. This is incredible! Is this a Victorian? I'm new to the Bay Area, so forgive the dumb questions. But, wow, this place is beautiful."

"Yeah, 2828's a classic Vic. It was built in 1888. It's what's considered a Grand Victorian, specifically a Queen Anne style—did you notice the curved towers on both sides? We took one look at the place and bought it, probably for less than a three-bedroom condo in Hunters Point would cost today. That was back in 1981. Bree's in the kitchen—she's getting some lunch together for us."

He followed me down the hall, stopping to look at the huge double parlour, the enormous formal dining room, the crown mouldings over the doors, the curve of the solid mahogany stairs leading up to the five bedrooms. Wolfling came around a corner, stopped and stared, and then curled between Ormand's ankles.

"Hey, there." Ormand stopped, bent, and scratched Wolfling under the chin. He hit precisely the right spot, and Wolfling rattled for a moment, purring, closing his eyes. This was someone who knew cats, and got them. That made it even harder to keep the sort of distance I wanted. "Are you King of All Tabby Toms? You're a very handsome guy."

"Come on, Wolfling, stop trying to seduce the nice policeman, okay? He's the king tabby, yeah, but that's because he's the only tabby. But he thinks he's king of all cats. Of course, the reality is, he can't compete with Bree's Siamese, and Simon, the third cat, is too dim to notice. So we let him believe whatever he wants, and leave shattering his illusions up to the other cats." I led the way back to the kitchen. "Bree! Company, love."

We had lunch out in the back garden, in the gazebo. Bree had put together cold cracked crab, a dressing with fresh garlic and the juice from lemons off one of our trees, warm bread in a basket, and salad from our own vegetable beds. She offered Ormand wine—even as a reformed drinker, I was safe around wine. It never appealed to me in the first place, and it was the only booze of any sort we ever had in the house, that and the bubbly, which is the only alcohol Bree's willing to touch.

After lunch, she got us coffee and accepted compliments on the food from both of us without a blink. That's one thing I never do, take her cooking skills for granted. It would be dead easy, and as I was learning the hard way, she'd probably let me do it and never once call me on it. But I was in no danger of messing up on that one, believe me. I've eaten too much road food to ever not know just how good I have it at home. Besides,

I love watching our friends' reactions to what she cooks. People knowing how cool my old lady is makes me happy.

"Okay." I stretched my legs out, relaxing into the afternoon. "So, let's get down to business, all right? I didn't get any details about what happened—you rang me up just a few minutes after Tony Mancuso did, to let me know, and he hasn't rung us back. All I know, so far, is what Tony told me, which is that Damon— that's the Bombardiers' sound engineer, Damon Gelb—had gone down to Freelon Street this morning, business as usual, and found Vinny dead in the studio. He said someone had smacked Vinny over the head with his own guitar. Is that right?"

"Bare bones—but, yes, that's it. First off, can I ask you a couple of questions?"

I felt myself stiffen up. He must have seen it, because he held up one hand. "No, literally, just questions. I'm not asking for anything in the way of gossip. But a few simple facts, that would save me a lot of confirming of the information I've already collected. You can always tell me to shove it if you think I'm being too personal."

"Right." I grinned at him. "I will, too. Carry on."

"Thanks. First things first, I already have statements about times yesterday—that is, what time rehearsal ended, who left in what order—but if you could confirm? . . ."

"We quit at half past six." I was thinking back, trying to be as precise as possible. "We'd been working on a particular song, and we'd got a brilliant version recorded. Normally we might have gone an hour or so longer, but there was no point. We were happy with the version we'd done, and anyway, it was very late in the day to start working on a new one. That gave Damon plenty of time to burn CDs of it for us. I was feeling pretty dodgy, so I suggested we call it a day. The rest of it—well, sorry, mate. I can't help you with that, I'm afraid. I was first one out. Bree picked me up—I don't drive."

"Great, thanks. Now, the studio itself—who owns it? We could easily spend a full day tracking down a landlord, but—"

"The band does. The Bombardiers. They bought it—crikey, when was it, Bree? Back around 1983 or so. Back then, the area was an industrial wasteland. You wouldn't know that now, of course, not with the ballpark a few blocks away. It's gone very gentrified and upscale. They couldn't afford to buy the studio now, not in today's market."

"It's an interesting part of town." Ormand accepted a plate of pastries from Bree and took one. "I work at Homicide, which seems to be right in the middle of it—we're at Seventh and Bryant. When the call came in about Freelon Street this morning, we were maybe three minutes away by car. So, the Bombardiers own it? Good. You're sure?"

"Hell yeah. We had a party there, to celebrate the acquisition—it was one of Bree's first professional catering gigs. Anton found the place, and the entire band kicked in some dosh for a down payment. I think the actual purchase price was something like seventy thousand dollars, and they were all freaked at taking on such a huge debt load, especially already owing their record label."

"Anton? I don't think I've heard that name."

"Anton Hall, the Bombardiers' founder and lead vocalist. He died of liver disease a few months back."

"He's the guy Vinny Fabiano replaced." Bree, who'd been listening in silence, spoke up. "Anton drank himself to death, basically. Not uncommon in this industry, Lieutenant— Damn, I have no idea if I just dropped a brick or not. Do we still call you Lieutenant?"

"Nah, call me Patrick, both of you. We can always get official again if we need to, right?" He settled back in his chair. "So what you're saying is, this guy Vinny Fabiano was a relative newcomer to this particular group? Is that right?"

"Newcomer? Yeah, definitely—they'd seen his solo act a couple of days after Anton died, and for whatever reason, they asked him to front the band. I've been rehearsing with them because they asked me to sit in on a few songs. Between the original members of the band breaking in Vinny, and me guesting, I'm amazed the rehearsals have been as shit-free as they have been. He's also a newcomer locally. I don't know that anyone really knew him up until a few months back. He's—he was—a transplanted New Yorker."

"Good to know. I can set some wheels turning back East and see what we come up with at that end."

I had a sudden chilly moment, envisioning all the wheels within wheels, the grind of the state machinery. Not for the first time, I got just how bloody lucky we'd been that my wife had opted for a way out that didn't involve lethal injection.

"Was he easy to deal with? On a personality level, I mean."

I opened my mouth, and closed it again. Patrick caught my look. "I'm not asking for specifics, JP, just basic personality stuff. My problem is, I know nothing about this guy. I've got his corpse, with a guitar-shaped dent in the skull, and I have no way of knowing who might have wanted to sock him with a guitar. If he was a mellow, easygoing guy, it's going to make my job easier, if a bit more interesting. Was he?"

"He was a menace." I grinned at Patrick. "Sorry, mate. If you want me to sugarcoat it because he's dead, you're out of luck. He was loud, conceited, self-absorbed, he made no attempt to adjust his style to the band who'd just hired him, because he honestly believed the entire universe should be adjusting to him, he treated women as if they were trash or property or commodities who ought to be ready to drop their knickers for—"

I stopped suddenly. Inside, I was cursing. What was it about Patrick Ormand that always made me say too much?

Bree, managing a smile, reached out and patted my hand.

"It's okay, John. I was about to suggest I tell him anyway. God knows, there were enough witnesses. I'd rather have him hear it from me."

She looked up at Patrick. He was watching, looking back and forth between us. If he'd set a trap, if he already knew all about it and was trying to catch us out, he was a brilliant actor; he just looked puzzled and interested. Bree took a deep breath and met his eye.

"I suppose—if the amount of mousehole-watching you did after Perry Dillon was killed is anything to go by—that you're going be asking around, seeing who'd had disagreements with him recently. Right?"

He nodded.

"Well," she told him, "let me save you some trouble. Last Saturday night, we went to a party in Sausalito—it was a house that belongs to a guy called Paul Morgenstern. He owns a club in Marin, where a lot of the local bands play. John had gone hunting in the crowd for some chairs and I went to load up a couple of plates at the buffet."

Patrick waited. Bree patted my hand again; I must have looked worried or something. "Anyway, Vinny came up behind me and grabbed me—I mean, grabbed me, solid grip on my ass. He was reaching around front with the other hand. I told him he moved his hand or I cut his nuts off and wore them as earrings. I was not amused."

"Jesus." Patrick gave a long whistle. "No, I can see how you wouldn't be. What happened?"

"He took a swing at me, a real swing, full fist. John was halfway across the room, trying to get through the hordes. Vinny was looking to inflict some serious damage and show me who was boss. So I kneed him in the balls."

"You—um—so, what? Kicked him?" Ormand was staring at Bree with a new respect. "Did it work?"

"Kneed him, good and hard. It's the old reliable standby: You grab the asshole by the shoulders, jerk him forward, and bring the knee up. I sort of had to—the top of John's head was about to explode. I figured nailing Vinny myself would calm things down, and it did."

Ormand opened his mouth, and closed it again. He looked absolutely fascinated.

Bree went on, sounding serene. "Don't get all excited over it, though. It's a nonissue and a nonmotive. He showed up at rehearsal day before yesterday with an armful of really expensive white roses—Vendelas, I think they are. Three dozen, and they probably set him back about a hundred bucks. As an apology, it really wasn't something I could refuse. Besides, I don't do stuff that's likely to make John's job trickier, and since the rest of the guys in the band wanted John to sit in, smoothing it over was the only way to go. John came out and gave me the heads-up when I picked him up at Freelon Street the other night. He asked if I could cope, and I said sure. I went in and made gracious lady noises, Vinny grovelled, and that was that—end of story. Anyway, I'd already kicked his ass publicly. The swing he took at me didn't connect, but my knee?" She smiled sweetly at Ormand. "That connected. Oh, man, did it connect."

"From the sound of it, this guy might have had people lining up for the pleasure of playing El Kabong on his cranium." Ormand's head had tilted over to one side. "Did he do that a lot? Grabbing women and trying to deck them when they objected?"

"He didn't know I was John's old lady." Bree made a face. "The thing is, he had no clue. Did he, John? He was just totally clueless when it came to dealing with people. There was no point getting outraged at him, because he just didn't speak Civilised Human Male language. He honestly saw his behaviour towards me as an offence against John's property. And he was scared to death of John, what with John being a rock star, and Vinny himself being nobody that anyone had ever heard of."

"Right." I decided it was time to grab the reins. "Look, Lieutenant—Patrick, I mean—tit for tat, yeah? What the hell happened? I actually am concerned in this, and not just because they're my mates. This is going to put the Bombardiers into deep shit, because we were rehearsing for their new CD and it's already late. It's a mess—their record label's been getting progressively more threatening, and this is going to blow it sky-high. I mean, the reason it was late to begin with was because Anton checked out, and now they've got no lead singer. What's the story?"

He gave it to us, clear and concise. At half past nine that morning, Damon Gelb had gone down to Freelon Street. I was able to confirm to Ormand that Damon did that every morning after a rehearsal, to make sure the entire sound file from the previous day's rehearsal had downloaded to the server during the night. It was standard operating procedure.

This morning, Damon had told Patrick, he'd got down there and found the alarm system turned off. Well, of course, he freaked. After all, the studio at 49 Freelon was opposite a construction site, the building was full of expensive equipment, and they'd put the security system in for a reason. Damon had apparently stood and cursed for a few minutes, then used his keys and let himself in.

The first thing he'd seen was a guitar, the neck cracked and half-broken away from the body, and the peghead dangling. The next thing he'd seen was a puddle of tacky blood, mostly dry. And beyond that, poking out from behind the Korg, was Vinny Fabiano's leg. The rest of Vinny was on the floor behind the other side of the Korg, with one side of his forehead thoroughly caved in.

Bree had turned pale, and the fact that Patrick was telling us all this in a calm, flat voice somehow made it worse. Right now, though, one thing was really upsetting. Right, I know—it sounds cold, okay, but I'm being honest here, and it *was* the most upsetting thing for me.

"Shit. The guitar was damaged? That blue waterfall PRS is worth a metric fuckload of money, and it's also a gorgeous instrument—there's not another one quite like it. It's one of the Private Stock axes—custom from top to finish. The neck cracked, and the peghead as well? Bloody hell. Someone must have really flipped their shit, to have swung that hard. I hope to hell it can be rebuilt."

"Blue?" Patrick was staring. "This guitar wasn't blue, it was red, and I mean *red*. It's incredibly fancy—gold wire, fancywork with different woods, a lot of inlay work. The maker's logo looks—I'm sorry, Ms. Godwin, it's the only way I can describe it—like two pairs of breasts, back to back, rotated. In mother-of-pearl, I think. What is it? What's wrong?"

"Damn." I heard my own voice, sounding grim. "Those are the luthier's initials, double *B* for Bruno Baines."

"Who?" There it was: the hunter behind the grey eyes. I knew we'd be seeing it eventually—there's that whole bit about leopards not being able to change their spots, or whatever it is. I was just damned glad that this time, neither of us was a suspect. "Who's Bruno Baines?"

"A local luthier. You've got a problem, because when we closed down for the night at a quarter of seven yesterday, that guitar wasn't on the premises. Vinny'd been playing his PRS Private Stock yesterday—that's the blue guitar I was talking about, the one I thought you meant. The day before that, he'd had a pearl-top Zemaitis in the studio. But Bruno Baines hadn't been paid yet. Vinny owed him nine thousand dollars, or he did as of Saturday night. That guitar wasn't at Freelon yesterday."

"Are you sure?"

"Yeah, I'm sure. You might want to trust me on this one, Patrick. I'm a guitar player, and I notice this stuff, all right? I've never seen Vinny with more than one electric guitar at a time in the Freelon Street studio. He wasn't big on switching axes midsong, and he didn't need to, not with the effects and pedal array in his setup. I don't see him making one-off exceptions to it; musicians tend to be really addicted to their own habits. Anyway, there really isn't a lot of room for equipment storage at Freelon. So I'd say you need to have a word with Bruno Baines."

"Bullshit!"

Patrick and I both jumped. The word had exploded out of Bree, forceful and furious. "That's the stupidest thing—John, you can't honestly think that boy would beat someone's head in with his own guitar. That's ridiculous. It's insane! No way!"

"Only one way to find out." Ormand got to his feet. "Thanks for a fantastic lunch, folks. I need to get back to work. I don't suppose you'd happen to have this guy's number? . . ."

CHAPTER FIVE

Later that night, poor Bree ended up having to cook for unexpected short-notice guests yet again. This time, it was the remaining members of the Bombardiers, Damon Gelb, their two roadies, and Rosario. The occasion was an emergency meeting, to discuss not only Vinny's murder, but also what they should do next.

It was unnerving, how shaken everyone was. The band members all looked to have aged since last night, and Rosario looked like a ghost. I'm not certain it's possible to lose weight in just a few hours, but he seemed to have got visibly thinner.

It was my idea to call a meeting, and Bree's notion to feed them all. So when they arrived within a few minutes of each other, they found hot food waiting for them, a gorgeous spread of it out on the big round dining room table, and Bree making sure that everyone got what they needed in the way of good sustaining nosh. In Bree's head, food equals comfort, and I'm damned if I think she's wrong. I suspect no one had got much to eat during the day after the news broke, because they all came in saying they weren't hungry and of course, once they'd taken a few bites, they all ate like ravening wolves. So, yeah: comfort, or maybe solace. My old lady gets it.

Conversation during the meal was sporadic, but the bulk of it seemed to be focused on the immediate problem: trying to figure out how to finish an already-overdue CD without a lead singer. When everyone had had enough food, I raised the topic on my mind. An idea had been simmering away all afternoon, and I thought, right, bring it up now and see if they shoot it down.

"I think I've got a solution to the main operational problem. We need a singer, yeah? This CD isn't going anywhere without one. Well—I think I can get us a pretty good one."

That got everyone's undivided attention. There was total and immediate silence. Everyone's head turned; everyone's stare fastened on me, and that included Bree. Since I hadn't brought this up yet, not even to her, she was about to be as surprised as they were.

"Man, that would be a lifesaver." Billy, of any of them, looked to be the hardest hit. Not too surprising, really. He was the realist of the group, the one who always seemed to handle shit when their manager wasn't about. The manager in question was on the other side of the planet at the moment, in Australia, and he wasn't due home until next month, when recording time had been booked. He'd probably come roaring back once he got the news. To be fair, he hadn't actually been needed during rehearsals; in fact, he'd have been in the way. The last thing you want hanging about while you're trying to work the knots out of a song is a bureaucrat.

"Speaking just for me, I'll listen to any and every idea

anyone's got right now," Kris told me. "Because if we don't pull something out of our asses pretty damned fast, we're hosed. What do you have in mind, JP?"

"Someone who'd get the suits off your arse in a hurry." I grinned at Billy. "What would you say to me asking Mac?"

Bree, quiet and nearly invisible in a corner now that we were talking band business, had been sipping prosecco with some fresh raspberries in it; as I say, dry bubbly is the only booze she drinks. When I dropped my little bombshell, she promptly swallowed a raspberry down the wrong pipe and choked. Tony thumped her on the back until she'd got control of her airways, but he wasn't really paying attention; his attention was on me, not Bree.

"Mac?" Kris sounded stunned. "Is that—do you mean—are you seriously offering to ask Malcolm Sharpe to fill in for Vinny Fabiano? Mac the Knife? Blacklight's Mac?"

"That's the only Mac I know, and hell yeah, I'll ask him if you want me to." I looked around at the band, the roadies, Damon. Bree had slipped out into the kitchen and was scrubbing at her shirt, which now had prosecco all over it. She was probably swearing and calling me rude names under her breath. "Why the hell not, Kris? All he can do is say no. But I'll tell you what, I don't think he will. He's a singer, mate. He loves it—it's what he does. And you know, he's actually a damned good bloke. Plus, Blacklight's resting at the moment, and so far as I know, Mac's not doing anything—okay, right, he's probably doing some twenty-year-old with pouty lips and a collection of French ticklers, and he's probably doing her even as we speak. But musically, I hadn't heard he was booked for anything. So the question is, do you want me to ask him? Because I'm not a member of the Bombardiers and it's absolutely your call. Not something I'd do without an okay."

"Holy *shit*." Tony had a huge moony grin on his face. "Oh,

man, holy shit, holy shit, that's fucking perfect, dude. Mac—perfect. If there's a faster way to get the label suits off our case, I can't think of it—maybe Mick Jagger, but that would be the only way to top it. Malcolm Sharpe! And hell, it's not like we don't know the guy—we sat in at Oakland, on 'Long Day in the Hot, Hot Sun,' and he was digging it. JP, would you? Really? Because I totally vote yes."

There seemed to be general agreement. I looked at the clock and did a sum in my head. It was half past six in the morning in the UK. "Right. I'll ring him in the morning, and let everyone know, all right?"

Bree had come back in, having changed into a T-shirt. She didn't generally wear that sort of thing—she's not a T-shirt and jeans sort of woman—so this one caught my eye. It was a stylised drawing of a cow with distended teats, directly under her own breast line, and the words MOO, MOTHERFUCKER! above it. I couldn't imagine where she'd got the thing, or why, but it was bloody funny.

"Hey," she said. Her voice was very gentle, and I realised she was looking at Rosario. "Did you get enough dinner? There's plenty left, if you're still hungry."

"Yeah. Thanks. I—I'm okay."

It was pants, that statement, total rubbish. Following Bree's lead, glancing over his way, I realised how completely not okay he looked. This was the first time he'd opened his mouth all evening. As if Bree's noticing him had hit some sort of switch, the rest of us all looked his way.

"Rosie, man, this has to be extra hard on you—we lost a bandmate, but you lost family. I'm sorry. It sucks." Billy patted Rosario lightly on the shoulder. "Be straight—does this leave you up a creek for cash? For work?"

"Kinda, yeah." Rosario looked around at us, and I realised he must have been crying. Either that, or he'd drunk himself halfway to oblivion and back, and then recouped before dinner. Whatever the reason, his eyes were red-rimmed. "But—damn. *Vinny*. Who the hell would do that to Vinny? I know he could piss people off, but he never meant to—it was just that sometimes he didn't know he was being a jerk, or scaring people. And he was my cousin, my only family. I've been working for Vinny since he first picked up a guitar and played his first gig. If I get my hands on the motherfucker that took him out, there's gonna be blood spilled. You can pretty much count on it."

We were all silent. His shoulders started to heave. "Man, this is fucked up."

That did it, of course; everyone began making motions towards leaving. The party would probably have broken up right there, but I had something else I wanted to say, and I held up a hand. "Okay. One more thing. I'm going to ring Mac in the morning, but there's one thing I can't tell him, not without checking with all of you. Here's the deal: 49 Freelon is a crime scene, and it's probably going to be one for a bit. That means you're not going to have any access to it, except maybe to get an instrument or a microphone or something out, and that would be with a couple of coppers to make sure that's all you did. There's no way you're going to be able to rehearse there."

"Shit!" Tony sounded almost panicky. "You're right, JP. We can't afford this. We can't afford the delay."

"No, I know you can't. The band hasn't got the time to wait, not even a couple of days, not considering how narked your label's getting. So if Mac says yeah, cool, love to help out, if he hops a plane and gets here day after tomorrow—where would we be rehearsing? What do I tell him?"

Of course, I knew what I wanted to do: I have a perfectly good rehearsal and small-scale recording studio in the basement of our house. Okay, it wasn't up to the level of Freelon. That one's a full warehouse, with storage and full thirty-two-track digital-recording capability. Still, my little studio is a good space, and I was willing to use it—I was even willing to augment it with some bells and whistles—if it would make everyone happy. But I was damned if I wanted to simply drop that on Bree. If anyone in the band had another option to offer, I wanted to hear it first.

And of course, Bree took my legs out from under me on that little notion. She got up, stretching—MOO, MOTHERFUCKER!—and looked at me, doing an uncanny echo of my one-raised-eyebrow look. And I realised she'd known just where I was heading, with my question about rehearsals. Of course she knew. She always does. She always has.

"Why don't you all just rehearse here, John? We have a perfectly good studio downstairs—it might be a bit cramped, but it's there. And if it needs anything to tart it up, well, I'm sure we can do whatever's necessary." She smiled at me. "It's not as if we're low on cash right now. Well, I am, a little, because I haven't been working. But John's not."

She began gathering plates. I exchanged a look with the others.

"You sure you're all right with that, love? I mean, Mac in an enclosed space could be tricky enough—he's got a lot of energy and he's quite a bit larger than life. Having the lot of us underfoot, well. I'm pretty sure we'd all understand if you stood at the front door with a crossbow to keep us all out." I caught the shadow of a grin as she ducked her head, and added, "Right, well, not keep me out. I damned well live here. But everyone else. You sure, love? Don't be brave about it—it's your house and you're in the middle of planning the wedding. If having us working here is going to make things harder to cope with, we can rent some space somewhere. I'll pay for it."

"Nope—I'm fine with it. That's why I suggested it." She stacked plates expertly, looked at the wineglasses, and Rosario jumped to help. "Oh—thanks. Seriously, I'd love to have you rehearsing here. It'll keep you all out of trouble."

"Bree, are you sure about this?"

She'd been drowsing next to me, dozing as my heart did its usual post-coupling stutter, trying to regulate. There was a lovely sheen of sweat along her collarbones, and her eyes were closed. She was damned near purring.

She opened her eyes. "About what? Recording downstairs? Of course."

She stretched, and a few joints cracked. That always made me jump, her doing that. She's so much younger than I am, and I'm such a mess physically, I sometimes forget she's in her forties now. It scares me—in my mind, she's always going to be too young for anything to go wrong, and I didn't want that vision messed with, not now, not ever. "Why not?" she asked. "I mean, especially if we're going to have Mac involved. The less he has to go out, the less likely we are to have paparazzi camped out in the bearded irises, or local musicology types leaping out from behind the recycling bin, asking him who his early influences were. No, seriously, I'm fine with it, John. Besides, wasn't that where you were going with that whole spiel in the first place? Wasn't that supposed to be a cue?"

I grinned into the darkness and ran one finger along her lips, tracing them. "You know me too damned well, lady. Yeah, it was—but I did want to see if anyone had anything else to offer up first, you know?"

She snatched a kiss at my wandering fingers. "They wouldn't have. Really, John, think about it—they've had that studio for at least twenty years. Have they ever had a reason to go waste the label's ill-gotten gains paying hourly rates somewhere else? This isn't the good old days of the Record Plant or Wally Heider Studios. Musicians don't do that anymore, do they?"

"Not very often, no. Even Blacklight, we just head straight for Luke's mobile, down in Kent." I spared a thought for the glory days of rock and roll in the Bay Area, when people would record sample tracks at the Record Plant all night and sleep all day at the Sausalito houseboat that was kept for the bands, and maybe go for a spin in the studio owner's purple Rolls. I'd got there at the end of all that, but even so, I'd still had a taste of the experience, just enough to make me sorry I missed it.

There was something else I wanted to run past Bree, and assuming she agreed, it would involve a lot more putting up with the probability of bullshit in close quarters than just having the Bombardiers in the basement. I took a good deep breath, and went for it.

"Bree, look, love. I want to beg a favour, okay?"

That got her up on one elbow, staring down at me in the darkness. "You want to what? Did you say beg? Beg a *what*? Well, you just blew my mind, John. This must be one honker, if you're calling it a favour. What in the world can I do for you— no, screw that, wrong question. What in the world haven't I done for you, that you could possibly think you had to ask me for?"

She reached her free hand out and traced my lips with her fingertips. Something about that gesture made me go soft inside. Maybe *tender* is the word I want. I wondered for a moment if she had the same reaction to it, just wanting to wrap us up in one tight bundle, and stay there.

"John? Come on, ask already. I'm dying of curiosity."

"It's about Mac. Probably Domitra, as well. If they stay at the Mark Hopkins or the W or anywhere, the press can set up camp, we'd be defeating the whole purpose of recording in the basement. The paparazzi would just follow them, from there to here. But this is your house, love, not just mine, and there's no way in hell—"

"Oh. My. *God*." There was a very odd note in her voice. "Oh, man. You want to invite Malcolm Sharpe and his bodyguard—well, bodyguardess—to stay with us?"

"I know, I know, it would be a total drag for you. Sorry. Silly idea. Just forget I ever—"

"Are you kidding? Of course you should ask him! I'll never forgive you if you don't." She was biting back giggles, like a bloody schoolgirl. "Oh my God, I can hardly wait. I wonder what excuses Katia will come up with, for suddenly developing a passionate interest in Tony's rehearsal habits? Sandra won't bother with excuses, of course—she'll just fix me with that editorial death glare and order me out of her way so she can stare at Mac and salivate." She went off into gales of laughter; she flopped back down, she was laughing so hard.

It was my turn to sit up and stare down at her. "Are you joking?" I demanded. "Bree, for fuck's sake! That's—Sandra's nearly fifty, and Katia's already passed that one. You telling me they'd be standing about, drooling over Mac, like a couple of teenaged groupies? No way!"

"Oh, hell yeah, way." She wiped her streaming eyes. "They'll be seething with envy. This is so damned funny—how early can you call him?"

"Funny? It's *obscene*." I wasn't stopping to ask myself why I was so outraged. "Mac's fifty-eight years old!"

Bree patted my hand. Her voice was very kind. "He's also hotter than the surface of the sun, baby. Most of the women of my acquaintance would not only do Mac in Macy's window—they've been fantasizing about exactly that since Blacklight's first album. Every female I know—including my mom, probably—will be ready to claw my eyes out with jealousy."

"Bree Godwin." I was talking through my teeth. "Are you telling me you've been secretly whispering Mac's name under your breath all these years while I was doing you?"

She snuggled up next to me suddenly. "No, darling. As it happens, I haven't. You were it, first sight. All I ever wanted, just you. But don't begrudge me being the envy of all my friends for a few weeks, John, okay? It's a very small side benefit, and it's not as if I've ever taken advantage of the others."

"True. You really haven't." I felt a bit cold suddenly, I wasn't sure why. "Right. If you're really okay with it, I'll ring him in the morning. And thank you, love. You can make soothing noises all you want, but it really is a favour and don't think I don't know it. The wedding planning, all this, Mac and rehearsals underfoot, it's a bit much to ask."

I was nearly asleep when she murmured something, and I got my eyes open again. "What? Sorry, love, I didn't catch that."

"Oh, damn, I woke you—I'm sorry. It was just, well, I'm worried about that kid. Vinny's cousin, or whatever he is. He's really messed up right now, isn't he? Is there anything we can do for him?"

"Rosario?" I yawned; for once, the MS was staying all the way back, and nothing actually hurt. That meant a decent night's sleep and, as much as I admire Bree's desire not to see anyone too hungry or messed up, a good night's sleep is a rarity in my life these days, and I was eager to get on with it.

"He just seemed—wow. I don't know."

"Yeah, he seemed pretty broken up, didn't he? Surprising, really. Vinny mostly bullied the hell out of him." I patted Bree's thigh. "Not to worry, love, it's certainly going to be on the Bombardiers' docket, you know? The band's going to need to figure this out. I'm wondering if Damon Gelb can find something for him to do—he's a damned good guitar roadie. I don't need one, but they'll need a guitar player at some point down the road, as well as a lead singer." I yawned suddenly, a huge cavernous yawn. "Bree, baby, I need to sleep, okay? G'night."

I rang London right after breakfast the next morning. Mac shocked me by answering the phone on the third ring.

"JP? That really you? Cheers, mate. What's going on, then?"

"Hey, Mac—yeah, it's me. Nice to know your caller ID works. Look, are you busy? I need to run something past you."

"Busy? Just the usual—writing some lyrics at the moment, actually. I spent the morning filming a telly spot for the World Wildlife Fund, and I figured that after all the Good Works, I either got laid or got creative, and there's no one in the house but me right now, so creativity won out over sex this time. What are you laughing at?"

"Nothing." He seemed to be in a very good mood. I took a deep breath. "Mac, listen. I want to ask you for a whacking big favour. I'll completely understand if you tell me to sod off. No pressure, mate, okay?"

I ran the situation past him. I gave him the entire story, including Vinny's encounter with Bree's knee—Mac began snickering halfway through that one, and then making exaggerated whimpering noises, and I had to give him a couple of minutes to get over it. In the interests of complete disclosure, I also added the fact that Patrick Ormand had gone from a nice safe distance of three thousand or so miles to next door. Mac, who'd done an hour with Patrick back in New York, was less amused by that tidbit. While we were talking, Bree came in and sat down, watching me, listening to me.

". . . so that's the situation. If there's any news, it hasn't got to me yet." I took a long breath and snagged a sip of Bree's coffee; my throat had gone dry as a bone with all the talking. "I know it's a bit much to ask, Mac, but they played with us at Oakland—"

"Come sing on the Bombardiers' new CD, is that it?" Mac sounded enthusiastic. "Fucking brilliant, mate! I'd love to. Tell you what, I'll ring off and get hold of Carla—she can book us flights and a hotel—"

"Well, actually, Mac, that's the other thing. Bree says to tell you you're coming to stay with us, and Dom as well, if you're bringing her. You are, yeah? And by the way, fucking brilliant is right—fantastic of you to come."

"Of course I'm coming, and so is Dom. I barely leave home without her, especially since that stupid git boyfriend of the paternity suit dolly bird thinks he can smell money."

"Christ, that paternity suit." I'd forgotten about that whole mess—Dom had been nice and vigilant during the tour, but that situation got thoroughly swamped by Perry Dillon's murder backstage at Madison Square Garden. If the boyfriend was still on it, there was a chance he'd be around, and I wasn't having anything that could make Bree's offer to host Mac something she'd regret later. "Mac, if you don't mind my asking, why in hell don't you just use a condom?"

Bree snorted out a mouthful of coffee and sat there, spluttering and glaring at me. I grinned at her. "Seriously, man. That would cut back on all these little bits of mystery and their paternity suits, right? Worth a shot."

"Wouldn't stop them. Besides, I don't need a damned Reggie and Ronnie anywhere near my willy, mate." He sounded cheerful. "Not for that sort of protection, at least. Truth is, I had a vasectomy back in 1995. All these paternity suits, they're just wishful thinking."

"You had a vasectomy? Bloody hell, Mac! Then why do you let these people try to pick your pocket?"

He sounded honestly surprised. "Are you joking? I'll take the free sex symbol reinforcement any day of the week. You couldn't buy that sort of PR. After a while, of course, it wears thin, and then I have my bloke take their bloke aside for a spot of clueing in. Brilliant publicity while I play it, though, and really not a problem. It's nothing Domitra can't handle for me—she can tell a troublemaker from fifty yards away, and she's got this whole 'I can eat you alive and still be hungry' thing going on that scares off the worst of them. Anyway, tell Bree we're delighted to accept, and no worries, I promise to behave myself. No rogering twenty-somethings in your best guest bedroom—word of honour."

"Good job, mate—I'll tell Bree. She'll appreciate not having to wash the sheets twice a day."

"Cheeky sod. Look, I'll ring you back as soon as I get hold of Dom, and Carla gets our flights booked. What's today? Right, Friday. Call your mates back—with any luck, we'll be there by Sunday, in time to buy you dinner."

CHAPTER SIX

As it turned out, Mac didn't buy us dinner. The moment I re-layed that comment to Bree, about him taking us out, she went into overdrive on the whole food-preparation thing.

Their flight got in early evening, right after Bree had nearly suffered a nervous breakdown. The problem was, she couldn't figure out how to be in two completely different places at once. On one hand, she wanted to be the perfect hostess: welcome our guests, be nice and gracious at the front door, all those gorgeous dinner scents wafting down the hallway, the cats wreathing around her ankles, show them to their rooms, fresh flowers in vases, all that, you know? Just short of putting mints on their damned pillows.

And of course, she also wanted to pick them up at the airport. She didn't have much choice on that one, since she's got the driver's license, not me. If there's any driving to be done,

Bree does it. She'd already told Carla not to bother with a limo, we'd be picking up our own guests, ta, cheers, bye. That led to Carla being narked, although of course she wasn't too noisy about showing it.

So, when Bree realised she'd painted herself into a corner, she got completely panicked, nearly hyperventilated, and threw a sort of mini-meltdown tantrum. I finally decided I'd had enough of that little lot and put my foot down.

"Knock it off, love." I kissed her, hard. "Dinner can simmer or warm or whatever the hell dinners do when the people planning to eat them have other things to cope with first, okay? You're flipping and making yourself nuts and I won't have it. Set the table if it makes you feel better—"

"I did that already." She was tense as a board in my arms. "The damned cats had better stay off it—damn, I should close off the dining room. And I made up the two bedrooms with the private baths. Oh, shit, I forgot to find out what they like for breakfast—and does Dom need an adjoining room, with a way in? To protect him? Because—" I shook her a bit. "Ouch! Hey!"

"Right, that's it. You're starting to make me as crazy as you're making yourself." I slid one hand off her shoulder and patted her bottom. "If you don't knock it off right now, I'll put you over my knee and take a hairbrush to you."

"Promises, promises." She managed a grin, and some of the stiffness went out of her stance. "Okay. I know, I'm being a pill and an anal control freak perfectionist pain in the ass. But—except for Luke, when you first got diagnosed? This is our first real houseguest, John. And it's Malcolm Sharpe! So of course I want everything to be perfect. Who wouldn't? Why are you rolling your eyes at me?"

"Bree, love, when it comes to Mac, I've spent a quarter century listening to the moans and screams from the hotel room next door. I really haven't got much interest in offering up perfection, all right? Besides, unless you've got an eighteen-year-old with double-D cups and no gag reflex in the guest room closet, you haven't got what he considers perfection anyway."

I put on as innocent a face as I could manage. "Of course, if you were serious about Sandra and Katia and maybe your mum all wanting to rip his clothes off, you might have a passable substitute. He'd love an orgy. And personally, I'd pay to see Miranda—"

"*John!*"

"Ah, the whole shocking-you thing worked. Good." I resorted to an old trick of mine, one I hadn't used in a good long time, designed to make her feel her youth: I bent my index finger at the knuckle and chucked her under the chin with it. "Seriously, Bree, relax. Mac's going to have a roaring good visit. And he's here to work, remember? No need to worry about Dom, either—while he's safe indoors, Dom gets to wander off and find people to beat up, or whatever she does in her free time. It'll be fine. Put things on simmer or warm, and let's get to the airport. By the way, what *are* we having for dinner? Smells brilliant."

"Poached salmon in citrus. Homemade bread. Salad. Oh, shit, I should check the warming drawer and make sure the veggies aren't overdone." She was beginning to look distracted again. I got her by the shoulders, turned her around, and pushed her towards the door leading down to the garage.

"Okay, got it, chill out, knee, hairbrush, daddy spank, yada yada. You are *so* full of—Jesus! Their plane lands in half an hour! Why are we standing here? Let's go!"

We decided to meet them at customs, catch them on the way out. And of course, we ran straight into the media circus that always seems to materialise in Mac's general vicinity. There was the usual crowd of people outside customs, families and friends picking up their loved ones. There were also about ten reporters and photographers. I recognised a few of the reporter types; one of them, Bob something or other, was a rock journalist out of L.A. He'd actually covered the West Coast leg of the most recent Blacklight tour—I'd seen him last at Oakland.

"Shit." I glanced at Bree, who was looking spooked. "Sorry, love, but it looks as if someone dished to the press that Mac was on his way here. Did you want to slip down and wait in the car? If they've cleared customs, they've already got their bags, so it'll just be a matter of shoving them into the lift and getting the hell out of here before the press descends on us."

"No, that's okay. As long as they don't come over and start asking me things, I mean." She understood my raised eyebrow—this was the same woman who used to panic at the sight of a reporter, and who literally tried to shrink and hide from anyone with a camera. I watched her set her shoulders. "I think it's time I got over some of this stuff. I mean—it's just—" Her voice died, and she turned her face away.

"I know what it is, Bree. It's okay, you can say it. No, sod that, I'll say it for you."

People were beginning to emerge from the customs exit; used to be you could meet people at the gate, at least for domestic flights, but that was a thing of the past, after 9/11. I put my lips to her ear, keeping one eye on the doors. "It's all right. I'm not a married man anymore, you know? You're not anyone's 'other woman.' I'm a widower. And if you ever find a place to host this wedding, you can put as much of the Cilla years behind you as you think is possible. I do get it, Bree. I'm honestly not heartless. It's like I told your mum—I may be lazy, but I'm not cruel. I'm not dim, either. Okay?"

"Okay. Yes. You do get it. Thank you, John."

There was a sudden commotion, a surge forward among the press corps. I snatched a quick kiss. "Right. Here we go. Showtime."

Someday, I may figure out what it is that Domitra Calley gets across to strangers without a word spoken, that gets them to stand back five feet and not ask questions. Whatever it is, it's silent, and it works.

She came out first, in jeans and a soft stretchy shirt the colour of blood and a leather jacket. Mac was three steps behind her, pushing a baggage trolley. And every single person who'd started towards Mac—including a few who'd just been waiting for people to get through customs and had recognised a rock and roll superstar—stepped right the hell back again. I'm damned if I know how she does it. No flash clothes, no gear, nothing obvious. Pheromones, maybe.

Even Domitra couldn't keep them from taking his picture or flinging questions at him, though. And Mac being Mac, this was his meat and drink, being noticed. I pulled Bree back a bit, and we settled down to watch and wait.

"Mac!" The L.A. reporter, Bob Whatever, got his question in first. "Welcome back to California! Is it true that you're going to be taking over for Vinny Fabiano as the vocalist on the upcoming Bombardiers CD?"

At my side, Bree stiffened. "How the hell did he—?"

"Shhh. Listen." I knew how this worked, and Bree didn't. Mac was a master at this stuff; unless I'd got it totally wrong, he was about to quell any possibility of unfortunate rumour and get the Bombardiers' label off their arses at the same time. I wondered who'd let the press know for the Bombardiers. Tony? No, Billy, most likely. . . .

Mac stood forward, easy and relaxed. It wasn't a pose; with Dom there, he had no reason not to be relaxed. Besides, there's really damned near nothing out there that can ruffle him. "That depends on what you mean by taking over for Vinny Fabiano. I'm sitting in on the CD, just doing the vocals as a favour—I'm not deserting Blacklight, no worries there. Tony Mancuso and

Kris Corcoran sat in with Blacklight at Oakland, when we closed the tour—you were there, right? So, JP Kinkaid and I, we're returning the favour." He glanced around and spotted us. "Oi! Johnny! Bree! There you are!"

He pointed and waved. And, of course, every head in the place swivelled round in our direction.

Kicking a habit that's based on reflex actions takes a lot of practise, apparently; Bree made a tight little noise at the back of her throat and started back, trying to get behind me. I had hold of her hand, though, and I wasn't having any. She'd just told me she thought it was time she started learning to cope. If she was going to be Mrs. Kinkaid in a few months, she could damned well get used to this. It didn't happen to me nearly so much as it did to Mac, or even the other members of Blacklight—I'd made sure of that over the years—but it did happen now and then, and she was going to have to learn to deal with it.

So I held on to her hand, good and tight, keeping her at my side and not letting her slip and hide behind me. She gave me one beseeching look, but I shook my head at her and waved back at Mac with my free hand.

"Cheers, Mac. Welcome back to Baghdad by the Bay."

I saw a few of the reporters head for the lifts that led to the parking garage. Damn. We were going to be followed home. Ah well—nothing to be done about it. "You two ready, then? Let's go. Supper's waiting."

Of course, half the press corps followed us back to Clay Street. Dom sat up front, and I got in back with Mac; we were rabbiting on like a couple of schoolboys back there, except that it was all about band business. You'd have thought we hadn't seen each other in a year, instead of a month.

I filled Mac in on the Bombardiers' work in progress: the progress on the CD, length, the balance of blues to rock and roll and country, the sort of guitar work I was doing. He was every bit as enthusiastic as he'd been on the phone, but halfway through, I saw a crease forming between his bows, and I lifted one of my own.

"Mac? What?"

"Johnny, I may be dim, but I may be missing something here. You said you were sitting in on three numbers, right? And that Vinny was their rhythm guitar player, as well as being their lead vocalist?"

"Right." Bree and Dom were quiet up front; each of them kept taking looks in the outside car mirrors, and I realised they were looking to see if the press was still on our tail. "Rhythm guitar, the occasional lead, some slide stuff and backing vocals. They brought me in to add some texture and complexity. It helps, being an old session bloke. Why?"

"Well—Vinny's gone off to the Endless Jam in the Sky. So who's doing the guitar on the other seven numbers?"

"Gordon *Bennett*!" I hadn't stopped to consider that, not once, and none of the Bombardiers had brought it up. "Mac, ta, mate— we'd have sat down in the studio day after tomorrow, and we'd all have been sitting there with our willies in our hands, and no gui- tar parts worked out. Hang on—I need to ring Tony."

Turned out Tony hadn't thought about it, either. It was a damned good thing we had the solution to hand; bless Damon and his insistence on burning CDs of every rehearsal the band did. Tony had almost a full set, and offered to come by that night with them, for me to listen to.

"Half a mo, Tony, will you?" I leaned forward. "Bree, can we have Tony come by after dinner? Offer him something to nosh and maybe some coffee? Turns out I'm going to need to learn the guitar parts to seven songs I haven't even heard yet, and Tony's got the CDs with all Vinny's guitar bits on them."

"Sure." She sounded distracted. Still fussing over the pa- parazzi, no doubt. "Tell him about nine, okay? Oh, and tell him to bring Katia along. I don't think she's ever actually met Mac before, unless it was at the party."

I bit back a grin over that one. "Tony? Yeah, that would be perfect. Bree says to come about nine, and bring Katia along. Sorry? No, I don't know whether Mac will still be awake—eight hours is a major time difference."

Both Mac and Dom had been at our place before, at the wrap party a month earlier. Thing is, for the party, we'd locked all three cats in the bedroom with a sign on the door saying off-limits, since the doors to the garden had been open, and none of the cats are allowed out of doors. So we were both surprised when Dom stopped halfway down the hall, interrupting Bree's explanation about how we were probably going to have a lift installed at some point, and ideas for doing it without trashing half the original woodwork. Dom had tensed up.

"What the hell was that?"

"What was what?" Bree, leading the way towards the stairs, stopped and stared. "What's the matter?"

"Something just went—oh!"

Farrowen had come round the corner of the front room. She sniffed at Mac's shoes, accepted the ritual scratch under the chin I gave her, and turned her attention to the two new humans on her terrain. She checked Mac out first—he's not much for animals, generally, although he's pleasant enough about them. She then turned her full attention to Domitra, who was staring at her.

"Huh." Farrowen was staring back. She'd settled in front of Dom—there was a definite bit of turf war dominance going on, there. I wondered if I ought to explain to Dom that she couldn't hope to win on this one, not a chance in hell, since Farrowen was well beyond territorial and nicely into closed borders if she doesn't like you, but I decided to just shut my gob and wait to see what happened next. "Blue-eyed cat," Dom said. "Intense. What's her name?"

"Farrowen. Named for a Native American goddess of the hunt. She's a lethal little hunter—insects in this house don't stand a chance, and any mouse coming near the place would have to have written a suicide note first. She's the only queen—the other two cats, Wolfling and Simon, are boy cats. Of course, they've all been fixed anyway." Bree looked towards the stairs. She wanted people seated and settled and fed; the control thing was rearing its head again. "How'd you know she was a queen, not a tom? I'm curious."

"Girl vibe." Domitra had locked stares with the cat, and the cat wasn't giving an inch. She was sitting straight up, she had her tail wrapped round her feet, and she looked like something you'd find guarding an Egyptian tomb somewhere. "No male of any species ever gives me that look."

At just that moment, Wolfling came out behind us. He glanced at me, pure cat on the verge of causing shit and letting me know in advance so that I couldn't claim ignorance later, and walked up behind Domitra. He gave me that look again—Mac had seen him, and caught my headshake—and then went to full stretch, with his front claws lightly against Dom's trouser leg. He didn't dig or break skin; he just let her know he could. This was going to end in tears. I just had no clue whose tears we were talking about.

Dom went straight up, almost too fast for me to follow. When she landed, she turned, also at speed. She was crouched and ready and looked extremely dangerous, but Wolfling never budged; he just looked up at her. I swear he was grinning.

"Silly cat," Bree said. "Isn't anyone hungry? Because I made dinner. I hope you're okay with fish."

Mac managed to stay awake long enough after dinner to head down to the studio and listen to all seven of the CDs Tony brought with him. And after about the third song, I began to realise we had a problem. If I was going to be of any use at all, stepping into Vinny's pricey shoes, I was going to need something beyond my Les Pauls and a couple of tube screamers.

Tony saw the crease between my eyebrows. "What's up, JP?"

"The guitar sound. The effects, really. I think we've got something needs solving. Here, listen to this."

I slipped in a CD. The song poured out, a solid driving rock number, thundering bassline and Billy's drums mixed up hot. Vinny came in on the vocals, and Mac grinned in appreciation. The song was right up his alley—he was going to have some serious fun with it. Unfortunately, I wasn't quite so happy.

"Listen to it." I shook my head. "You and Kris structured your own bits specifically to match what Vinny was doing, yeah? From the sound of it, he was playing the pearl-top on this one, heavy on the effects. The sound he was getting here is crucial. The song's going to feel completely different without it."

Mac was listening, fingers tapping out the rhythm, lips moving. I nodded towards the Bechstein. "Tony, do me a favour. I'll plug in and let's run a little bit of it live together, with my setup as is, okay?"

Less than two minutes into it, Tony lifted his hands from the Bechstein's keyboard and stared at me. "Shit."

"No, but it will be, if we run it this way. I've got two PRS axes upstairs—they were sent on spec, part of an endorsement deal that never happened. I can probably figure out his effects sequence, but that's only the tip of the problem. He played other axes besides the PRS."

"Can't you just use Vinny's gear?" Mac asked. "Because I'm no guitar player, but I can hear the difference. The entire feel of the song, it's different. JP's stuff is really vivid, and it's really signature. And that's the issue here, isn't it? Because this isn't a Blacklight CD, it's a Bombardiers CD, and I think we need to keep the integrity of it. Johnny, would your copper chum let you borrow Vinny's stuff, do you think? I mean, it's all locked down tight at the studio, right?"

"Yeah, Freelon Street's off-limits. But it isn't just the PRS and the effects, Mac. He'd been playing a Zemaitis pearl-top on some of this as well, heavily customised, and I don't have one of those. And I didn't see it at the studio that day. I've got no clue where it might be."

Mac was gaping. "A Zemaitis pearl-top? What, like Ronnie Wood's old one?"

"Yeah, very similar. This one was an early eighties—Vinny said he'd got it off a Japanese collector. Customised for miles, and way more tarted up than Ronnie's was, electronically. God knows what sort of tats and bobs he had added on—unless Tony Zemaitis actually did the originals himself."

Mac gave a long, low whistle. "Bloody hell. Where did this bloke get his dosh, then?"

I caught Tony's eye. "I've been wondering about that myself. Anyway, more to the point right now, how the hell do I get my hands on the gear that'll make this sound like the Bombardiers and not like a watered-down Blacklight copy? I'm damned if I want to do the material anything less than justice, you know? Bottom line is, I haven't got a Zemaitis, and as much as I love my Pauls, the sound is totally different. If the cops have got their hands on Vinny's rig, I can ask Patrick Ormand to open the evidence locker, but if they don't, I'm hosed, mate. I can probably use my own PRS and get close to what Vinny was getting on those numbers, but I can't hope to duplicate the Zemaitis sound on my gear. No damned way."

"Rosario will know." Tony got up. "Damn, my cell won't work down here. Let's head upstairs and I'll call him. I'll leave the CDs with you guys—and Mac, I really appreciate this. We all do. You and JP are saving our asses."

He grinned suddenly. "By the way, speaking of asses? If my wife drools into your lap, don't worry about it. She can't help herself. If you blow her a kiss, ten bucks says she keels over or starts giggling like a fifteen-year-old. She's probably dying up there. She's been hot for you for thirty years."

So Bree had been dead right. Once again, she'd seen stuff I didn't.

"What, Katia has? Oh, that's sweet, because she's a hottie." Mac gave Tony a light punch on the arm. "I'll do better than blowing kisses—I'm always up for a good harmless flirt. You don't mind? You're okay with it?"

"Are you kidding?" We were almost up the stairs. "Why would I mind? Bottom line is, when we get home, she's all turned on. However she gets there, I reap the benefits, dude. Besides, she'd love it, and I love seeing her happy. Go for it. Feel free to flirt like a mad thing."

Katia was settled in the front room, drinking prosecco with Bree, and while she couldn't stop glancing at Mac, she was decently dignified about it. Tony grabbed a mouthful of leftover salmon, said something rhapsodic to Bree about how good it was, and rang Rosario.

And Mac went straight over and proceeded to make damned sure Tony would have several hours of fantastic sex when he got Katia home. He plumped down next to her on the sofa and began the kind of cheerful flirting he generally uses on the wide-eyed nymphets he invariably brings back to his hotel with him. I'd seen the technique a thousand times before; this was tried-and-true. It rarely fails.

What floored me was that Katia—as tough as old boots, completely sensible, absolutely level-headed, middle-aged Katia—was lapping it up with a spoon. It was ridiculous, and also very distracting. Between watching Mac seducing Tony's wife on Tony's behalf, and trying to keep some attention on listening to

Tony trying to find out what I needed to know, I damned near developed whiplash. And of course, Bree noticed the whole thing. She had it pretty well banked down, but she was desperately trying not to dissolve into helpless laughter.

"Rosie? Hey, man, it's Tony. Listen, do you know where Vinny's gear is right now? No, not the PRS—what we really need is the Zemaitis and Vinny's effects rig. No, JP needs it, if we can get our hands on it—yeah, he wants to stay true to Vinny's sound, and he says he can't do that with his own rig. . . ."

Mac was whispering into Katia's ear. Even from where I was standing, there was something intimate and playful about it. I watched the ear, the cheekbone, and the entire side of Katia's neck go vivid scarlet. Tony, with one eye on his wife and his borrowed rock star, listened to Rosario on the other end of the line.

"Warehouse? No, I don't— What? Where in San Rafael? Oh, wait, hang on a minute, Rosie. Are you talking about Paul Morgenstern's place? Okay, no, I did know he has that small warehouse—I just didn't know Vinny kept stuff there. Do you have a key, or do I need to ask Paul? Okay, cool—tell you what, I'll call Paul and I'll get back to you, and let you know where to meet us and when."

Mac leaned back on the sofa and stretched. He let the tip of one index finger brush the back of her hand. And I'm damned if she didn't start giggling. It was ridiculous. She sounded younger than Luke Hedley's daughter Solange, and Solange was barely eighteen. Hell, even Solange wouldn't giggle that way. She's too sophisticated for that.

Bree got up in a hurry and excused herself, heading into the kitchen with a tray of empty cups. I followed her in. By the time the door had closed behind us, she was shaking with suppressed laughter.

"Amazing." I was snickering as well—couldn't help it. It was disturbing, but mostly, it was funny. "And in case you're wondering, yeah, Mac cleared it with Tony first. In fact, Tony suggested it. Apparently, he's expecting some serious sex."

"Are you kidding?" Bree looked as if she couldn't decide whether to be outraged or howling with laughter. "That's just—it's so—"

"Wrong? That the word you want?" I opened the door a crack; Tony had wandered out into the hall. He was still on the phone, but Mac and Katia were still side by side on the sofa. I was just in time to see Mac kiss Katia's hand.

"Oh, Christ, Bree—he's gone way the hell over the top. Sex? Poor Tony—Katia's going to cripple him, she's so turned on. I can't bear to watch."

"I was going to say sleazy, but—oh my *God*, this is so funny." Bree set the tray down and succumbed, leaning against me to muffle the giggles. After a minute, she got control of herself and wiped tears off her cheeks. "It really is a little creepy, too. I'm not sure why. Thanks be, Domitra's gone up to bed. I wouldn't want her beating Katia to death, in case Katia decides she can't take it and tries to rape the poor man."

"Knowing Dom, she'd probably rip Tony's leg off and use that as the weapon." I pulled her into my arms and kissed her. "Bree, you superstar, I'm sorry to put you to such trouble. I'll help clear up when everyone's sorted out, okay?"

"Don't worry about it—it's mostly done. It's one of the first things you learn as a caterer: Clear up as you go. There's not much left to do. I'll run a dishwasher load overnight." She cracked the door and peeped through. "Oh, good, Tony's off the phone. Let's go rescue poor Katia—or maybe poor Mac. Never underestimate an avid woman, especially one of a certain age. Oh, Jesus, John, would you look at her? I swear she's about to climb into his lap! Is he always this big a slut around susceptible women?"

"You mean there are women who aren't susceptible?" She shot me a look, and I corrected myself. "Other than you?"

We got back out to our guests just in time to see Mac stretch his legs. They were—as Bree mentioned later—very long legs, and at the moment, they were encased in very tight trousers. Katia was doing her best to not look, and she was making a bad job of it. Tony was in for a long night, but if he knew it, the idea didn't seem to worry him much.

"Hey, JP—I called Paul Morgenstern. Turns out Vinny has all his stuff stored at Paul's warehouse—you know, that little converted garage thing next door to the 707. Vinny's apartment is just down the road. I didn't even know he lived in Marin, did you?"

"Paul Morgenstern?" Mac's attention had been caught, and Katia, limp as overcooked pasta on our sofa, finally got a breather from the arc lamp charisma that Mac had turned her way. "I've met him. He's the producer from New York, right? Nice bloke. He's done some charity work with Amnesty music spots. What's the 707?"

"Paul's club, up on Francisco Boulevard in San Rafael. It's about half an hour north of here—holds about a thousand people, small bar, licensed for beer and wine, in-house PA. I played it last year, just sitting in, and I know Vinny played there as well, before he was asked to front the Bombardiers—that's right, isn't it, Tony?"

"Yep. That's it."

Both my legs had begun to throb a bit. I had the uneasy feeling that I was in for a long bumpy night myself, not nearly so much fun as Tony's was likely to be. I didn't need the complication of the MS right now; the police investigation was going to be a major drag, without any help. "Tony, sorry, mate. It's been a long day, and I'm really knackered. I really need my night meds, and I promised I'd help Bree clean up. What's the story for tomorrow?"

"Shit, man, you should have kicked us out an hour ago." Tony looked guilty. "Bree, we're sorry. Mac's probably jet-lagged as hell. Anyway, Paul says no problem—he's at a recording session at the Plant right now, but he's up for going with us tomorrow. We'll stop off and get him in Sausalito, and he'll let us in, and we can borrow any of Vinny's stuff that we need. We should be cool—Rosie and Paul both said the Zemaitis and most of the stuff that isn't at Freelon is up there. I can drive, if Bree's busy. Katia, honey, you ready to head out? Mac, thanks again for helping us out. This is going to be one kick-ass CD."

CHAPTER SEVEN

Bree ended up driving after all. We did a simple sum, added up the number of people wanting to go to San Rafael, and compared it to the number of seats available in Tony's Range Rover. Mac, Domitra, me, Tony, probably Katia, a stop to pick up Paul, plus the reality of having to load the back of the Range Rover with guitar cases and whatnot. It was clear the truck wasn't going to hold all of us.

Bree had given our guests breakfast. In fact, she'd got up an hour early to do it; when I padded downstairs at half past nine, the kitchen smelled like heaven and she'd just pulled a cherry streusel out of the oven. I think the smell had some sort of secret magnetic thing happening, because Mac came down moments after, with Domitra right on his heels.

Of course, Bree had no earthly business being this anal. It

was damned irritating. I helped myself to streusel, brushed her ear with my lips, and whispered "Bloody perfectionist" around a mouthful of cinnamon crumbs.

She shot me a look and turned back to our guests. "No problem. I'll drive you up there."

"You, madam, are sensational." Mac got hold of her hand and began kissing her fingers, one by one. The man's indecent sometimes, you know? No one should be able to flirt that effectively at half past nine in the morning. If Katia'd been there to see it, she'd have either gouged Bree's eyes out or hurt herself. Talk about the best butter . . .

Mac shot me a look, pure mischief. "I've never been farther north than the bridge. Gorgeous, sexy, capable, and kind. Johnny, you're a jammy sod. Mind I don't steal her from you."

The cheeky bastard knew exactly what he was doing. I grinned at him, probably not for the reason he thought I was; if he thought he was going to get the same reaction off Bree that he gets from everyone else, he was doomed to disappointment. I know my old lady.

"That's all right, Mac, no problem. There's no way you're all going to cram into Tony's truck—John doesn't do well all mashed in. The MS gets touchy." She smiled a bit absently and patted Mac's hand. You'd have thought he was someone's uncle she was obliged to be kind to. "Anyone want eggs? More coffee? . . ."

We ended up putting Mac and Dom in the Jaguar with us, with Tony and Katia leading the way in Tony's truck. It was another postcard of a day, everything sparkling, the East Bay hills and Marin looking green and lush, and the Transamerica Pyramid shining in the morning sun.

"Wow." Dom had a camera with her. I'm not into photography at all, but even I could tell it looked expensive. She handled it with the kind of assurance I use with guitars. This was someone who knew what she was doing with the tool she had strapped round her neck. "This is some killer geography. Bree, you mind if I put the window down and take some pictures?"

"Feel free." Bree sounded distracted, a bit edgy. I had no idea why.

She took pictures all the way across the Golden Gate Bridge. We followed Tony through the rainbow tunnel and down into the hills, to Paul Morgenstern's house.

No parking issues this time—Paul was waiting for us. He hadn't been expecting Mac, though, and of course there was no way he wasn't showing Mac his house, his view of the Bay, and his artwork.

"Wow!" Mac reacted, but probably not the way Paul thought he would. He was staring at a solid wall of framed paintings. He seemed to be focussed on one in particular. "Is that a genuine Picasso drawing?"

"What, the horse?" Paul looked pleased. "Yep. I bought that about twenty years ago. And no, before you ask, not everything on the walls is genuine. Man, don't I wish! About a dozen pieces are, though. You picked one of my favourites to notice—isn't that horse a kick-ass little monster? So stylised. I really love it. And up there, second from the right—that's a Goya drawing. Part of the Age of Reason stuff."

I always forgot that Mac, before he opted for as much sex as he could take and untold wealth instead of academia, had been a fine arts major at university. His own London digs, a period house in Knightsbridge near Sloane Square, has a nice little collection of paintings. He's actually got a reputation as a patron of up-and-coming artists, but he's spent a lot of lolly on things like the Georgia O'Keeffe that hangs over his bed. He knows his stuff, does Mac.

I let him salivate for a minute, but we had an errand to run and a CD to rehearse, and anyway, Bree was getting fretful and impatient. I slid an arm around her waist and held her back a few steps as we trailed the others through Paul's house.

"What's up, lady? You're in a hurry to get out of here. Got a hot date?"

She turned a bit pale. Now, that startled me—I mean, I was only teasing, yeah? I pulled my head back and lifted an eyebrow. "Got something to tell me, Bree?"

"Sorry. I'm just being antsy." She slid a hand into mine; Mac was waxing lyrical about Jasper Johns, Paul was nodding respectfully, and Katia was looking at Mac as if she thought he might be nice to lick. "I really did want to get some work done today, and I need to call a place back about the wedding reception later. I told the woman I'd try to call before five."

"That's masses of time, love. But I wish I'd known you weren't really up for this—you don't need to be a damned martyr every time. Katia could have driven."

"No, that's fine, I'm up for it. I'd just like to keep it moving. Long critical discussions about art really aren't my thing. In fact—John, would you mind if I went and sat in the car? Maybe they'll take the hint and hurry it up."

It was another ten minutes before I finally managed to get everyone out of doors, and Bree was just putting her cell phone away as we came out to the cars. Good. If she'd got her venue call done, she might be less edgy.

It took nearly half an hour to get from Paul's house to his warehouse; we ran into some sort of traffic cock-up on Highway 101, road work between Larkspur and San Rafael. It's damned lucky the Jag is such a comfortable car, and even luckier that it's got effective air-conditioning. The day had gone quite warm, and fender-to-fender stop and start is no fun anyway.

We actually managed to get something of our own accomplished on that drive; Bree remembered that the last rehearsal

CD the Bombardiers had done of "Liplock" was still in the CD player, and we played it for Mac, three times running. By the time we followed Tony's blinking right-turn indicator and got off the freeway at Francisco Boulevard, Mac had the feel of the song down, and most of the lyric memorised, as well. He was singing it, not loud but with different emphasis points, as we pulled up and killed the engine.

I'd been to the 707 only once before, to sit in on a couple of guest sets, and that had been after dark. Looking at the place in daylight, it reminded me of Las Vegas, somehow. That's a place that sparkles at night, but it looks peculiar, almost undressed, during the day. Sort of sad, really. The club at night was fun and funky. Right now, it looked like a girl caught covering old acne scars with Pan-Cake makeup—you could see where new paint was needed around the edges, especially since it had already had some recent work done, and the new bits just threw the old dodgy areas into high contrast.

"So, here we are." Paul had a key ring in one hand and was waving us towards the garage a few hundred feet east of the club itself. "Hey, did anyone call Rosario? Tony, didn't you say last night he was going to meet us here?"

"I tried him this morning, before we left the city, but he didn't answer." Tony held a hand out to his wife, and she took it, carefully picking her way around cracks and ruts in the driveway. Katia had a sleepy, relaxed look to her this morning, and when I thought back to the probable reason, I found myself wondering. Tony had said he didn't mind what got her there, so long as he got to reap the benefits. And, see, I just couldn't sort that out. If I thought Bree was wrapping her legs round me because she was turned on over someone else, the top of my bloody head would probably explode. . . .

About ten feet from the garage, Paul stopped in front of us. "That's weird." He was staring ahead. "What the hell?"

"What's wrong, mate?"

"The door—it's open. There's supposed to be a padlock on it." He started forward. "Jesus, did we have a break-in? There's fifty grand' worth of PA in there! And Vinny's stuff!"

He was right—there was no padlock. The roll-up door was actually open; I could see a thin line of shadow at the bottom, where it was meant to actually sit on the cement lip. It wasn't sitting anywhere. It was a good inch up in the air, as if someone had pulled it down in a hurry but hadn't bothered to check and make sure it was done properly. There was no lock in sight, either. Something really nasty moved down my back.

"Mac." It was Dom, interposing herself between Mac and the building. "Stop right there, and don't go anywhere until I tell you it's safe."

I haven't got a clue what she did, but the difference in her stance was as obvious, and as immediate, as the change in her attitude. She just looked ready, suddenly, ready for trouble and completely dangerous, too. Mac did precisely what she told him to do. So would I, if she'd used that tone to me.

"Wait a minute." Tony got one end of the roll-up and called over to Paul. "Okay—grab it. One—two—up!"

The door went up, smooth and easy. It was a corrugated metal loading door, about twelve feet across. I got in front of Bree, trying to block her, making sure that if anything got near her, it would have to go through me first.

We saw him right off. He was sprawled out on his belly, his face turned sideways, towards the door. His eyes were half-open. It was almost as if he'd been hoping for a last look at the sun, you know? But he hadn't been granted that. By the time his face had landed in that position, his neck couldn't possibly have been in one piece. Human heads simply don't turn that way, not unless the neck that holds them up has got genuinely fucked up along the way.

Behind me, Bree sucked in her breath, and without thinking, I wrapped her up in both arms, turning both our backs towards the garage, blocking out the picture in front of us. I hoped she hadn't seen enough to register; she'd been the one to find Perry Dillon's body in Blacklight's Madison Square Garden dressing room, and I hadn't even had to glance at that. This one was on me. It was my turn to deal.

"Don't look," I whispered, and put a hand up to turn her face away. "You don't have to look, love. It's all right."

"Bloody hell." Mac, obedient behind Domitra's outstretched arm, craned and stared. "Who the hell is that, then?"

"It's Vinny's cousin." Tony had gone sallow; holding the door up, he couldn't get to Katia, who'd backed up fast and was retching her own breakfast into the scrubby grass at the side of the driveway. "Vinny's guitar tech. Rosario."

If you asked me to sort out what happened over the next few hours into any sort of logical sequence, I couldn't do it. Bits of it stand out in my head, of course, moments, scenes from that day. And I'd have had to be nearly unconscious to miss Bree and Dom going toe to toe.

Dom was doing her job, of course, and her job is protecting Mac. In Dom's head, that meant getting him the hell out of there. And of course, she couldn't. You don't just leave the scene of a crime, not without all hell breaking loose. But when Dom smells any threat to Mac, she's ruthless. Right now, ruthless meant getting the hell out of it, and taking Mac with her, before the media or the cops arrived.

"Hey! You! Paul—it's Paul, right?"

He'd been staring down at Rosario, his own face nearly as bad a colour as the bloke he was staring at. "Yeah. My name's Paul." He swallowed hard. "Wow. Shit."

"Is there any other way out of that place?" Dom's voice was

driving, urgent. "Or are we looking at the one and only? God damn it, pay attention, dude, I asked you something! Yes or no? Any other way out besides this one?"

"No—this is it." He suddenly put a hand up to his mouth; a moment later, he was adding his own breakfast to the side of the driveway.

"Mac." Dom caught his eye. "Do you need to be here? Because if you don't, I'm thinking we should go, like, now."

"Oh, hell the fuck no. I don't think so."

I jumped about a mile. It was Bree, and I'd never heard that tone of voice from her before. Hell, I never knew she could sound like that, just as dangerous as Dom. "He stays right here. So do you."

The two women stared at each other, brown eyes meeting green. My stomach did a flip-flop, and I stepped backward; I honestly couldn't help it. Mac stayed right where he was.

"You think?" Dom's face was masklike. "Because my job is to keep Mac out of trouble. He doesn't know these people. He's here as a favour. He doesn't need to be involved in another murder investigation. So, are you planning to try to stop me doing my job? How?"

"Stop you?" Bree snapped. "I don't have to try to stop you. Feel free—head right on out, honey. Shit, I'll call you a cab. Five seconds after the cab pulls out, I'll be on the phone with Patrick Ormand so fast, it'll make your head spin. You won't get as far as the bridge. Have you got a brain? Try using it. It's illegal to discover a crime and leave the scene. You think Mac doesn't need to be involved? Stop talking like a fucking idiot. He's involved. Period, end of story."

They were locked up, the pair of them. Behind me, I heard someone gulp—I have no idea who.

"I have a job I get paid to do." Dom sounded very much the

way I figured she'd sound if she'd been announcing her intention to kill something. "Deal with it."

"Just for the record, honey, you aren't the only one with a job; I'm willing to do whatever it takes to stop you, or anyone else who gets in my way. Deal with *that*. John doesn't need to be involved, either. And my job is protecting him. There's no dodging this one, so I suggest you try for a little sense. You split now, it makes it worse. For Christ's sake, Dom, wake up and smell the dead guy."

"Bree, I do think you could have put that a trifle more poetically." Mac sounded almost amused. "Smell the dead guy? Remind me not to collaborate with you on lyrics. Dom?"

She glanced at him. He shook his head.

"We stay right where we are. Sorry, love. The lioness is right—it's illegal to leave the scene of a crime. Even if I were willing to nip out the back and leave my mates to cope with this particular mess, it wouldn't be feasible. I'm sorry it's going to make your job a bit trickier than either of us would like, but sod it, that's life, right?"

Dom shrugged. I took that as a yes—she still looked irritated, but not actually murderous. Mac looked at Paul.

"We need to ring up the police, don't we? Soonest would be best, yes?"

"Jesus." I let my breath out. "Dom, Bree, would you both back off a bit? It'll be fine. And Mac's right, we need to get the police. Paul? Do you know any of the locals?"

"Casually. They cruise by and keep an eye on the club for me, and on the warehouse." He gave Rosario another fast look, shuddered, and turned away. Slowly, carefully, Tony let the door roll down to where he'd found it. "My cell phone's in Tony's truck." Paul sounded seriously shaken up. "God, what a mess."

He headed for the Range Rover. Dom and Bree were looking at each other; I was reminded of Farrowen, getting Dom to break her stare first.

"Problem solved." I swear I caught the glimmer of a smile on Dom's face. "My boss wants to hang out and be a pain in the ass. The man signs my cheques. He says stay, we stay. Like I said, doing my job. No grudge over here. You?"

Bree had relaxed. "Nope. Don't get me wrong, Dom—I totally get it, wanting to have nothing to do with this. Shit, I was Patrick Ormand's Number One with a bullet for Perry Dillon's murder, and it sucked decayed salmon on toast points. But there's no hiding from it. We're in it. And speaking of which . . ." She fumbled for her cell. "I'm going to call Patrick. He asked us to call if we had information that might have any bearing on Vinny's murder, and I'd say this qualifies."

She turned away, the cell open in her hand. She was keeping her voice down. "Patrick? Listen, it's Bree. There's something I need to let you know about. . . ."

She moved away, dropping her voice, her back to me. And for the first time since the day I'd met her, I felt something down in the pit of my belly, and I identified it right off.

Bloody hell. Jealousy. I was jealous.

She'd rung his number without a moment's hesitation. That meant it was either fixed in her memory, or it was fixed in her phone's memory. What the hell? She had no earthly reason to know Patrick Ormand's direct number, and no reason to have programmed it into her phone, either.

And what was that rubbish, about him asking us to call if we had any information? News to me, that was. If he'd said it to her, I hadn't been there. When, since the afternoon we'd had him over and given him lunch, had she seen Patrick Ormand? What the fuck was going on?

So there I was, on low simmer, with the police showing up

any moment, suddenly having to push away a picture of my old lady and Patrick Ormand. There was sod-all I could do about it, not at that point. It didn't help that one of the pictures that kept insisting on me looking at it was a real memory and not just one of those nightmare shots of naked lovers: I was remembering being onstage at Blacklight's Oakland show, turning round and seeing Ormand dancing with Bree. He was about her age as well—at least ten years younger than I was. Healthy and fit. The bloke looked like he worked out. . . .

It didn't matter that I knew I was being a prat, you know? It didn't matter that I could look back over twenty-five years and see nothing but loyalty, love, protection, her being there for me every time, covering my ass, forgiving me when I messed up, saving my life on more than one occasion. It didn't matter that if anyone had cause to understand about jealousy, it was Bree, not me. My brain turned off, at just the time when I really ought to have been on at full capacity.

I've been a junkie, addicted to everything from bourbon to cocaine to heroin. All of that stuff messes with your perception of what's real and what's not. But jealousy, that seemed to be the worst of the lot. And it was new to me. I'd never doubted Bree before, not for one second.

"Johnny?" Mac touched me on the shoulder, and I jumped. "You all right, mate? You're looking a bit fragged out."

Bree'd rung off. "John, come and sit. I'm going to. The car's unlocked—there's no reason to stand around like a bunch of garden gnomes. SFPD is calling the San Rafael police, and they'll be here in a few minutes—Ah. Speak of the devil." Off to the other side of the highway, we heard distant sirens, getting closer by the moment. "What was that, four minutes? Man, these people scare me. Really efficient."

The next few hours were nuts, basically. The local blokes—they arrived in three squad cars—got us all separated, asking questions, and I watched a few eyes go really wide when they landed on Mac and realised who they were about to demand an alibi from. I also watched a few jaws tighten up when they got round to talking to Dom. She'd gone into full professional mode. I think she was scaring them.

In the meantime, they had evidence people and yellow tape and all the stuff I remembered from Madison Square Garden. I remember the cops sealing off the block, merchants from the neighbouring businesses coming out to ask what was going on, being shooed off.

I remember Bree telling the cop who was asking me questions that we'd be delighted to answer anything at all but we weren't criminals, we'd all come up in a group, that I had multiple sclerosis and needed to sit, yes of course the car would be fine, yes ours was the pale green Jaguar, door's unlocked, help yourself. She also asked if it might not make more sense to wait for Patrick Ormand and the SFPD guys to show up, since this had pretty much a 100 percent probability of being connected to Vinny Fabiano's death, and that was City jurisdiction. The cop and I both glared at her for that one.

Eventually, the City cops got there as well, Ormand leading the pack. He took the cop in charge of the locals aside. I watched them talking, heads together, pointing, nodding. I hadn't noticed what a good-looking bloke he was before. . . .

"John?" Bree sounded nervous. "Is something wrong? I mean, something other than what's wrong?"

"Don't know, do I?" My own voice actually shocked me. I sounded as cold as summer in Antarctica, and ominous with it. "We'll talk."

It was a stupid, spiteful thing to say, especially said in that tone of voice. I watched all the colour disappear from her cheeks, watched the muscles round her eyes and mouth tighten up, and heard her breathing shorten. The tone of voice I'd used was one she'd probably never heard from me before, and right then, I told myself she was never going to hear it again. She doesn't like surprises, not from me, and she's got good reason not to.

Thing is, it scared the shit out of me. The power that reaction of hers gave me—it was all wrong. Christ, how wrong was it that one remark from me could reduce her to a state of waiting for calamity?

I didn't want that kind of power over anyone's life or anyone's happiness, especially not Bree's. I seemed to have it, though, and even worse, I seemed to be abusing it. I bent over and kissed her ear.

"Sorry, love. I'm being a self-indulgent berk. I'm edgy—there's no reason to let me take it out on you. You ought to thump me."

That seemed to reassure her. I dropped an arm around her and held on until Patrick came over and took her aside. I spent the next couple of hours alternating between watching every move Ormand and Bree made and making sure that my awareness of them didn't ride me into doing something stupid.

They'd brought a medical examiner along with them, a calm-looking woman with an entourage. When we left, to go sign statements at the local cop shop up the highway in Terra Linda, she was directing traffic, arranging for Rosario's body to be taken elsewhere.

Ormand waved us off towards our cars. I gathered that, for whatever reason, none of us were being regarded as suspects, and as I was reading over and signing my own statement, I asked Patrick why.

"Timing." He wasn't paying any attention to Bree at all. "It's not carved in stone, but the ME told us that, at first look, he'd been killed around eleven last night, with a two-hour window either way. You guys alibi each other, in a group. Mr. Morgenstern was in Sausalito, down at the Plant recording studio, handling a session—he got there around eight and didn't leave until nearly three in the morning. We called down to the people who run the Plant, and they confirmed that. So, provisionally, you're in the clear."

"Lovely. Ta. Look, Patrick—" The name nearly choked me, saying it right then, but I managed. "I need to ask you something. We came up specifically to get some gear. Rosie getting his neck broken doesn't make our problem go away—the Bombardiers still need to record a CD, and their record label's looking for an excuse to drop them as it is. Mac flew in from London as a favour to sing Vinny's stuff, and we need to rehearse and record. I was slotted to sit in on three numbers, but with Vinny gone, I have to do guitar on all ten songs, and I can't make it sound like the Bombardiers instead of Blacklight without Vinny's gear. We are—we were—totally different guitar styles, you know?"

Patrick was nodding. "Yeah, I can see how it would be a problem. What was it you came up to get, exactly?"

"Vinny's stuff. Paul says Vinny lived just down the road, and he's been storing his stuff in that warehouse, or garage, or whatever it is, since he moved out here from the East Coast. Specifically, what we came up to get was a handful of pedal effects, a couple of particular amplifiers, and one very flashy guitar. Very pricey, too, fifty-grand in fact."

"Fif—" His eyes went very wide, and then snapped down into thin slits. I'd noticed before, I didn't much care for the bloke's eyes. "Whoa. What is it? And was it his?"

"So he said. It's a custom Zemaitis with an inlaid mother-of-pearl top—there are maybe three of them from that vintage in the world, and Tony Zemaitis built them by hand, but he died a few years back, so they're a collector's wet dream. And the one Vinny was using has some heavy modifications to the electronics, and I can't duplicate his sound without it. Any chance we can get what we came up for, and get on with the rehearsals?"

It turned out the forensics people were nearly done, and after that, they wanted Paul to go down with them and do a spot-inventory anyway. Paul said he had no problem with us coming along if the cops didn't mind, and Ormand said he didn't mind so long as the cops could be there as well, so we were all one big happy family, yeah, or at least on the same page.

It was nearly seven in the evening when we were shepherded out into our respective vehicles. This time, Mac and Dom rode with Tony, and Paul rode with Ormand, and I had Bree to myself. It was too short a drive to say anything useful, ten minutes at most, but I kissed her hard just before she started the engine.

"John?" Her voice was small, troubled. "Did I do something? Are you mad at me?"

"No. Jealous."

She jerked her head around. "Jealous? Of what?"

"Not what, who. I'm an idiot, that's all. Let's go nab a pretty guitar and get some dinner, yeah? Think we can get into Angelino, if we finish up at the warehouse fast enough?"

"Probably, but do you really want to? After all, this is Marin—the news is probably all over the county. We'd be eating in a fishbowl." We were out of the parking lot and onto Highway 101, and her attention was on the road. I couldn't read her look. "Jealous of who? Mac? Because, well, no. Really no. I mean, you'd have to be joking. He flirts the way he breathes, and I notice it just about as much."

"Not Mac, no. Patrick Ormand."

She opened her mouth and closed it again, but she didn't meet my eye, and I felt my stomach jump uneasily. I touched her knee. "Eyes on the road, lady, please. Like I said, we'll talk. I'm an idiot."

Bree had her lower lip between her teeth. We did the rest of the ride in silence. Tony and Ormand's people beat us to the warehouse by a few minutes; they'd already begun taking inventory as we pulled up.

The warehouse was a weird place. It had obviously started out as a garage, but Paul decided to store valuable sound gear in it, and he'd covered the windows with Sheetrock, and now there were intact walls with no windows. There was the roll-up door, and that was all.

There was a lot of gear stashed about the place, most of it with CLUB 707 stencilled on it. Paul went from corner to corner with Ormand, but they stopped when they got to a peculiar metal trailer, right in the middle of the room.

"Is the trailer yours?" Ormand was studying it. "Or was it Vinny Fabiano's?"

"You mean the Bambi?" Paul looked surprised. "Oh, that's mine. I actually had all my worldly goods in it when I moved out here from New York, about twelve years ago. It's been parked here ever since. Did you want to check it out? Feel free. I've got the key, but it may be unlocked already."

My attention was wandering. I looked around and found the pile of amps that I recognised as probably being Vinny's.

They emerged from the trailer—it really looked like an old-fashioned silver cigar tube with wheels on—and continued checking things over. There didn't seem to be anything missing; whatever the motive was that had left Rosario's neck in its final condition, it didn't look to be theft.

Finally, Paul led the way over to the amps in the corner. "Here we go. This is Vinny's stuff, amps, guitars, all his musical gear. He stored everything here. A ten-year-old kid with a lollipop stick could have broken into his apartment. Much safer here. Like I told the police, though, I can't help with an inventory of this stuff. It wasn't mine. Vinny just asked if he could keep it here, I said yes and gave him a key, reminded him to make damned sure he locked up whenever he was in and out, and that was it. JP, Tony—come take what you need, man."

"Love to." I was moving through Vinny's pile, moving things aside. "But we've got a problem. The amps are here, and so is his PRS case." I knelt and snapped it open. "Good, the PRS is where it belongs. That's an acoustic case over there—looks like a Martin D-28. Most of the effects pedals are here, as well."

"Shit." Tony had been peering behind road cases, pushing them aside. Now he straightened up. He was chewing his lower lip. "Not good, man. Problem is fucking right. We're hosed."

"What is it?" Paul looked bewildered. "What's wrong?"

"The Zemaitis." I met Tony's eye. "It's not here. And if he wouldn't have kept it at his place, and it isn't at Freelon Street, then someone's nicked it."

CHAPTER EIGHT

We got home just before midnight, and by that time, I was not only in a really bad temper, but I was also in the middle of a relapse as bad as anything I'd dealt since early on in Blacklight's last tour. Nothing was working—not legs, not hands, nothing at all. If I'd had any real motor control over my body, I'd have been swearing. This was working up to be a monster of a relapse, and of all the shitty times for it to be coming in, this was hard to top.

Bree got us home and locked down for the night. Tony had loaded what there was of Vinny's gear into the Range Rover, and he'd followed the Jag into our garage and unloaded it there, carrying everything into the studio. By this point, I was barely coherent. Bree had concentrated on getting us home as fast as she could while not getting us a speeding ticket; once we were safely indoors, though, I managed to grab Tony's attention.

"Tony. The PRS." It hurt to talk; I was gritting my teeth, slurring my speech even worse. "Vinny's. In the case?"

"Safe and sound." He couldn't hide how disturbed he was, and I didn't blame him; he'd already seen a dead bloke today, and he'd never seen me this messed up before. "It's cool, man. Only thing missing is the Zemaitis. Everything else was there—we grabbed the amps, the effects array, the PRS. It's all here. We're getting it into the studio, ready whenever you are." He caught a look from Bree and added hastily, "But not tonight."

Mac and Dom were carrying smaller items from the truck to the studio. I ignored them and focussed on Tony.

"Look. In the case—how? It was—at Freelon. It got to Marin—to the warehouse—how? Vinny was dead—Rosario said, no key. Why we needed Paul—remember?" I rubbed my jaw; there was no feeling there and nothing being communicated from fingers to face to brain. Shit. Maybe an extra dose of Neurontin or pain meds? "Sorry—talking not on. Don't feel well."

"Whoa." Tony was staring at me. "Good question, about the PRS. When I called Rosie, he told me Vinny had a key, but he didn't, and Vinny's was probably tagged as evidence or some shit. That's right, that's why we needed Paul to let us in, in the first place. How the hell did the PRS get up there? Vinny used it on 'Liplock' that last night—I remember how good it sounded. This is some weird, weird shit. Maybe I should call the cops and tell them?"

"I will. Tomorrow." I'd suddenly remembered, tonight being Monday, I was due for my weekly interferon shot. Thank Christ for that, anyway. I turned to Bree, who was hovering, impatient and helpless, and tried sounding less like a stroke victim. "Shot—it's Monday. Meds in the fridge. Forgot."

She disappeared up the stairs to the kitchen. Interferon is tricky stuff—it has to be kept cold until a few hours before you use it. If you leave it out too long, though, it goes off and you've just spent about five hundred dollars for something you end up pouring down the sink. Normally, I'd take the shot just before bed, which meant getting it up to room temperature at right around seven o'clock, but we'd got home several hours later than we'd expected, and it was still in the fridge. And shooting myself up with something ice cold? Not bloody likely. I already felt like death warmed over.

So I was another hour away from my bed and knockout meds, at the very least. Damn. I tried going Zen, concentrating on other things, things that weren't the immediate pain. Right. Tonight was interferon, and an extra dose of muscle relaxants, and antispasmodics, and a good long kip with my old lady there beside me. And maybe tomorrow, this exacerbation would have eased off and I'd be able to cope, to deal, to play. . . .

Bree sent Tony and Katia off, telling them she'd call in the morning and let them know what was going on. Then she armed our own security system and herded our guests upstairs to their respective rooms. She made it clear she wasn't taking no for an answer, but luckily, jet lag had finally caught up with both Mac and Dom, and they were quite ready for some sleep.

And finally, at half past one in the morning, we were alone in our room and she brought my interferon and my painkillers and I was able to give myself the shot and climb into bed, with Bree beside me and my body trying to decide whether it wanted to function or not, and, unfortunately, a very busy brain that didn't seem to want to shut down for the night.

The more I thought about the situation at the warehouse, the more bizarre it seemed. None of it made sense. If everyone had been telling the truth, there was no way that damned PRS should have been where we'd found it. No matter how I looked at it, I couldn't work out an answer.

I'd been first out of Freelon the night Vinny got bashed, but there was nothing wrong with my memory. The picture in my head was very clear: Vinny had been playing the damned thing on "Liplock," fuzzing it out, getting some excellent grit off it, kicking in one of his distortion pedals. He'd been a "one song, one axe" bloke, and the one axe, for that one song, had been his PRS. I remembered the blue waterfall on the guitar's top, the inlay on the neck catching my eye as Doug, the roadie, handed me my jacket and some cold water for my meds. I remember thinking that, as good as the PRS sounded, the Zemaitis might work even better on that particular tune. . . .

There was no way I was going to believe Vinny had left Freelon Street, driven to San Rafael to put the PRS away, and then driven all the way back to the City, just to do—what, exactly? The idea was ridiculous. So, the odds were good that someone had taken that PRS and returned it to Paul's warehouse after Vinny was dead.

But that was just as ridiculous as the fact itself. Why would anyone do that? The PRS wasn't as valuable as the Zemaitis, but it was still worth a good twenty thousand dollars, and maybe more. The two guitars were both very recognisable, and either one would be really hard to sell off without people noticing. So why nick one and put the other tidily back in its case and leave it there? It didn't make sense.

I shifted a bit as the right leg spasmed and twitched and then settled down; eight years of this, and I'd learned how to do it so that I didn't wake Bree. My body wanted sleep, but my damned head wasn't cooperating. Right. The best way to deal was to let the head finish doing its thing, and hope for sleep at the end of it.

Okay—so, for whatever reason, someone had taken the PRS up to San Rafael. The likeliest person for that would have been Rosario. If Paul had given Vinny a key, and Vinny wanted the PRS up in the warehouse, he'd have had no problem tossing the key and the guitar to his cousin the guitar tech, and sending him on his way. But if Rosie had Vinny's key tucked in his pocket when Tony had called him, why had Rosie lied about it? And where in hell was the Zemaitis?

There was another big unanswered question keeping me from sleep: Bruno Baines. Where did he, and his gorgeous red guitar, come into it?

Because he did, quite obviously. I wasn't about to say so to Bree, but truth is, I was surprised he wasn't behind bars already. After all, he'd obviously gone to Freelon Street and he'd obviously been let in. He definitely had his share of explaining to do, but even though I couldn't summon up Bree's fierceness on the matter, I agreed completely about the basic fact: no one who had spent three months of their life on a labour of love that intensive was going to smash it over someone's head. According to Ormand, the guitar had been damaged, possibly beyond repair. And there was just no way the man who made the guitar had risked damaging it. It would be like trying to imagine Leonardo da Vinci smashing someone over the head with the *Mona Lisa*, or something.

There was something else, something that was trying to grab me, but this one, I knew what it was and I'd already decided I wasn't looking at it tonight. My own reaction to Bree dealing with Ormand was going to have to wait. I wasn't coping until I felt stronger.

The brain was beginning to slow down, finally. About time; I'd taken extra antispasmodics and a TyCo for the pain, and everything was beginning to kick in.

One by one, the nerves responded, doing their thing, slowing down. The twitching stopped, first in the left leg, then in the right. The left hand eased up, and I felt the fingers uncurl; the right hand took longer to ease up, but it finally stopped the restless jerking and spasming. And then, finally, the lungs evened out their rhythm, signalling the beginning of sleep.

At the edge of unconsciousness, I felt Bree slip out of bed and head for the bathroom. I hadn't realised she was still awake; her breathing had been even and regular. She wouldn't turn the light on, because the light in our master bath activated the ventilation system, and that was really loud; the damned thing sounds like a 747 prepping for takeoff. I was always reminding myself to get a contractor in to fix it, make it quieter, but I always forgot in the morning.

Relaxed, easy, quiet, heading off into sleep. Just before I got there, I thought I heard something, a strange choked-off noise from the bathroom.

I tried to open one eye, but there was no way; I was too close to unconsciousness. Stuck in that weird little place between waking and dreaming, I couldn't be certain, but it sounded for all the world as if she was crying.

The meds completely saved my ass that night. When I woke up, I'd stopped shaking and I had some control of my jaw back again. Bless that interferon, it's good stuff. And the TyCo, left over from the heart attack I'd had in Boston during the Black-light tour, had done the trick as well.

The problem with anything that's got codeine in it is that it knocks me all the way out, and doesn't really want to move on next day. I slept until nearly ten, which was something close to a record. Bree had got up well before me; I stood under the shower and tried to wash the codeine haze away with the showerhead set to needle-pulse. It didn't work very well.

When I got down to breakfast, I found Mac waiting for me. He was perky and focussed, which didn't help my general feeling of being left out in the rain somewhere.

"Johnny! Good, you're alive. You look human again—well, almost human. You all right?" He was drinking bottled water, something he does a lot of on the road; he says staying hydrated helps him not get buried by jet lag and general exhaustion. He's disgustingly healthy, is Mac. "Because I've done something useful before breakfast—amazing, I know. I had an idea, and I rang up Luke. I asked him about the Zemaitis. He hasn't got one himself, but apparently there's some sort of club, the Zemaitis Collectors Club. It sounds like a cult, but he got on to them and told them what was needed. They tracked down Vinny's guitar and told Luke what all the fancy electronics were. And . . ."

"Come on, mate, get on with it." I had a cup of coffee of my own in hand, and I was beginning to wake up. "Brilliant idea, yeah, but what's the story?"

"It turns out there's a bloke down in Santa Barbara who's got two of the damned things, and one of them has been tarted up, quite close to what Vinny had on his. Not a pearl-top—it's a maple-top." Mac sounded triumphant. "So I rang him up and explained what was going on, and asked to borrow it. And he said yes, provided he got to watch us rehearse and record with it."

My jaw dropped. "Mac, you fucking hero! You absolutely rock. Brilliant job, mate. When can he get here?"

He grinned. It was a damned good thing none of Bree's horny middle-aged girlfriends were lurking about; Mac, when he's feeling triumphant, radiates a kind of charm that's noticeable even by his old geezer mates.

"Hang on a minute, before you finalise those plans to carry me around the streets of Rome—there's one small problem. He says the peghead is cracked, and he wants to get it fixed."

"Cool." I finished my coffee and reached for my cell phone. "I know a good luthier, assuming he's not in jail. Mac, have you seen Bree this morning? She let me sleep in, bless the girl."

"Yeah, she went out—that was about half an hour ago. Said she had an appointment. Since I was going to be safe indoors most of the day, I shooed Dom off to go play for a few hours. Bree said something about dropping her off at some martial arts supply place. Damned if I know why—it's not like she can pick up a couple of *sai*, and maybe a nice new *kama* to play with, and stuff them in her carry-on when we head back to London. They frown on sharp objects on airplanes these days."

"I don't know what any of that is, but it all sounds lethal. Of course, assuming it's Dom, I suppose the whole lethal thing comes with the bodyguard."

I punched in Tony's number, but my mind was showing an irritating tendency to fixate on the wrong thing.

An appointment? Bree hadn't said a word to me about an appointment today. In fact, she'd told me she wasn't going to take any catering work until after the wedding.

That had actually led to an interesting situation. She sees my money as mine, period, and doesn't like using it for stuff that's just for her. She handles the chequebook, she pays the bills, she knows down to the penny how much I've got, but she uses my money willingly only for stuff that's mine, or that's for both of us.

The big Sub-Zero fridge in our kitchen, for instance—that had been a corker of a row. We'd gone furniture shopping for a new dining room table and chairs. She'd watched me write a cheque for nearly four thousand dollars without a blink, because the dining room table was both of ours, see, and we'd be using it to seat all our friends, not just mine or hers.

So, when I spotted a Sub-Zero fridge on the way out and suggested we get it, I was really narked to watch her stiffen up and say, no, she'd be mostly storing catering stuff in that, so she should pay for it, and she couldn't afford it right now. Of course, I could afford it easily, so we had words. We were really lucky none of the salespeople were secret gossip columnists, because we'd ended up having this huge pissy row, right there at the store. I'd finally announced I was buying it because I wanted a giant pricey fridge to store my interferon in, and she would damned well have to live with it. She got me back by putting the entire take from her next catering gig into the house account, so she ended up paying for it in the end, anyway. There really are days I could cheerfully thump her.

Tony was home, and he had Bruno Baines's number. I told him to ring up the rest of the Bombardiers and Damon, and get them over to our place; even without the Zemaitis, we could save some time with Mac working out the vocals to the point where the band was happy with it. I rang off and got Bruno on the phone.

More good luck: he wasn't in jail, although he sounded a bit depressed. I gave him a quick rundown of what had been happening, and it turned out he knew Rosario had been killed, because he was one of the first people Ormand had dragged in for questioning. I didn't ask, but I got the impression he had no alibi—not for either of the killings—and of course, there was the murder weapon and how it had got to Freelon Street.

So yeah, he was nervous, but the prospect of coming to our house and working on a vintage Zemaitis cheered him up enormously. I told him I'd ring him as soon as I knew when the collector with the guitar was coming, and hung up.

The band showed up together, with Damon and the roadies right behind them in the Bombardiers' equipment van. We pulled it inside, and I watched everyone unload; the studio was going to be cramped, but we could at least get started.

By the time we broke for a rest, it was three hours later, and Mac had the Bombardiers in the palm of his hand. I was feeling shaky, but it was mostly the legs, and I'd been sitting. It was past time for a stretch and some fresh air, I thought, and maybe something to eat. Besides, I could see if Bree had got home yet.

The Jag was out in the driveway. Shit. I'd forgotten to get them to move the van, and she'd had to park outside. Still, she was home. I left everyone out in our back garden and headed upstairs in search of her.

She wasn't in the kitchen; in fact, she wasn't anywhere downstairs. That surprised me, because the kitchen was where she tends to hang out when I'm down in the studio, it's where she feels at home, and comfortable.

I rummaged around in the fridge and got some cheese and some leftovers and took them out to the garden. I left them to it and headed back inside. But I was feeling uneasy.

Something was up. Bree wouldn't interrupt a rehearsal, but it wasn't like her to just disappear, either, not with guests in the house.

"Bree?" I noticed her computer was up and blinking, in its alcove off the kitchen. She'd been using it, and left it up.

Out of nowhere, I was genuinely edgy. Leaving the browser open, that's something else she never does, not with the cats and their fondness for walking on her keyboard and locking up her operating system. Something must have taken her away from the computer in a hurry, for her to do that. What the hell?

I walked over and looked at the browser window she'd left open. In the window seat, Farrowen lifted her head from her front paws and blinked up at me.

If You Have Been Recently Diagnosed—Information: Cancer of the cervix is the third most common gynecologic cancer in the United States today. Fortunately, however, cervical cancer, when caught early, has a high success rate in both treatment and post-five-year life expectancy.

For a minute, an hour, a lifetime, I stood there, just staring at the screen. I was dizzy, heart revving like a race car engine, sick at my stomach.

I closed my eyes. The words, the fucking words, didn't go anywhere. They were still there when I opened my eyes:

If You Have Been Recently Diagnosed. . .

Voices broke through the haze inside my head: I could hear Mac and Billy laughing about something, out in the garden.

I took the stairs two at a time. By the time I hit the top, I was calling her. It was tricky, because I was fighting an ache in my chest and a huge stabbing stitch in my side, and I had no breath available. But I was calling her anyway.

She was where I knew she'd be, where she sits when the shit is piling up and she just needs a tiny corner of the universe where she can stop and breathe. I heard the squeak of the rocking chair as I opened the bedroom door: back and forth, back and forth, just sitting there, rocking.

"Bree?"

Silence. Nothing, not a word—just the quiet, rhythmic squeak of the chair. I reached over her shoulders and got her hands in my own, and held hard.

"I was going to tell you." Her voice was flat, completely un-inflected. Oh, God. "I wasn't trying to hide it, or keep it secret, I swear I wasn't. Don't be mad. But I only got it confirmed yesterday—that was the phone call I made, while I was out in the car at Paul Morgenstern's house. And then there was Rosario. I was going to tell you, I promise."

I swallowed hard. Things—hands and legs—wanted to

130

shake, but right now, the multiple sclerosis could fuck off. What I was feeling wasn't allowing much room for anything else. "I know. It's okay. Do you want to talk about it, love? Would it make it easier? Can you tell me what I ought to know, to help?"

"I had my Pap, ten days ago." Rocking forward, rocking back, taking me with her. I was off balance, but I held on to her. "It came back abnormal. That's not uncommon—I'm in my forties, hormones, things change. I went back, and she took another look. That was the day Vinny got killed. She didn't like what she saw; she tried to hide it, but she couldn't. They did a full biopsy and sent it off for priority testing. Sometimes it's useful, my mother being who she is. Anyway—it's malignant." Her voice hadn't changed. "They don't think it's metastasised, but they won't know until the surgery."

"If they've caught it nice and early, it's quite curable, right?" I heard the words come out. I was gobsmacked at my own voice, soothing, calm. I didn't feel that way.

"That's what the surgeon thinks, that where it is, it's survivable. But it could be much further developed than she thinks it is." She shuddered under my hands. "Apparently, I have some weird interior angles they can't see behind without doing some major digging."

"It's going to be okay. You're going to be okay. I'm right here. I won't let anything happen." Rubbish, I thought, total bullshit, bollocks. I was helpless, worse than useless. She couldn't get sick. I wouldn't allow it. What if she died? Oh, Christ, what was I going on about? "*Is* it early, Bree? I mean, did they catch it early on?"

"They think so—she said stage one. She scheduled me for surgery on Thursday. They want me in fast, because of that ovary they took out when I miscarried."

The past, the bloody past—it never seems to let go. Just grabs like a leech, sucking away joy, sucking away hope. Too many memories: Cilla, the ovarian cancer, the muddle, the mess, and Viv, Luke's Viv, getting the diagnosis with a toddler and Luke left alone behind, a bare month left to her life. . . .

I let go of her hands and rubbed her neck, tilting her head forward. The rocking stilled as she relaxed under my fingers. "What do you want me to do? Get Mac and Dom a hotel? I'll tell the band what's going on, let them know I can't—"

"No, don't do that, John. There's no need. Keep the sessions going, please."

She tilted her head up and looked at me. I remembered that look, too damned well. Somewhere inside the middle-aged lioness was a frightened teenager. And there was nothing—not one damned thing—I could do to help, not this time. The feeling was about as bad as it gets in this life, and I suddenly found myself thinking, *This is what she lives with, this feeling, dealing with my MS, with my heart murmur, with all my health issues. This is what she lives with, every day, waking and sleeping. How does she do it? How the fuck can she deal? . . .*

"Are you sure, Bree?"

"Yes. The doctor says it's about ninety minutes of surgery, unless they find more than they think they will. That's always possible." She steadied her voice—it seemed to want to jump. "My mother is going to be there, of course—they don't want me driving afterward, so she's going to pick me up and drive me home afterward. You don't need to not get the work done, John."

Her voice wavered suddenly, out of her control. "But will you come to the hospital with me Thursday? Please? I know it's a drag, but I'd like to know you'll be there when they knock me out. And when—when I wake up."

A memory, a bad one, and recent: a phone call in the small hours of the morning as I waited in a Miami hotel, not knowing where she was or why she'd gone. What had she said? *I never ask you to do anything, and I sure as hell never ask you not to do any-thing.*

"You don't need to ask that, Bree. Not now, not ever." I kissed her hair. "Look, I'm going back down and let them know, unless you'd rather I kept quiet about it."

"No, you can tell them—Katia already knows, and so does Sandra. Just—I'm staying up here for now. I just don't feel like seeing a lot of people. Okay?"

"Right." I came round the front and knelt in front of her. "We'll get through it. We will. You're going to be okay."

CHAPTER NINE

I know this sounds peculiar, but the news of Bree's cancer did something to me musically.

If I'd thought about it, I'd have imagined news like that would stop me in my tracks. Instead, something about the situation pushed me into high gear creatively. Of course, I didn't know that right off; the plain fact of the word, *cancer*, pretty much filled my entire horizon just then.

I also got organised, in a way I'm not, mostly. I think it was probably just the feeling that I had to have control of something, anything at all. And my mind had turned off.

The job of telling the band came first. I kissed Bree one more time and went back out into the garden. It was weird, you know? I thought I was okay and I hadn't said a word, but everyone had been talking, laughing, pulling on the beer Kris had brought along, and when they saw me, they went dead quiet.

"JP?" Tony was staring at me. "What's going on, man? What's up? What's wrong?"

"Bree." I'd been a fucking idiot, thinking I was calm—my voice was all over the place. "She's got cancer. Surgery this Thursday morning. She's only just found out—they want to deal with it fast."

"Oh, Jesus." Kris put his beer down. "JP, oh shit. How bad—do they know—?"

"They think it's early on, but they won't know for sure until Thursday." I looked around at all of them and suddenly realised that my legs weren't going to hold me up. "She wants me to go on with the sessions. I need to sit down."

"Too right you do." Mac was there, pushing me into a chair. He looked stunned, and I suddenly remembered 1989, Viv Hedley's diagnosis, the chemo, it not working, her cancer spreading into brain and spine and stomach.

I'd been in hospital myself, in San Francisco, while that particular bit of hell was going on. Mac had been there for Luke, doing what little he could; they never talked about it, but from how I was feeling right now, I got just how scared Luke must have been.

"Here, take this." Mac handed me a paper napkin. I couldn't imagine what I was supposed to do with it. Then something splashed on the back of my hand, and I realised I was crying. I hadn't known before.

Of course, everyone wanted to pack up and leave, but there was a CD that needed rehearsing, and anyway, Bree'd been really clear about wanting us to keep going. It could have been a complete clusterfuck, but out of nowhere, there was Bree herself. I wondered if she'd been watching from the window seat, seen what was going on. She was so calm about it, and so firm about wanting them to keep on with it, that there wasn't any room for argument.

135

It was another revelation, that encounter in the garden. No one knew how to react to her at first—it was as if they'd all decided she was already dead, past hope, and no one knew how to deal. I had a really black moment, wanting to kill every last fucking one of them, before I realised that their reaction was just what most of the world would do in that situation.

That kind of fear, that feeling guilty because you're so happy it isn't you who has the problem, that only really transmutes when it's someone you care about under the gun, you know? It's one thing to be in the soup yourself, but when it's someone you love, the reactions are much sharper. Mine were, anyway.

She offered everyone a scratch dinner, but I put my foot down about that, and we decided to send out for a few pizzas instead. Bree was really working at it, trying to get things back to relatively normal, at least on the surface; while she bantered with Billy about whether pepperoni was actually edible or not, I told her what I wanted on mine—artichoke hearts and mushrooms—and went back inside in search of my cell phone. If Bree could be this organised and on top of it, then damned if I wasn't going to do the same. It was time to get the guitar business worked out.

So I rang the collector with the Zemaitis in Santa Barbara— the bloke's name was Magnus Mattsson, which I suspected he might have made up, because really, it was far too much of a good thing, that name.

As soon as I convinced him that no, it wasn't a hoax, yeah, that really had been Malcolm Sharpe on the phone and now it was JP Kinkaid, he was ready to grab the guitar and get on a plane. I told him I'd have Blacklight's PR person get him a flight and a hotel and transportation booked to get him into and around San Francisco, and asked if he could be up here on Friday.

"Oh, definitely. My schedule's wide open. Besides, I'd reschedule pretty much anything. If I said I wasn't excited about this, I'd be lying."

"Good. That's brilliant. You're doing us a huge favour, you know?" I was having difficulty trying to wrap my head around the squeaky little voice coming out of the phone at me being attached to someone with a name that would have been perfectly at home sacking Constantinople in a longboat or something.

"But—look, did Mr. Sharpe explain? About the crack in the peghead? I mean, it's totally playable as is, but I really want to get the peghead fixed. The Zemaitis is the most valuable instrument I own, and I'd really feel better if—"

"Not a problem. We've got a world-class luthier lined up. He'll be here to fix it." Bree had come indoors and was filling the kettle for tea. "Right. So, expect a call from a woman called Carla Fanucci, with flight and hotel info, okay? Of course, we'll cover any costs—this is band business. Like I said, without the Zemaitis, we'd be in deep water, trying to get this CD recorded. We owe you for this one, Mr. Mattsson, so anything we can do, or Carla can do, let us know, yeah?"

"No, it's my pleasure. And please call me Magnus—no one ever calls me anything else." He was quiet for a moment. "You know, I own a lot of guitars—eighteen of them, actually. This particular one, I had built for me, but I don't play it as much as I used to. If I knew then what I know now, I probably wouldn't have asked Tony Zemaitis to put in half of what's there, electronically. But under these circumstances, I'm glad I did. It should do the job for you, Mr. Kinkaid. And I'm really looking forward to hearing you play it, it's a wonderful guitar and it deserves to be played by the best. See you Friday."

"Tea?" The electric kettle had whistled, and Bree turned it off. "Or do you want coffee? Everyone's back downstairs, by the way. I said I'd let them know when the pizza got here."

"Tea, love, please—whatever you're having. Hang on a minute, okay? I need to call Carla."

The phone call to Los Angeles was nice and quick. I didn't mention Bree being sick at all—I just told Carla what was going on about Vinny getting bashed, added the news about Rosario—she hadn't heard about that yet. Of course, she already knew about me and Mac helping out, having butted heads with Bree about the limo deal. This one was easy; I asked her to get an open-ended flight and a hotel for a bloke she'd never heard of before, and this time, she got to book the town car as well.

Carla's a professional. She must have been burning to know what the hell was going on, but she didn't ask a single question, just took all the numbers and whatnot for Magnus Mattsson, said she'd book everything and let people know when she'd finished up, and told me to say hi to Mac and Dom for her. I think she was still a bit stewed about Bree insisting on picking Mac up at the airport, because she did have a pointed few words about that. Knowing Carla, it was a safe bet she'd have flights and hotels booked and paid for within ten minutes, and everyone concerned notified two minutes after that. Like I said, she's a professional. She earns her pay, Carla does.

So there I was, organised and trying not to freak out, and then Bree sat down at the table next to me. She didn't say anything, just set both teacups and the little pot she'd bought in Chinatown down on the table and sighed. It was a long deep sigh, and for some reason, I opened my mouth, and something incredibly stupid came out.

"Bree. Look, love, I need to ask you something. Is there something up, with you and Patrick Ormand?"

Fuck. Bloody unbelievable. I heard the words, heard my voice putting them out there, and wondered if I'd gone nuts. Of all the things to say, and of all the times to say it . . .

"No." She sounded very tired, dispirited, no energy at all. "I mean, not if you mean what I think you mean, which, by the way, would be just about the most insulting question ever asked by anybody in the history of the universe. If you mean something else—something professional—then, yes, something is going on. I called him to scream at him, because he seemed to have it stuck in that rat terrier brain of his that Bruno Baines might actually have been capable of destroying his own guitar on Vinny Fabiano's skull. There are times I think the man is an idiot." She looked at me over the rim of her teacup. "But then, there are times I think all men are idiots."

I gaped at her. She went on, still sounding tired, a bit remote, as if nothing was really worth bothering about, you know? It scared me, because it wasn't like her at all. Me thinking she was doing another man, even hinting I thought that, should have sent her into a major slap-down. Instead, all she had left was weariness. She didn't have enough left to get angry. For a moment, I wanted her to take a good solid swing at me, deck me, throw something, scream, anything at all that would show me she was still my own healthy Bree. . . .

"He also seemed to think that a cell would be a good place to stash Bruno while he and his cop buddies thought about it." She took a mouthful of tea, and then there was that sigh again. "So I called him a couple of times to tell him he was an idiot, and to let him know just why I thought he was an idiot."

"Okay." There wasn't much else I could say. "Got it."

"No, it's not okay. Because that's not what you meant, was it? You thought I was sleeping with him or something. And really, John, I'd like to know what I've ever done to make you think I'd be capable of cheating on you. Because I can't think of anything, no matter how hard I try. I guess I just don't have enough imagination."

I sat there, feeling like the most complete berk that ever breathed. She was looking at me, watching me, just holding her teacup, waiting for an answer.

It was a peculiar moment: The basement studio was full of my mates, singing about sex and loss and love and whatnot, and I was up here with her, and I just gave her the truth. I gave it to her straight as it came into my head, no filtering.

"Of course you can't think of anything," I told her. "There isn't anything, nothing at all. You've never once not been there for me. You've never once done anything that gives me any right at all to doubt you. You've been a rock, and I'm a fool and I don't think I deserve my own good luck. And you really are the only thing I've ever loved in my life, besides music. I haven't got a good answer to why I thought that, Bree. I haven't got a bad answer to it, either. Unless, maybe, I'm beginning to feel my age, and maybe I'm just looking at what life would be like if you were gone. And I can't look at it. The idea eats me alive. I can't do it."

"I'm not going anywhere. And as for your age—you're no older than me now than you were when I forgot about the zipper on my blue velvet dress and let you undo all the buttons that first night at the Miyako. We were eleven years apart then, and it's still eleven years—and even if I'm not seventeen and telling myself not to let you see how scared I am, I've never loved you any less. I've never known how to turn that light off, even if there have been a few times I've wanted to."

I stayed quiet. I mean, what was there to say?

She set her cup down and leaned forward to kiss me. "Just— don't think such stupid stuff about me, please. It isn't fair, and I don't deserve it from you. It hurts, John."

"I know. And I won't, I promise." I cleared my throat— there seemed to a lump that didn't want to be got rid of. "I should go back down, if you're okay with that. I'm the only gui-tar player they've got right now."

"It's fine. You go play. I'll let you know when dinner gets here."

I don't really remember much about the next day and a half. The whole idea of time, about how it marches along and does its thing, and shit happens along the way? That went west. It was like being in a bubble, away from anything that anyone could call normal. All I remember is waiting for Thursday morning.

And that's nuts, because actually, I did a lot. I got word from Carla that Magnus Mattsson would be arriving on Friday, early afternoon; she arranged all of it, had him booked in at the W, Mercedes town car with a driver at his beck and call, the lot. So Carla doing what she does best, that was one thing.

And I know I managed to take possession of a small package for me, delivered by FedEx. I got it and signed for it and slipped it into my pocket before Bree ever saw it. I'd literally closed the front door and got my hand out of my trousers pocket as Bree came out of the kitchen. I remember thinking that at least something had gone right, even if it was just the timing.

I remember Bree heading up the hill to the hospital for her pre-surgery screening, telling me no, she honestly didn't want to drive, that she wanted to feel the burn of her muscles taking the hill. I remember her smiling at me, that the smile made it possible to accept that she wanted to go up alone.

I remember the phone call from Luke. Of course he'd heard—Mac let him know, probably the moment he'd been alone with his phone. So Luke had rung me.

That's Luke, you know? Talking about it, asking if I needed him to come out, offering me backup had to be harder for him than I could even begin to understand. Those memories, Viv dying—that had to be the stuff you find in nightmares. But he offered, and he meant it. I remember holding it together while we talked, remembering knowing just where each of us was coming from, of slipping into the small back bedroom we use as a storeroom for my guitars, fighting off a crying fit. Bless my mates. They're my family. They're the best.

Also, the Bombardiers came back on Wednesday, and we spent several very productive hours down in the studio. Damon actually took some good mixes, the band plus me and Mac working on three more of the songs we both needed to learn. And I'm fairly sure I'm not hallucinating or having an acid flashback or something, remembering that Damon was doing a sort of restrained bitch and moan about how much he missed the big Korg at Freelon Street, with its capability for the overnight downloads for backup, and me telling him, well, go buy what you need, then, no problem, whatever, I'll pay for it.

I remember that Mac insisted on taking Dom out for dinner Wednesday night, and that I knew, right off, that he wanted to give me a few hours alone with Bree. We spent the time in the living room, making music, me playing for her. And really, that's the only bit I do remember clearly, because she actually sang that night, when I started playing "That's What Love Will Make You Do." It's already important to me, that memory, because she just doesn't sing, usually, and when she does, I remember.

So I played some wailing slide, leading into it, not really thinking offhand what I was playing, just making music, making her happy, me and Bree and the cats. She twigged it before I did, and out of nowhere, she was singing it, strong and true: *"When I speak your name / I start to shake inside / When I see you stroll / I lose all self-control. . . . "*

She had her eyes closed, but when we got to the chorus, she opened them again and looked straight at me, singing: *"That's what love is, baby / That's what love will make you do. . . ."*

I joined in on the last line and heard us, both together: "*No matter how hard I fight it / Baby I'm still in love with you.*" And her voice faltered there, just for a moment, but I kept singing, and so did she.

So, yeah, a gorgeous iconic little bubble, those few hours. They got me through a night of never closing my eyes, going over memories, trying to convince myself they'd caught it early enough and they weren't going to go in and do whatever they had to do and then find out it was stage four, repeating over and over inside my head, *This is Bree, it's not Viv Hedley, this is Bree*, over and over, making sure she was asleep, remembering, trying to pretend it was an MRI all over again, a place where the only one in any trouble was me, and I could go Zen. But the Zen never came, not that night.

Bree had been told not to eat or drink anything after eight o'clock Wednesday night, so I got out of bed at five, went down-stairs, and fed the cats and did their litter boxes. I made myself a piece of toast and got some coffee before Bree could come downstairs. No need to torment her with the smell of it, since she'd be snarling over not being able to have a sip.

Miranda showed up at half past seven. She looked—I don't know—less collected than usual. And yeah, I'm not dim and I know she was worried off her nut over Bree, but that wasn't it. She just looked more tired, less resilient than usual. That got to me, because she was used to working two days at a stretch at hospital. Hell, the night she'd let it slip about Bree's miscar-riage, she'd been on for two solid days with only a handful of short kip breaks on the sofa in her office, and she'd looked as if she'd just come from a beauty salon.

"John, you're staring at me." She managed a smile, but it looked too much like hard work. "Is there something caught between my teeth?"

"No, but you look knackered. Here—espresso. Drink it

before Bree gets down here and tries to sneak a cup. She's not allowed, not this morning."

"I *am* really tired. It's been a worrying week. And let's not forget that I'm sixty-four years old. Not quite as perky as I was when I was Bree's age." She accepted the cup and took the caffeine at one swallow. "You look exhausted yourself. Did you get any sleep last night?"

"No. Also, I had a bad relapse Monday night. I'm fine, I'll cope. Bree was taking a shower when I went up to get dressed, she ought to be down in a minute. Miranda, a question—we're just a few blocks from the hospital. Any reason for us not to walk over? I know it's a hill, but I don't mind that if you don't. You can park right here in the driveway and drive over when— when she's ready to come home."

"Excellent idea." If she'd caught the slight break in my voice, she wasn't letting on. "Let's do that, if Bree's up for it. It's a very nice morning, no fog in sight. Walking's always a good idea— very healthy. And if they want her to stay there, I can—"

Her own voice stopped suddenly, hearing footsteps on the stairs. "Morning, Bree, is that you?"

"Hi, Mom. Is John down here? Hey, baby, good morning."

Bree came down in nice loose yoga trousers. She had her hair pulled back in a ponytail. She looked about twenty this morning, which did odd things to my heart. "Oh, man, let's get out of here—I can smell the coffee. Sadists, both of you, you both suck. Hey, I had an idea. Would it make sense to walk over to the hospital, instead of having to deal with the parking? What are you both grinning at? . . ."

She was the calmest of the three of us. We'd given Mac the house security code, so that he wouldn't be stuck indoors all day. With Magnus Mattsson and his Zemaitis arriving tomorrow and Damon off buying me a new Roland for my studio, today was a rest day from rehearsing.

You'd think, after eight years of multiple sclerosis, a heart attack, emergency room visits at obscene hours and in too many cities, relapses and exacerbations and MRIs and weekly shots of interferon, that I'd have been able to deal, yeah? Truth is, I was on the verge of a major meltdown. If Bree felt anything like this when it was me in the frying pan, how the hell did she handle it? I wanted to smash things, yell, anything at all to make this not be happening.

The oncologist was waiting for Bree when we got there. "John, you haven't met Elizabeth, have you? This is Elizabeth Nelson, Bree's oncologist. Elizabeth is the best in the Bay Area—Bree's in very good hands. Elizabeth, this is Bree's fiancé, John Kinkaid."

It was all incredibly civilised, you know? The women all seemed so easy about it. I said something conventional and shook the doctor's hand. Beside me, Bree suddenly reached for my other hand and held it, hard. And I suddenly got it, understood it—she wasn't easy at all. She was scared half out of her mind, and her hand was ice cold.

"You're staying here, during surgery—aren't you?"

"Too right I am." I slipped my arm round her shoulders and pulled her close. "Right here, lady. Not going anywhere."

That morning—I don't know. It's very clear because nothing happened, but a lot happened, too. They took Bree off and put her in one of those miserable little hospital gowns. We were let in to see her, and she had an IV patched in to the back of her hand. I didn't ask what was in it. Then the doctor came in, told Bree they were just about ready, and followed us out into the waiting area.

"I just want you to know, I really don't think the cancer has spread." She sounded the way doctors always sound to me: calm, competent, on top of it. It didn't stop me wanting to kill something. "But I don't want to sugarcoat anything, either. There's a

145

chance I'm wrong. If I am—well. We'll know more in about an hour. You're both staying? Good. I need to go scrub up—I'll see you in a while."

Then she was gone through the swinging doors, and I was alone with Miranda Godwin.

I don't think either of us said anything for a good bit. There was no one else in the waiting area; she sat back with her eyes closed, and for a minute, looking at her, she really looked like a woman in her sixties. I'd never seen her that way, but I was beginning to understand that there was a lot I hadn't seen.

I couldn't sit still, and after the first ten minutes or so, after I'd checked my watch about a dozen times, I couldn't take it anymore. I got up and went to the door, and peered out. An orderly in scrubs turned a corner, glanced at me, kept going. Nothing, no one in the corridor. The hospital was silent as a—

"John, there won't be any news yet. Right now, Elizabeth is only just beginning to—" She stopped suddenly.

Christ. I hadn't thought about that. Miranda was a doctor, a surgeon. She would be able to envision exactly what her chum was doing to her daughter.

"Sorry." She really did look exhausted. "Do I seem a little detached? It's the only way I can stay sane right now."

"Jesus. Hang on—I'm going to go get us both a coffee."

I headed out into the hall—there was a Starbucks cart, right there in the lobby, and I got two black Venti dark roasts and headed back. "Here. Drink this. Miranda, have I ever said how sorry I am, about some of the earlier stuff that happened?"

"No. But I'm not really certain what you're apologising for, John. You didn't know about her pregnancy, so you really can't blame yourself for not being here to cope with it. That one's on Bree, not you. Or did you mean something else?" She took a mouthful of coffee. "Good. This was a good idea."

"That's the problem, Miranda. I don't know what else there

is. I'm only just starting to realise how much shit I don't know about. Bree got into the habit of not telling me things, of keeping secrets. I've got no way of knowing where the land mines are."

We looked at each other over the cups. I was closer to her in age than I was to Bree. Scary.

"Well," she told me, "you aren't alone, John. I'm still pretty angry over her letting me think she'd told you about the miscarriage—I don't like being unfair to people. If she never told you about the miscarriage, then I suppose she never told you about the suicide attempt, either?"

I set the coffee cup down, very slow, very careful. I've got no idea why I was being so delicate about it; the table was littered with the usual waiting room magazines, and it was already covered in dried rings where Christ only knows how many frantic people had set their Venti dark roasts, waiting for a miracle, waiting for the bad news to hit.

"What suicide attempt?" Good. My voice was steady. "Because no, she didn't. Care to remove another land mine for me?"

"Yes, I think maybe I'd better. Be warned, though—this really is a land mine, John. It wasn't a schoolgirl yell for attention, and it wasn't a 'you'll be sorry when I'm dead' thing. She meant it."

"Christ." The smell of the coffee had suddenly stopped appealing to me at all. "Right. Okay. Yeah, I can't see Bree doing that for attention, even back then. Demanding attention, just not her thing. What happened?"

"It was about three weeks before you came home from London, that first long stay away." Miranda was looking back, staring at the memory; I could see it in her face, her remembering with all her senses. "I decided to stop off at Clay Street and see if I could talk Bree into cooking me dinner. She'd been

147

very listless, too quiet—I knew she was missing you, rattling around that enormous house like a ghost. She was unhappy. I thought she could use cheering up. Cooking always distracts her, doesn't it?"

I wasn't saying a damned thing. I couldn't trust myself, my voice, my choice of words, anything at all.

"She had no reason at all to expect me. I was on call that night and she knew it, but I traded off with one of the other doctors just before I was due to go on shift. I don't know why—maybe it was intuition. I rang the bell, there was no answer, but the lights were on. The security system wasn't installed back in those days, so I just used my key and let myself in. Halfway down the hall, I smelled alcohol. The house simply reeked of it."

Memory, crying with my head in Bree's lap, watching her empty my carefully stashed bourbon bottles, watching her heft one, hearing her voice, fierce and straight, telling me, *You wanted my help, we're doing this my way, and if I find another one of these in the house, I'm going to christen your skull with it like you were the fucking* QE2. . . .

"Bree hates alcohol." The words were out, without any effort. "Always has. She got me off booze when she was barely twenty. She never drinks anything except bubbly stuff. Are you saying she was drunk? What kind of alcohol, for Christ's sake?"

"As it turned out, tequila." Miranda took another mouthful of coffee; her voice had gone scratchy and dry. "She'd got her hands on an entire bottle of it somewhere. She'd drunk most of it, too. There was nothing in it but dregs. What was left of it was the wrong colour. It was cloudy—she'd doped the bottle."

"What—?" I stopped. *Oh, bloody hell.* I tried again. "What was in it?"

"Prescription pain pills, about forty of them. Yours, if I remember correctly—wasn't that after you'd had that problem with back spasms? You'd left them behind, in the medicine chest. She was well into the no-perspiration and ultra-slow heartbeat stage when I got her to the hospital; we were lucky there was no organ damage. There easily could have been. Another half hour, there would have been a complete shutdown of all cardio and pulmonary functions, and irreversible brain damage. Another ninety minutes and she'd have been gone."

She raised those cool blue eyes to me, and I wondered why, how, she hadn't wanted to fucking spit every time she heard my name down all these years. "And that was exactly what she was trying to do. She meant to die, John. She nearly pulled it off, too. There was no note. Knowing my ridiculous daughter and her Joan of Arc complex, she'd have considered that melodramatic, or unfair, or traumatic. As if finding her half-decayed body wouldn't be, the little idiot. I pumped her stomach myself—that close to the whole mess with her helping herself to that heroin, I wasn't going to risk having her put into a mental institution. Not exactly a mother–daughter bonding moment for the family scrapbook."

My hands were shaking. "Miranda—right. Okay. First off, just in case you're wondering, yeah, this is the first I've ever heard about this. But I want you to tell me: What else do you suppose I could have done? Cilla's mother died of ovarian cancer. She turned out to have a form of it herself, even if it was curable, and she didn't know that when she called me and begged for help. It was the last thing on earth I wanted to do, but she was still my wife, damn it!"

"You're preaching to the choir, dear. And keep your voice down, please—this is a hospital." Miranda yawned suddenly. "You did just what you had to do. I knew it, and I kept telling Bree that, over and over. I suppose I told her once too often and she couldn't bear to listen to it anymore. I'd like to get my hands on whoever sold her that bottle of tequila, though. She was still underage."

There wasn't one hint of blame or dislike in her voice. If I'd learned anything at all over the past few weeks, it was that Bree's mum had every reason on earth to hate my bloody guts. And here she was, looking me dead in the eye, and she blamed me for absolutely nothing.

"You know how much I love her, don't you?" I suddenly needed to hear her, hear that she knew. "I'm a lazy sod, but you do know what she means to me, yeah?"

The blue stare was honestly puzzled. "Why do you need validation from me? I'm Bree's mother, John. I'm not Bree. You're both adults. However I may have felt about it when I thought she was far too young to be doing what she was doing, I don't feel that way now, and I haven't for a very long time."

Out of nowhere, the facade cracked, and so did her voice. "The simple truth is, Bree's just like her father. It's not stubbornness, or doing the reverse of what you want her to do. She has Ben's insularity of vision: She wants this, she wants nothing else, and everything else disappears. He wanted to help out in Vietnam, all those children, not enough medics. It didn't matter what I said. That's what he wanted, that's what he got. I could have talked myself hoarse, and he would have listened to every word, and you know, in the end, it wouldn't have made any difference. He wanted to go. He went. He died."

She closed her eyes, and I could see her fighting for control. "Just like her father, except that it isn't for herself. Tell me something, John. Have you ever wanted anything that she didn't make happen, if she could? Have you ever not wanted something, and had her not do her best to prevent it?"

"No." It was something I understood now; I just hadn't known where it came from. "Not a damned thing, Miranda. Domitra—you'll meet her later, she's Mac's bodyguard—she called Bree a big dope for enabling me. She doesn't have a lot of patience for it."

"She doesn't have to, does she? It's not her business." Miranda patted my hand. "But honestly, it's all right, John. If I had doubts, I've come to feel differently over the years. You've been together a very long time. And after all, I'm not naive—you're not a nobody. You're famous, you're wealthy, you're a celebrity. You are who you are. You could have traded Bree in for a younger model pretty much any time, and believe me, there were times I expected you to. You make her happy, you make her miserable—but that's what love is about, even if she seems to demand the extremes. No matter how hard or how often I've expected the worst, all I've ever seen is love."

I could feel my eyes stinging, burning. They were damp and gritty; maybe it was lack of sleep or maybe not. I opened my mouth. What she'd said was generous, it was perfect, and it demanded I give her an answer, but I didn't have a clue what to say.

And then the door to the lobby was swinging and Elizabeth Nelson was back, and she was smiling.

"It went perfectly. Stage one, one small area, completely contained. We've removed the affected tissue and a percentage of the surrounding tissue, just to be sure. Thirty days, you two get to pretend you're a monk and a nun—no sexual activity. I want her back in here in thirty days; we'll do another check then. If there's anything showing then, we can talk about chemo as a follow-up. But for right now, I'm going to say we got it all."

CHAPTER TEN

Friday afternoon, Magnus Mattsson arrived at the house in a town car, and I rediscovered the true meaning of the phrase "guitar lust."

Bruno Baines had got there in time for lunch, along with the Bombardiers. Bruno looked worried, a bit thinner than he had last time I'd seen him. Bree fussed over him, sat everyone down, and got everyone fed. I'd been prepared to get heavy about her not resting, but she probably saw that coming. She'd just pulled some homemade soup out of the freezer, dumped it in a pan to heat up, and told me to make a salad. I'm completely useless in the kitchen, so that was a good effective way of sandbagging me, since she knew damned well that anything I made was likely to be well below her standard. I did manage to shake the cruet and mix the oil and vinegar together, and make a basic salad dressing, once she'd told me how much stuff to mix.

"Bruno, dude, how you doing?" Tony forked up some salad. "What the hell happened with Vinny's guitar? Are the cops going to give it back to you? Can you fix it?"

Bruno looked miserable suddenly. "I don't know. The cop in charge, the one with the iceberg eyes and all the teeth? I really thought he was going to charge me with taking out Vinny. I mean, I was there that night. I didn't deny that—I was delivering the guitar and picking up a cheque."

Right. This was one of the things I'd been wondering about. Since he was here, eating my old lady's soup, I decided to just ask him. "Bruno, I'm curious about something. Vinny's PRS— the blue waterfall—was it there, at Freelon Street, when you got there? Do you remember?"

"The PRS?" Bruno thought about it for a minute. "No. No, I'm sure it wasn't. It wasn't sitting on its stand, anyway, and he always had his stand in the same place, right next to his pedal array. And I do remember that when Vinny opened the case and took the red out, he actually made a crack about how I'd pulled it off, how I'd outfancied the fancy. See, when Vinny first commissioned the red, he just held up the PRS and told me, top this. But the PRS wasn't there to compare it with."

He looked at me. "The cop asked me about that, too. Officer Big Bad Wolf, whatever his name is, asked me that three times. I don't know why."

"Because the PRS is sitting downstairs in the studio. We picked it up from the 707 warehouse Monday night, after we found Rosario dead, and there doesn't seem to be a good explanation for how it got there." So, Ormand had been asking himself that same question? Right—that was probably just as well. I'd meant to ring him, and bring it up, but Bree's cancer scare had pushed everything else out of my frontal lobes.

"The cops say I had opportunity." Bruno sounded depressed. "Well, yeah, I did. But I gave them a full statement and

153

signed it. The thing is, they know Vinny was a pain in the ass—sorry, the dead are sacred and all that crap, but he really was a complete asshole sometimes. I bet that if they could find a real motive, they'd lock me up. I guess they aren't looking for a handy scapegoat yet. Maybe the press hasn't made enough noise about it. I bet that as soon as the papers start getting loud and putting it front page, they'll try and nail me. But in case anyone's wondering, I didn't do it."

"Hang on a moment." Something was bubbling away at the back of my mind. "Did you say Vinny paid you?"

Bruno nodded. "He gave me a personal cheque, for the whole nine thousand he still owed me, and asked me to wait a couple of days before I cashed it. Something about how he had to do something at his bank that would take a couple of days to clear. Of course, the cops won't let me cash it yet anyway. Hell, they wouldn't even let me hang on to it. They took it away from me—evidence or something, I guess. Officer Big Bad Wolf says I'll get it back, assuming they decide I didn't kill anyone. And right now, maybe they really don't think I did it. Otherwise, why am I still walking around? Because I don't have an alibi for Rosario, and I was right there the night Vinny got it."

"Maybe they were smart enough to figure out that if you'd wanted to go upside Vinny's head with something, the last thing you'd have used was the guitar you spent so much time and work on." Kris ladled more soup into his bowl. "Bree, this is really good. But why are you running around? Aren't you supposed to be resting?"

She shot him a look. "Don't you start with me. I'm fine, thank you. I rested all morning. I'm bored with resting. And once everyone's settled downstairs, I'll go back to bed for a while and keep John from screaming at me. As soon as the guy with the fancy guitar gets here, I'll rest some more. Okay? Everyone want to get off my ass about resting now?"

The chauffeured Mercedes with Magnus Mattsson in it arrived about forty minutes later. Until we welcomed him inside, and he was actually shaking hands with Mac, I think the bloke honestly believed someone had been taking the piss, you know? He looked so shocked to see we were just who we'd said we were that he must have believed someone was playing some huge bizarre joke on him.

"Wow. This is an honour. JP Kinkaid is going to be playing one of my guitars!" He wasn't what I'd been expecting, not after a few minutes of that squeaky voice on the phone. The voice was just as squeaky in real-time, but he actually did look like his name: he was very tall, very blond, very bony. He was rail-thin, too, and I caught Bree looking at him. Give the girl half a chance, and she'd be strapping him to a chair and shovelling food down his throat.

I herded him indoors. "Boot's on the other foot, mate. We'd be dead in the water without the Zemaitis. Look, if everyone wants to head into the studio, I'll be down in a few minutes, yeah? I've got a couple of things I need to get done first. Why don't you all get set up? Bree, love, don't even think about the washing up. I'll do that. The doctor said rest. Off you go; I'll get you tucked in. Besides, I want to ask you something."

I marched her upstairs. She didn't say a word, not until I'd got her settled in bed with her MP3 player and a few cold bottles of spring water on the nightstand, right within her reach. Just as she was reaching for her headphones, I stopped her.

"Hang on a minute before you dive into the Rolling Stones or whatever, okay?"

I reached down into my pocket and pulled out the package I'd been carrying with me since the FedEx people had delivered it Wednesday afternoon. I'd got rid of the outer wrapping. "I've got a question for you, lady."

Her eyes had gone very wide, and very green. She still

wasn't saying anything. She just looked at the case I was holding, and then up at me.

I opened it and took out the ring.

They'd done a beautiful job with it. The stone that had warmed my skin was set up high, as a solitaire, in dull gold to match the simple wedding bands she'd chosen, with both sides of the main stone inlaid with tiny emeralds, adding a bit of extra sparkle. No diamonds mucking things up, either.

I reached out and got hold of her left hand. I wasn't sure she was breathing.

"Ball's in my court, yeah?" It felt good, you know? It felt right. I'd thought about doing this yesterday, while I waited for her to come out of the post-op anaesthesia in recovery, but Miranda had been there. This way was better, here, in her own house, her own bed. "There's an inscription, or at least there had better be, since I was really specific about it. Can you see, in this light?"

She tilted the reading lamp and held the ring under it, moving the band. She seemed to be having some trouble swallowing. The inscription was there, etched deep into the gold: *B from J: The light's always burning.*

She looked up at me. "I'm giving you back your question," I told her. "Marry me, please?"

So, I didn't make it down for another ten minutes or so. We didn't talk, either, not after the one breathless yes she managed, but it felt like a moment for just being in the same place for a few minutes, blocking out the world I'd invited in, doing what seems to come so easily to her: pretending to be invisible. It lasted only a few minutes, but it made up for a lot, at least in my head.

"Look, love, I should go back." I got to my feet. "I'll tidy up in the kitchen at the first break. Okay?"

"Okay—the dishes need a rinse before they go into the

dishwasher, but the dishwasher's empty. If you can just get the dishes in the sink and run some water over them, that'll be plenty. Be warned, if I get too bored up here, I'm relocating to the sofa. Don't worry, I know, resting, yes, but the oncologist didn't say bed rest, just rest. I can do that on the sofa, too."

So, having proposed to my old lady of twenty-five years, I stacked the dishes and headed back into the studio.

I love the space, I really do, but it simply wasn't designed for this many people. Ideally, five working musicians do quite well down here. At the back of my mind, when I was working with the architect on the layout, I was thinking about Blacklight, considering the possibility of the band coming to me for a change, instead of me heading to the UK every time. And Blacklight's a five-piece.

Right now, looking around, it felt about the size of that damned MRI machine they slide me into every year. I did a fast headcount: There were eight of us, plus an extra guitar case, plus the new Korg and server Damon had spent the morning setting up, plus some of Bruno's tools—the rest were locked in the boot of his car. What usually seemed plenty of room suddenly wasn't anymore. In fact, it was really claustrophobic, and we were actually missing a few people.

"Where's Domitra, Mac?"

Mac looked amused. "She's off with one of the roadies—Doug, is it? He's taking her to a krav maga workout over in the Castro. The boy seems to be smitten; I'm laying odds on him trying to seduce her somehow. Hopefully, he'll use his eyes and realise that trying to put a move on her would hurt worse than love itself. Of course, you never know. Poor Dom's always so busy guarding the door while I'm getting laid—it would make a nice change for her, wouldn't it? I could stand guard outside and offer to smack intruders with a gold record or something."

"Little Doug's hot for Dom? Heaven help him." I turned to

Magnus. "Right, let's get some work in, yeah? Okay, so, this Zemaitis. May I?"

"Of course. Be careful, though—there's that crack in the peghead. It's not bad, but it's there."

"No worries, I'll be careful." I opened the case and lifted the guitar free. "Here, let's have a butcher's."

As most of my fans know, I'm a Gibson bloke. Hell, I'm actually famous for being a Gibson bloke. I've been in more magazine pieces about Gibson guitars, especially the Les Pauls, than I can count. I've been interviewed and filmed and asked my opinion. I've endorsed them. I love my Les Pauls, every damned thing about them, from the deep curve of the necks to the classic PAF pickups. They're perfect and familiar; my sound is signature, and anyone who knows anything about guitars hears four bars coming from me and says, right, JP Kinkaid, Les Paul, or sometimes my 345 or my SG. Bottom line, though? If it's electric, it's almost always a Gibson.

This was the first time since my teens that I'd picked up a guitar that wasn't a Gibson and had this kind of reaction to it. It was a case of instant guitar lust, and that's despite the fact that the damned thing was loaded down with electronics. There were more knobs and controls than I'd expect on the control panel of a bloody passenger jet. It was indecent.

Well—okay, then, not instant lust. It was more like instantly being impressed. The lust came in after I plugged it in, turned it on, and discovered just what all those fancy electronics could do, in the way of sound.

"Bloody *hell*."

I examined the top, a red glazed maple flame; like all Zemaitis electrics, it was a single cutaway, so the body shape, similar to my Pauls, was already familiar. Everyone was watching me, and I began counting and identifying the electronics.

Three pickups, to start with: two humbuckers with a single

coil mounted between them. Okay—basic. I could cope, so far.

Right. So, for three pickups, there had to be six controls, and Tony Zemaitis—if Tony had done this particular layout, and I seemed to recall Magnus saying that Tony had built it for him, to his specs—had done it absolutely right: He'd dual-ganged the control pots, so that instead of having to deal with six knobs, there were only three, with two functions per knob. Cool.

I looked down at it, turning it faceup in my lap. It wasn't as heavy as I'd expected, but it was still heavier than my Paul Deluxe, by about a pound. Of course, the pearl-top version probably outweighed this one by a good bit.

"What in sweet hell? . . ."

There were six—*six*—toggle switches. There were also two extra knobs, and I was having to guess what they might be for. "Okay, hang on a minute. This is nuts. Why are there six switches? And what the hell are the extra two knobs for? I think I've sussed out the pickup switching, but don't tell me there's an overdrive built into this thing as well."

Bruno was gaping at the Zemaitis, and I didn't blame him. It wasn't gaudy the way the pearl-top had been gaudy, but it was bristling with extras. I suppose Bruno had just realised what it was he was going to be working on. Even though he wasn't going to be anywhere near all those fancy interior bits, it still must have been pretty intimidating. This was beyond custom and into decadent. It was gorgeous.

"Yes, there's an overdrive. There's a preamp, too. It's pure *Spinal Tap*: This guitar goes to eleven." Magnus began explaining the electronics. "It's actually a compressor-overdrive combination. These two knobs, here? One gives you overdrive, the other gives you compression—the compression knob combo is also the master volume. The toggles are for the different combinations you can get from the pickups. Here, why not try it? Play with it? See what you like."

I suppose, really, that I was doomed from the moment I plugged that damned guitar into my 50-watt Marshall stack. I honestly should have seen it coming. The neck was gorgeous—unlike the PRS scale, this one worked well in my hands—and the body shape was really comfortable. It was a pity about the weight, but it really wasn't all that heavy, just a bit more than my beloved Pauls. It could have been a lot worse; I didn't even want to guess what the missing pearl-top must have weighed.

I stood up, the guitar strapped round my neck. As I say, it was heavy, but beautifully balanced. Zemaitis guitars have that reputation, everyone from Ron Wood to George Harrison loved theirs, but I was still surprised by how easily it sat, how nicely balanced between the neck and the body weight. I'm not a big bloke, after all.

Right. Time for me to learn to fly the plane.

I took a breath and touched one of the extra knobs. "This one's the compressor? And this switch?"

I tried the standards first, just going between the three pickups, seeing how it sang in all the voices. I left all the toggle switches and the two extra knobs neutral—this was just about me getting the feel of the basics. What came out of the Celestion speakers was excellent, but not all that different from what I'd get from one of my Pauls. The difference, the unique grit levels Vinny'd been getting, had to have come from all those toggle switches, from something in the pickup and distortion combinations.

"Okay. Let's give it a shot real-time, yeah? Damon, is that thing recording? Great, ta. JP, memo to self: Zemaitis maple, compressor full on, boost on, bridge pickup three-way setting on. Trying 'Liplock,' Vinny's bit, leading in."

I hit the strings. The single nastiest, ballsiest bit of howling grit I've ever played slammed out of the speakers.

Gordon *Bennett*. Instant lust. And I wasn't the only one reacting that way, either.

"Whoa." Tony made it sound like he was praying. He hit the portable Roland he'd brought, fingers taking the scale and nailing it, the perfect run. "Shit. Wow. Dude. That's so damned hot—Kris!"

"I'm on it, man. Billy, downbeat! Damon, is the Korg live?"

"Live and ready. On four, JP leads it in. One—two—three—*go!*"

We played the lead-in and never hit a wrong note. Halfway into where the vocals would be popping in, I shifted to the middle pickup and hit the overdrive toggle, and nearly joined Bree in the realm of the multiple orgasm. The burn coming out of the amp, the push, the sheer roaring over-the-top howl of the instrument—it was amazing.

Damon was mouthing something, not wanting to talk, just mouthing it—*keep it up keep it up keep it up*—over and over. And right on cue, here came Mac, and we stopped it for a breath, pure instinct, knowing that, unlike Vinny's take, Mac wanted a moment before he slammed it home, because this was all about sex, and the pause before the hips move is what gets the girl over the hill, and no one sings that better than Mac.

"Mama, pretty mama, honey lock your lips on me, slide 'em down lower, I'll be yellin' like a banshee. . . ."

The Zemaitis was screaming, snarling, doing a vicious little bebop with Mac's voice, and Kris had his P Bass in a rhythm like a pelvis in full *go* mode, feeding off the guitar, feeding off Mac's vocal. Magnus had his mouth half-open, and Bruno's lips were pursed up, as if he wanted to whistle. I was grinning like a maniac. It was fucking glorious.

"Lock 'em on me low, there's a fire down below, lock me down, honey, take it deep, take it slow. . . ."

Another switch; my fingers seemed to know the damned axe as if I'd been playing it since I'd stopped wearing nappies. Mac went with it, teasing the vocal up as if the song were one of his little groupies and he wanted to send her home with a night she could gloat over when she was a grandmother.

"Just a little nibble, honey, just a little touch, don't bother sayin' that I want it too much. . . ."

What he was doing with the vocal probably broke pornography laws in a few American states. He was standing still, but he might as well have been onstage, full audience. We damned near blew the ceiling off the studio.

"Wrap." Damon had this huge shit-eating grin on his face. "Holy mother—that, damn, that cooked. It just—wow, guys."

I unplugged the guitar and handed it over to Bruno. "Here," I told him. "For fuck's sake, take the bloody thing away from me before I cheat on my old lady and offer it my hand in marriage. Go fix the peghead—how long, do you think?"

"Two days, max. Probably less. It can be done here, if I have some space to work in. I brought my tools—I'm pretty sure I have everything I need, clamps and stuff." Bruno had turned it over and was examining the back side, the etched plate with the Zemaitis name, the quality of the wood, the perfect finish. He sounded reverent. "God, this baby's pretty. Beautiful, beautiful workmanship. It's a privilege to be asked to work on it."

"I think I need one of these." My hands were tingling, and this time, I wasn't certain whether it was the MS talking to me or just that my fingers wanted that guitar back. "And yeah, I know, Tony Zemaitis isn't around anymore to build me one, and I'm betting Magnus, here, isn't open to bribes or even offers big enough to pay off someone's national debt."

"Nope, sorry." He really did look sympathetic. "If it's any

consolation, hearing you play it has reminded me just how much *I* love playing it. I hadn't picked it up in a while, but I will now, once you guys are done. Hello?"

The studio door had opened behind us. I turned around and saw Bree. She was holding my cell phone in one hand.

"Sorry to interrupt, but you left this in the kitchen, John—Patrick Ormand wants a word with you, if you have a few minutes. He says he got word that someone's been trying to sell Vinny's Zemaitis guitar."

If I'd had any inclination to underestimate Patrick Ormand's brains, I got rid of it that day. I also got given reason to remember that, every once in a while, he can show a streak of genuine sensitivity.

It turned out that Mac and Luke weren't the only people who'd thought to check with the worldwide collectors' community. Patrick had got onto the Zemaitis club almost immediately—damn Mac, I was going to have to stop thinking about it in terms of it being a cult.

It turns out there are quite a few Zemaitis fanatics out there. Guitar collectors are just as bizarre as any other collectors; they have a tendency to obsess over details. That makes them tricky to have normal conversations with, but when it comes to the ins and outs of their particular lust objects, they can be very useful. So, good on Patrick Ormand for figuring that out early on.

I took the cell phone into the back garden. "Patrick? Hey. JP here. What's going on, then?"

"Hey, JP. I just got an e-mail from a guy who signs himself—wait a minute, let me get this right—Thor the Destroyer."

"Thor the what, now?" Bree had come out, and sat down beside me; the emerald on her left hand looked as if it had grown there. I reached out and touched it with my fingertip, and she smiled at me. "Are you joking? That can't be his name."

"That's what he signs himself." There wasn't a hint of amusement in his voice. I suppose there's nothing funny about murder, but crikey, taking a pseudonym like that seriously? Our pet copper needed a humour transplant, or something equally drastic. "He seems to be a sort of self-appointed watchdog over the movement of these guitars in the collectors' community. I'd checked in at their Web site this morning and posted up a notice of theft and a description."

"Right. So, what did Thor the Destroyer have to say?"

Bree's eyes were wide. She mouthed, *Thor the Destroyer?* at me, and I nodded. At that point, she started giggling, and I shook my head at her—it was a serious call, damn it. She stuck her tongue out at me and then made a horrible scowling face and mimed a pair of Viking horns over her head with her index fingers, and after that, the rest of the call got tricky for me to deal with.

"Hello? Are you still there?" He sounded even less amused than he had before. I wondered if he'd heard her giggling.

"Yeah, still here. Sorry. Bree's just out of hospital, and I think she's still on the giddy side from all the dope they pumped her full of. Anyway, tell me about Thor. What about the guitar? What's going on with that, then?"

Of course, that derailed him, straight off the track. I minimised the cancer scare as much as I could, since really, it wasn't any of his business, you know? Finally, after a while, I got him back on the subject of the e-mail from the watchdog named Thor, and got some actual information out of him, though not very much. There wasn't very much to get.

Bare bones, it seemed that a bloke in Osaka somewhere, a rabid collector of valuable guitars, claimed to have got a phone call from someone claiming to want to sell Vinny's Zemaitis. And yeah, it was definitely the missing Zemaitis: Whoever was trying to unload it had read off the serial number. Since this was the only pearl-top Zemaitis with this particular electronics package in the world, this one had to be Vinny's missing axe— there simply wasn't anything else it could be.

The Japanese collector had immediately posted word of the call up on the Zemaitis Club Web site, on the message boards, or whatever the damned things are called. This Thor bloke, who'd seen Patrick's original notice, e-mailed him straight off. And there we were, Bob's your uncle.

"You know, Patrick, I'm having trouble wrapping my head round this. From what I know about collectors, they aren't usually so honest—although the one sitting in our basement may be an exception that proves the rule. They're certainly not that noisy. Thing is, they're like most crazy obsessive people. They're big on the whole stealth deal, you know? So why would this bloke in Japan be so up front?"

"I'm not sure. I'm going to try and get him on the phone, and find out what's going on. But I thought you might have some ideas about it."

"Sorry, mate, I can't help you there. The only idea I have about Zemaitis guitars right now is that I've been playing one all afternoon, that I want one, and that I haven't bleedin' got one and it's breaking my heart. We've borrowed one from one of those crazy collector types, a very accommodating bloke from Santa Barbara called Magnus Mattsson—Swedish name, so maybe he's a chum of Thor. Anyway, he flew up here with it today, and I've been crooning into its pretty inlaid frets and trying to get it drunk and get its knickers off, basically."

Bree was still giggly. She mimed a sort of Victorian pantomime thing, betrayed damsel shocked by cruel rake or something, complete with gasp and a hand to her brow. I grinned at her—I couldn't help it, I was just so glad to have her sitting here, alive and well and laughing.

"It's a brilliant axe," I told Patrick. "If that pearl-top ever surfaces legally, I may have to bid on it, even though it's heavy enough to cripple me, most likely. The one that's been seducing me isn't a pearl-top, it's a clear red maple. But it's got very similar electronics to Vinny's, and it's almost as valuable, I imagine."

"Valuable—that reminds me, the value was something else I wanted to ask you about. We're talking about a lot of money here, aren't we?" Patrick was going to know more than he ever needed to about custom guitar collecting before this mess had got sorted out. "I mean, enough to pay off the mortgage on the condo valuable? Because the collector in Japan says the figure named by his mysterious deal-maker was seventy-five thousand dollars. That's even higher than what you originally told me you thought it was worth. Does seventy-five thousand sound too high?"

"Okay—that's interesting. Seventy-five thousand?"

"That's what he says, or what Thor says, anyway. Why? Does that sound out of line? I mean, it sounds preposterous to me, but I don't have any touchstone to gauge it with."

"Buggered if I know, mate. I'm not a Zemaitis expert, either. Check the Maverick Music Web site, and see what theirs are going for—they carry the originals. The chances of them having one with this electronics package are basically nil, but I'd personally pegged Vinny's pearl-top at fifty thousand, maybe more. If Tony did the electronics himself—and I can't imagine anyone else having the cheek to drill holes in that inlay— seventy-five thousand could be just about right."

"Maverick Music. Okay, I'll check. Thanks. Give my best to Ms. Godwin, and tell her I hope she's feeling better."

I sat there for a minute after we'd rung off, thinking. Bree, who seemed to have got over her fit of the giggles, watched me, not saying anything.

"Right." I got up, shaking my head. "Bree, that ring looks as if you were born with it on your finger. Did I pick the right stone for you, love?"

She held her hand away from her face, flexed her fingers, and squinted. It was the classic gesture of the girl looking at the engagement ring as if she can't believe her luck, and for someone as impatient of tradition as Bree is, it was weirdly endearing. "Oh, hell yes. Sandra and Katia are coming over later to pick the guys up, so be warned, there will be much showing off and gushing and high-pitched squealing and girly stuff in the front room after dinner. I'm kind of sorry I can't turn the ring inside out, though. As perfect as the stone is, I wish I could see the inscription all the time. Still, this way? It's against my skin, twenty-four–seven. And that's just as cool. Win–win!"

She stretched forward and kissed me suddenly, full on the mouth. It was a long, serious kiss, and I had to remind myself that the oncologist had condemned us to frustration for a full month. "Thank you, John. I'm feeling all giddy and bratty and teenaged again."

That made me really happy, especially since I'd been feeling so damned old, myself. I found myself wondering if she had enough of the teenage feeling thing to go round, enough for both of us. "You know," I told her, "I had a thought. If we've got to keep our hands off each other for a month—"

"I don't think she actually said anything about hands." Bree sounded very demure. "Wasn't it more a question of other body parts?"

I shot her a look. "It occurs to me, we're going to have a hell of a wedding night. You're not going to be able to walk for a week, lady. Prepare yourself."

"I can hardly wait." She got up, and winced, her face twisting a bit. "Damn. Time for some painkillers and a new pad. I'm gushing away, here, and these stupid cramps . . ."

"Are you all right?" I got up, fast. "Bree?"

"No, I'm fine—this is the normal result. She told me to expect it. If it doesn't ease up within seventy-two hours, I'm supposed to get back there, but honestly, it's already less than it was last night and this morning. It's just going to suck, until it stops. And I was due for some pain meds about an hour ago, anyway—I forgot." She caught her breath suddenly and reached for her stomach. "Whoa. TyCo time. Back in a minute."

I followed her indoors and headed back downstairs. Damon had just finished downloading "Liplock." He looked disgusted.

"You look like someone left your Aunt Sally out in the rain, mate. What's wrong?"

"I'm a fucking idiot, that's what. I bought the Korg, I bought the server, I forgot the multiple burner. The computer's got a burner setup in it, but it can do only one CD at a time." He shook his head. "Slower than shit. I'm an idiot."

"Just burn the one copy, Damon, and don't worry about it." Billy told him. "We can always spring for a multiple burner tomorrow, assuming JP doesn't object to one more piece of equipment cluttering up his studio. For right now, I just want to hear the playback and see if it sounds as good as I thought it sounded when we were playing it. Mac, that vocal? That was a bloodbeast, man. Totally killer. A whole generation of kids are going to lose their virginity with that as the soundtrack."

We headed upstairs. Dom had got back, with Doug in tow; Bree was looking a bit pinched, and had got herself settled in on the sofa, so I took over her usual role of being the gracious host, something I'm piss-poor at doing. Billy had something he needed to go do, so he took off, with Damon heading out not long after; Tony and Kris were waiting for their old ladies to show up, and neither Magnus nor Bruno showed any inclination to go anywhere, and I didn't have a clue how to dislodge them. I looked at Bree, and she smiled—it was almost as if she was saying, *Right, you think this whole host thing is simple? Let's see you do it.*

Sandra and Katia showed up eventually, and Sandra got her turn at being flirted with by Mac. It was bizarre, you know? Sandra's one of scariest professional women I've ever met in my life—she's an editor for a law review or something, and she's as on top of her shit as Carla is—but she might as well have been about fourteen for a while, there.

Mac turned the high beams down after a while, and Bree showed off her ring; the women did precisely what she told me they'd do, making *ooh-aah* noises over it. We played the CD of "Liplock" for everyone as well. At the first guitar notes, Bree's eyes went wide.

"Hot damn, that's sexy!" She stared at me. "Is that the Zemaitis you're playing, John? Because if it is, no wonder you want one."

Mac was singing along under his breath, swaying to it. The bloody CD sounded studio-ready. They could have mixed it, burned it, and sent it off to the suits at their record label exactly as it was, and the suits would have wet themselves with joy. It was unbelievable.

Later, in bed for the night, Bree brought up the Zemaitis again.

"John, are you serious about wanting one of those? It really sounded incredible on the CD—I've never heard your guitar, well, *growl* like that. It was really groiny."

"Yeah, I think I do. If that pearl-top ever surfaces, I might have to try for it; really, it's the combination of the electronics and the guitar itself that makes it. Tony Zemaitis—he really was one of the great luthiers—died a few years ago. I think his estate licensed the name out to a shop they trusted enough to do it right. I'll probably look into it, sometime down the road. But I'll admit to having a hard time wrapping my head around paying seventy-five thousand dollars for a guitar."

"Music is what you do, sweetie. It's a tool of the trade and hell, if it makes you happy? Anyway, it's your money, and if you want to spend seventy-five grand on a drop-dead guitar, you should. Besides, it's tax deductible." She shifted her weight, re-settling. "But isn't it really heavy? You said it was maple, and I know that's a pretty dense wood. Hell, half my cutting boards are maple, and they take some major abuse, not to mention our floors. And doesn't adding all those extra bells and whistles jack up the weight even more?"

"It's not that much heavier than either of my Les Pauls, Bree. If I had to guess, I'd say it weighs maybe ten pounds. Of course, if I'm being honest here, ten pounds is pretty damned heavy, especially with the MS. What I'd really love is a hollow-body version of that Zemaitis, with exactly those electronics. I love the neck on that, and the body size is really similar to your basic Paul. A hollow-body version, or at least chambered, would probably take about three pounds or so off the weight. And seven pounds is definitely doable."

"Cool. Maybe we can talk Magnus Mattsson out of it." She shifted a bit, onto her back, taking the pressure off her abdomen, and changed the subject. "Stupid pyjamas. Stupid pads. I feel like one of those dumb chicks in an early sixties song—you know, the ones where they're being bad by having sex and the car gets stalled on the tracks? He books it out of the car and then, wham! Here comes the five-fifteen local with Casey Jones at the wheel, and she's in heaven now, being an angel. I bet she got stuck in the car because she was wearing a stupid belt and a pad, and it got caught on the steering wheel while he was trying to feel her up. So she gets squashed into raspberry jelly all over the tracks and the front of the locomotive, and he gets all moony over it, and writes a really crappy song."

"Crikey, Bree, you weren't even born when early sixties necrophilia rock was going on. Here, roll over—no, not facing me. Other way, love."

I began stroking her back, teasing just the tips of my fingers over her skin. She calls it giving chills, and she loves it, but it's really hard on the arms, if you're the one stroking, so I don't do it often, and like so many other things, she never asks me to do it; she just waits for me to remember to offer. "Bree, do me a favour, okay? Small thing, really, and just for the next thirty days?"

"Mmmm. Okay." She was already relaxing. "God, that feels good. Sleepy. TyCo kicking in, too. What favour?"

"Don't talk about dying," I told her, very quiet, but she was already asleep.

CHAPTER ELEVEN

"On four—take one, 'My Way or the Highway'. Mac leads it in, a capella vocal—JP on eight. One—two—three—"

There are people out there who probably assume that Mac's a pampered star, spoiled half to death, a git with an ego so swollen, it wants its own entourage. He's not, as a matter of fact, and he could have proved that to anyone watching him squeezed into my incredibly crowded basement studio, working his arse off, digging it, not a word of complaint about the cramped quarters. Of course, anyone watching would have had to be out in the garage, because the studio was full. Bloody hell, we were stacked two deep, or at least it felt that way.

"Stop throwing those lies at me, baby, don't you waste my precious time. . . ."

I hit the chord, the neck pickup maxed, the overdrive redlined. The Zemaitis, with its repaired peghead, was staying in tune; Bruno had spent the weekend at Tony's place in Bernal Heights, doing the fix in Tony's workshop, with Magnus watching every move over his shoulder. I'd promised Magnus I'd stay aware of anything even remotely off about the repaired pearl-top and let him know.

This was the third song we'd done since I got the guitar back on Monday, and the only thing I had to tell Magnus was that I was willing to offer him damned near anything he wanted for the damned thing. Even at ten pounds of shoulder-wrenching weight, I was jonesing after it. It was addictive, that axe.

"This is just the way it works, it's tequila and it's lime. . . ."

Billy had his sticks and his high hat ready; the drums and bass were coming in together. Like everything else since Mac had got here and since I'd got my hands on the guitar, the song was roasting from the first note. Mac's vocal was really the biggest kick on this one—it was pure tomcat, a big alpha tom curled up in the sun. He sang it watchful, a bit lazy, but that's what the song wanted: It's the voice of a bloke who can't be arsed to deal with the lady's bullshit any longer. That's what the song was about, being tired of playing games. Vinny had tried for the throbbing emotion rubbish, and it really hadn't worked. This—hell, yeah. Mac had nailed it.

I smoked the second chord, stepping it up, making the Zemaitis sound like a second tomcat, an angry, pissy one this time, counterpointing Mac's voice, challenging his dominance, doing that heavy macho thing. It made the song really barnyard masculine, somehow. Mac grinned at me and punched it, taking the vocal and the lyric to their limit, leading bass and drums and keyboard into it: *"If you think I'm buyin' it, honey, guess again—it's my way or the highway."*

The bass and keyboard were both in, and Kris was scalding it, turning the bottom end up so that the bassline strobed, pulsing like someone in the middle of an orgasm. It was brilliant stuff, and Mac was loving it. He had his hands on his hips, and everything—the vocal, his stance, the lyric, the music—seemed to be saying, *Right, fuck off, then, things and people to do and you're not one of them. . . .*

Sensational. It was so good, it was almost enough to make me forget that we were due—all of us—at Paul Morgenstern's house that night, because Vinny and Rosario were being cremated today, and Paul was hosting a memorial service at his place in Sausalito. As Bree might say, not my sort of party.

"Yell about it all you want, baby it don't bother me, I just have to close my eyes, ain't gonna mind what I can't see, it's my way or the highway, baby, my way or the highway, do or die or let it lie, it's my way or the highway. . . ."

"Fantastic! Guys, why not take a break? I'll burn this."

Damon was seriously blissed. There was something about these rehearsals that just seemed to make everything go easily, painlessly, and he really wasn't used to that—he simply didn't have anything to measure it against. Anton had always been edgy and tricky to work with; serious boozing can turn anyone into a drooling wreck, with no clue about what they're doing to the people around them, and even less conscience or concern. Trust me, I ought to know.

From Anton, he'd fetched up having to deal with Vinny. Even for the short time they'd worked together, Damon had been dealing with a touchy bloke with at least as much ego as he had talent, and probably more. Not much of an improvement from Anton, you know?

And now, here was Mac—serious star power, miles above the sort of celebrity Damon had worked with before—and not only was he a joy to work with, but he was turning out to be the most professional of the lot. You could suggest things and he'd listen, and try it, whatever it was, but I think what was making Damon so happy was that he barely had to suggest anything at all. Hand Mac the lyrics and the music, and he runs with it beautifully, every time.

"Cool." I set the Zemaitis down in its stand. "I want to check my messages and get some nosh. Anyone want a cold drink?"

I was supposed to be ringing up my neurologist sometime this week, because the results of that post-tour MRI would be in by now. I kept putting it off. Truth is, after Bree's scare last week, I'd got into the head space of an almost superstitious terror. I just couldn't shake the feeling that, if I rang up, they'd hand me some bad news.

So I'd gone into ostrich mode, you know? Head in the sand, no news is good news. If there was any bad news, they could damned well ring me up and tell me. So far, no one had.

I headed upstairs. Bree promised me, before we'd locked ourselves in the studio this morning, that she'd take a nap—she was going to need to drive to Sausalito, after all, her first long drive since the surgery. Right, so, yeah, I was being as fussy as someone's middle-aged nanny, but it had been less than a week ago, that surgery. She was still pulled down and tired, still lethargic. Besides, it was fucking *cancer*, you know?

So even though she was healing up nicely, and all the various bits and pieces seemed to be doing what the oncologist had told her they were supposed to do, I was edgy. And she hated driving the bridges, but we didn't have a lot of choice, there. We couldn't skip out on the memorial service.

She was in the kitchen when we came upstairs, checking her e-mail with a cup of tea in one hand. She smiled at us.

"Hey, guys. There's a pot of soup on the stove—seven-bean with chicken, and some bread. Help yourselves. John, don't give me that look. I'm being good, I swear. The soup's out of the freezer; all I had to do was put the pot on the stove. And I slept for a while, and now I'm sitting on my ass doing nothing, being a lazy cow. So stop glaring at me."

"Yeah, right, lazy cow. Moo, motherfucker!" The others had headed straight for the big range, grabbing the bowls and spoons she'd left stacked for them. The kitchen smelled good, but then, it usually did. "What time are we leaving for Sausalito, love? We're going to hit rush hour traffic—I suppose it's lucky we're not going to the cremation. I really don't need to watch that, you know?"

"Ugh." I thought I saw her shoulders move. "The thing at Paul's is supposed to go from eight onward, so we should probably plan on getting out of here no later than a quarter after seven. Midweek evening commute on the Golden Gate Bridge? Nasty. But you don't have to worry about it, John. I worked out the logistics with Katia already. She's driving over in the truck, and she's bringing Sandra along. They're bringing Doug. Damon, I noticed that you drove over today, so there's another set of wheels. I haven't heard whether Bruno or Magnus are going to be there. So we've got Mac and—is Dom coming?"

"Hell yes." I jumped. She'd come downstairs, completely unnoticed, and gone straight for the soup. "If Mac's going, I'm going. It's my job."

We ate soup and hot rolls, and relaxed in the garden for a while afterward. The conversation was quite casual, nice and relaxed. And Mac brought up a subject that had been sitting on my mind as well.

"You know," he remarked, "about this CD we're working on. Unless I've lost my ear—and I don't think I have—these takes are pretty close to perfect. My thinking is that, if this keeps up, you could take these CDs into the studio, do a day or two mixing and overdub, add a few frills, and send them off to your record label. Hard to believe, isn't it?"

He lifted his glass in a general toast. "Cheers, mates. Here's to you. I walked into a murder already done, a murder about to

176

be done, a cancer scare, and Johnny here, having to learn all the guitar parts for seven songs he hadn't touched. And you know what, I'm still having a brilliant time, and I think—I hope—that I'm delivering my end of the goods for you. Thanks for having me in on this."

"Dude, the pleasure is completely ours. JP rocks for thinking of asking you to help. We owe both of you, big-time." Billy had obviously been thinking about it. "And shit, yes, guys—Mac's right. If we could just get ourselves back into Freelon Street, we could wrap it up, head over to the Plant, and start the mixdown. The CD's basically in the can. We've got four songs down, perfect, ready to go. If the other six come as fast and hot as the first four, we're ready to roll this sucker on out the door."

Everyone made noises of agreement, including me. Another week of rehearsing and recording, and Mac could head home with an entire CD side project under his belt, a brilliant job. It was amazing, the way this had gone. And that was despite two murders. Creatively, technically, we hadn't hit so much as a speed bump, much less a roadblock.

I looked around the garden, at my mates, at my family, and got hit with a stab of gratitude that damned near knocked me over. I'd had a few bad breaks, but taken all in all? There's sod-all about it I'd trade.

I found myself catching Bree's eye. That was something I'd only recently become aware that I did, looking around, having that moment of contact with my old lady, wanting it, needing it. I'd noticed myself doing it during this last Blacklight tour—someday, I might even ask her if I'd in fact been doing the same damned thing ever since that first meeting of the eyes, during the Hurricane Felina Benefit, back in 1979.

She caught my eye and smiled at me. "Well. I'm thinking it's time to go get out of these sweats and into something real.

Does anyone know what you're supposed to wear to a memorial service for someone you kicked in the balls? . . ."

Unlike Bree and her fleecy yoga wear, I didn't have to change clothes for the memorial. Ever since I'd outgrown my earliest rock star days with Blacklight, when Cilla had chosen my clothes for me, I'd settled on a nice minimalist look, basic black, mostly. These days, that's all I wore, onstage or off it.

Those bits of wardrobe, Cilla's choices, had been picked for maximum flash: silver, embroidery, clothes meant to be noticed from the back of the balcony by thousands of adoring fans. What she'd wanted, of course, was for me to outshine Mac, but it had taken me years to suss that. I wondered where all that stuff was now—I hadn't seen it in twenty-five years. If the Hall of Fame ever asked for a coat or a pair of trousers, I might have to find it.

The ride over the bridge was less crowded than we'd thought, and we got there quite early. Luckily, Paul was back from the cremation itself, and he wasn't alone. Even though I'd got over my bizarre little jealousy thing, my stomach did a nasty dodgy rollover move when Paul let us in, and I recognised Patrick Ormand standing just outside Paul's sliding deck doors, looking out over the view.

Paul looked completely knackered. His eyes were red-rimmed. I wondered if he'd got weepy at the cremation; after all, he'd known Vinny at least marginally better than the rest of us had. Truth was, my own instinct was to feel a hell of a lot sorrier for Rosario than for Vinny. Of course, I hadn't seen Vinny after he'd been thumped. I'd seen Rosario, though, dead on the floor of the warehouse, and I'm not likely to lose that little picture from my frontal lobes anytime soon. "Hey, guys, I'm glad you made it. Come on in. There's a few other people here already, and some food and drink, out on the deck. It's been a really long day—come outside and relax for a few minutes, okay? Watch the sun go down."

I headed for the deck. There was a handful of people I didn't know, standing about under all the artwork—I thought I recognised a couple of them from the 707, the bloke who ran their soundboard during gigs and their manager, Jeff something or other, but I wasn't sure. Mac had stopped inside, and was talking to Paul; he was waving his arms about, and they were both looking animated, so I suspected they were rabbiting on about Paul's collection.

When we first walked in, I'd seen Bree stop Paul and pull him aside for a moment. From the speed with which she'd disappeared off towards the back of the house, it looked pretty obvious that she'd gone in search of a loo. That had me feeling twitchy. She'd told me she was feeling fine, and things were healing, but she was quite capable of lying to me to spare me worrying. If I found out that's what she was doing, I was going to flip my shit. This wasn't something about which I was even remotely prepared to be lied to, not for my own good or for anything else.

"Hey, there." Patrick turned around and nodded at me. "Amazing view. How are you? How are the sessions going? And how's Ms. Godwin?"

I snagged some bottled water. "Hello, Patrick. Yeah, the view is amazing. I'm better than I was a week ago today. The sessions are going brilliantly—four songs down, six more to do, and the chemistry's been so hot, they'll be ready for a final prettying up in about a week, assuming you ever let my mates back onto the premises at Freelon Street. And Bree's doing quite well, thanks. She drove us over, so you can ask for yourself. In fact—hello, love. Patrick was just asking after you." I fixed her with a stare. "So am I, actually. Are you okay? Here, sit. Put your feet up."

"I'm okay. Tired, though. I'll be glad when this thirty-day

thing is over. Oh—hey, Patrick. How's the investigation going?" She looked around for a chair and pulled one over, staring out towards the Bay and the City in the distance. "Wow. This is one hell of a view. Last time I was here, I never made it out this far."

"No, you were busy kneeing Vinny in the nuts. And he damned well had it coming, so don't let the memory fuck up the pretty view for you, okay?" I kissed her hair and pulled my own chair over. I had my lips up to her ear and whispered, "All right? Really?"

"Mmmmm." She nodded, a tiny movement, but enough. "That reminds me, did we want to call down to Angelino and try for a dinner reservation? I don't know what protocol is for these things. I mean, are we supposed to be too grief-stricken to eat? Because I don't think I am."

"Angelino? Oh, yum." The deck was beginning to fill up; the Bombardiers had all found their way outside. Katia sounded enthusiastic. "What a neat idea, Bree. Oh, is there food out here? Awesome, but I'm going to want dinner later anyway. This is nice and light, but I think I want a humongous plate of pasta, or maybe an entire fish. Can I ask a question? Because I'm new at this—what do people actually *do* at a memorial?"

Patrick had a beer in one hand. He popped the cap and took a long chug. "Good question. Does anyone know?"

"I think everyone who knew the dearly departed takes turns eulogising him." Mac had come out as well, with Paul and Doug bringing up the rear. The deck was getting crowded. I found myself wondering how much weight the damned thing was rated as being safe to hold. "The guests who actually gave a damn about the dearly departed then say what a shining beacon of humanity he was, and how everyone's going to miss him, and what a terrible loss he is, and all that. After that, there's a bit of disagreement about the shining beacon assessment, a few fights break out, everyone gets thoroughly sozzled, and people start flinging themselves all over the dearly departed."

"That's a wake, not a memorial." Domitra wasn't smiling; there were people here she didn't know, which put her on the job. "You're thinking about James Joyce, or somebody like that. Especially that shit about throwing yourself on the dead guy, and the getting sozzled bit. With a memorial, I think you just remember the dead guy and talk about him. Maybe have a beer."

"Interesting." Patrick took a long swig off his own beer bottle. "Well—if we're talking about the dead guys, I can open up the memorial with some background. For one thing, did you know that Vinny Fabiano and Rosco Galliano were each other's only living family?"

There was a moment of silence. Damon tilted his head.

"Who the hell is Rosco? Are we talking about Rosario?"

"His name was Rosco, changed legally to Rocco at eighteen. Rosario was actually his fiancée, back in New York—they had some weird personal thing going on, where they promised to call each other Rosie until she'd moved out here."

I was blinking at Patrick. "Okay, right. Hang on a minute. So, what you're saying—Rosie was actually Rocco, and Rocco was actually born Rosco? And Rosario is actually some chick in New York? That can't be right."

Patrick had already finished his beer and was looking around for another one. "The nice Puerto Rican girl he was planning to marry, at least according to her. We're inclined to believe that, by the way—he actually had her name tattooed on his groin, complete with the bright red heart. That's in the ME's report. And hoo boy, is she mad. If she ever finds out who offed her boyfriend, she'll be up on charges of her own, and the forensics guys will be swabbing blood off the walls. When I talked to her, she was spitting blue murder and talking about rusty razor blades. She didn't give a damn that she was talking to a cop, either. The lady is seriously pissed off."

He'd found another beer and popped it. I thought for a moment about asking who his designated driver was, but I've never found that cops—no matter what country, or level of seniority—had much humour.

"By the way," he said casually, "since we're talking about girlfriends, it's a shame Vinny's girlfriend couldn't be here. I wouldn't have minded meeting her."

There was a long silence. He glanced around at all of us, one after another. And I suddenly understood.

Patrick Ormand wasn't tipsy at all. He wasn't sozzled. He wasn't being sloppy. And he wasn't casual, either; those damned light eyes of his were in full cold hunt mode. He'd shared the information deliberately, dropped it like a brick in the middle of a quiet pond. He was waiting for a reaction he could use.

The man was dangerous. I remembered the cold eyes and the way he seemed to be able smell a weakness, too damned well, from when he'd tried that with Bree in New York, in Boston.

This time, though, he didn't look to have struck it lucky. All the looks he got back were completely blank.

"Vinny had a girlfriend?" Tony looked at Katia, and then back at Patrick. He was shaking his head. "You're kidding, right? Because, no way, man. Sorry, but that's just a big hell-no. I actually assumed he was gay, didn't you, Katia? He never had a woman around him, never talked about one, never mentioned a woman in his life, nothing. Hell, the vibe I always got off him was that he despised women. Even when he was being flirty, it had this forced, artificial smell to it. I never got the feeling that he was even seriously hitting on any of the chicks he got next to. Katia, a little backup here, would you? Did you ever get a flash off Vinny that he liked women?"

"I'm not Katia, but I'm with Tony, at least in spirit." Bree was shaking her head. "I mean, I have no idea whether he was gay or straight or preferred corpses or chickens, but whatever he liked, I sure as hell don't believe it was women. He didn't like us much. He certainly saw us as having no status unless were attached to some guy as property—look at the way he backed down when he realised John and I were a couple. He had no respect at all. I mean, he apologised to me for groping me, he even bought me roses. But he didn't do that because he was sorry he'd done something offensive to me. He did it because he thought he'd pissed off John. And honestly, when I put him down in front of the party, he took a swing at me, and he wasn't kidding. He meant to mess me up."

"Not after you nailed him in the balls." Katia blew a kiss at Bree. "I know, I know, I'm supposed to be remembering all the good in Vinny, but you kicking his ass was so damned *pretty*. Anyway—I'm with Tony and Bree on this one. I don't believe in Vinny's girlfriend. I think she's a figment of your imagination, or of someone's imagination, anyway. If he had one anywhere, we'd have heard all about it, and we didn't. Who says he had a girlfriend, anyway?"

Patrick wasn't drinking; he was swirling the beer around and around in the bottle. "The psycho lady in New York, that's who. She says Rocco told her—I don't want to try and separate he-Rosie from she-Rosie, so I'm sticking with Rocco. Anyway, according to her, there was a woman. Rocco never mentioned the girlfriend's name, but the nice lady in New York got the impression Vinny's playmate might be married. Of course, that's easy to assume, but it's also unverified. I was hoping she might show up tonight."

No one said anything. That look again, eyes like the razor blades the girl in New York wanted to use on Rosie's killer. "Ah, well. Pity—I'm always in favour of saving work, and it was worth a shot. We'll find out who she was. It'll take some digging, but we'll find her."

I'd had enough of the manipulation the bloke was so fond of using. It was going to keep me from ever being able to really trust him, and at the moment, with my mates looking sussy and being jerked around, I wanted a bit of my own back.

"Right. Okay. Patrick, do you mind if I ask you something? Since you're being so forthcoming?"

That last word came out with more bite than I'd meant it to have. He shot me a look and waited. We locked up in a good hard stare.

"The night Rosario was killed, you told me they'd put a provisional time on when he'd got it. Remember? That was over a week ago. If anyone here's officially eliminated from the list, how about sharing the information? Enquiring minds wanting to know, and all that. We'd like to get on with our new record, not to mention sleeping a bit easier. Who has a real alibi? Come along, mate—crank up the volume."

I scored a hit on him, there. I'd said that to him, those exact words, the night he'd decided not to prosecute Bree as an accessory before the fact to Perry Dillon's murder. And he remembered. I could see from the way his face changed that he remembered. Good. I'd meant him to.

"Alibis? Let's see if I can remember, just off the top of my head."

He looked around at us, measuring us up, looking for anything to use. The bloody dangerous sod remembered, all right. If he ever forgot a detail of anything, ever, he wouldn't keep getting hired on in different cities the way he did. "The ME was able to be definitive—definitive enough to satisfy a jury—about the time of death. Her initial estimation turned out to be accurate: Rocco Galliano was hit with a blunt instrument, something hard and metal and with a square edge. He was hit hard enough to snap his head around, kind of a super-whiplash. That broke his neck. The weapon wasn't there in the warehouse, by the way; we've been over everything in there with the proverbial fine-toothed comb."

He paused, looking around at us, waiting for someone to say something. No one obliged.

"The ME says it happened no earlier than nine last Sunday night, and no later than one in the morning Monday," he went on. "So the group at Clay Street Sunday night are in the clear: Mr. Kinkaid, Ms. Godwin, Mr. Sharpe, Ms. Calley. Oh, and Mr. and Mrs. Mancuso—what is it, Mr. Mancuso?"

Tony was on his feet. "Wait a minute. I called Rosie, Sunday night. Remember, guys? When we headed upstairs, just before I called Paul—that was just after we finished up in JP's studio. My phone has no reception in JP's studio—it's too well shielded down in the basement. Shit! What time was that?"

"Right around ten, I think." Mac spoke up. "Hang on, let me sort this out. Dom and I got out of Customs at SFO right around quarter of six. There was a gaggle of reporters, we answered a few questions, maybe three minutes' worth. We got into Bree's car, ducked the media, got back to Clay Street, had dinner, and you and Katia came over. Dom went off to bed with jet lag, Katia went off into the kitchen to hang out with Bree, and the three of us went down to the studio to check out the CDs of the rest of the songs. Oh, good gods, I'm an idiot. What am I doing sums for? Tony, check your dialled-calls log, unless you've erased it by now."

"May I see that, please, Mr. Mancuso?" No hope of playing casual, not anymore—Ormand's voice was sharp and cold. He held a hand out, and Tony immediately handed him the phone.

I'd got hold of Bree's hand. Her fingertips were chilly, and I remembered, out of nowhere, that I'd thought that in Ormand's New York office and that I'd meant to gang up with Miranda and bully Bree into getting some blood work done. . . .

"Ten fourteen." The predator was right there now, completely visible. Any minute, he'd start a wolf howl, or something.

Christ, if it was a full moon, he'd probably be out on the prowl, looking for someone's lungs to rip out, like Lon Chaney's werewolf. "I need someone with a confirmed alibi to look at this, please, because I don't want to impound the phone. After all, I can always subpoena the records if I need them. Mr. Kinkaid? Would you?"

I let go of Bree's hand and got up to peer at the phone. "Yeah, that's what it says: Rocco Galliano, a Marin number, ten fourteen." I counted backward in my head. "And yeah, a week ago Sunday. So Rosie was alive at a quarter past ten?"

"If this is accurate, then yes, he was." Cautious bastard. "That narrows the field. We've checked alibis, very thoroughly. I can tell you that Mr. Morgenstern, for instance, got to the Plant studios in Sausalito at ten minutes to eight, and was there until after three in the morning; the session ran late and we have signed statements to show he never left. Everyone at the Kinkaid residence on Clay Street is essentially clear, short of massive collusion. Mr. Gelb has no alibi; neither do Mr. and Mrs. Corcoran, or either of the Bombardiers' equipment men, Mr. Hewlett or Mr. Jenckel. Mr. DuMont was cohost of an AIDS fund-raiser at a private club in Berkeley, and he's covered for the relevant times. And of course, we're looking at everyone and anyone who knew either or both men locally."

"Well." Bree got up. No one else seemed to want to say anything at all. Sandra looked outraged, Kris looked furious, both roadies looked uneasy. "You know, this is twice in a row I've had to say this. Paul? Would you mind very much if we headed out early? I had surgery a few days ago, I want some dinner, I'm going to have to drive back over the bridge, probably in the fog, and anyway, this really doesn't feel like our kind of party. But hell, it's still a memorial. I'd say we're all going to remember Vinny, whether we want to or not."

CHAPTER TWELVE

The day after the get-together Paul had held in Vinny's memory, I got a closer look than I wanted to at a very bad memory of my own.

Thursday morning started out with the first genuine annoyance of the Bombardier rehearsals with Mac. Everything had been going perfectly, but of course, that couldn't possibly last; I should have known it was too good to be true. The day something involving more than one person comes off without a spanner in the works is the day I'll know the last trump's been blown, and I didn't hear it because I was in headphones, doing playback on my own stuff, and swearing under my breath.

We had six songs left to get down. And yeah, okay, the first four had been beyond painless, they'd been spectacular. But here came song number five, and of course, it had to be one of

Vinny's. And the CD burn we had of it, the only one we had, was a partial. It was missing half the vocal.

"So you say you have to leave me, you say you have to go? Go for it if you want to, baby, who am I to tell you no? . . ."

Vinny's vocal, a bit too yearning, against nothing but a single guitar. This was a practice run. The band hadn't been there. The vocal, trying the line again, him forgetting the second half of it. A muttered "Shit!"

It was really strange, hearing his voice coming out of the speakers. Spooky, you know? It was really as if I hadn't quite got the full meaning of it until now, him getting his skull cracked, him being dead. Here he was, crooning and muttering, dicking with the guitar—the PRS, from the tone—and now, there he wasn't, and never would be again. It sent something crawling down my back, and the feeling wasn't pleasant.

I looked around the studio and saw my own discomfort level reflected pretty clearly on the Bombardiers' faces. Damon was especially creeped, from the looks of it, but then again, he'd been the one to find Vinny dead, so no surprise there.

"You say I've got no answers to the questions that you pose, babe I ain't your answer man, that's the way it goes. . . ."

It was uncanny, really. I hadn't much cared for the bloke, but shit, I'd worked with him, you know? I'd played my guitar, locking it up with what he was doing. I'd listened to him hit the occasional wrong note and swear under his breath or good and loud, and we'd both grinned, because it's something we all do. I'd nodded at the occasional moment of inspiration, when he caught the edge of something that worked, and went with it, riding the music. That's all part of the deal, when you're doing session work.

And here he was, doing all that, just him and the PRS alone at Freelon Street, with the Korg recording and downloading to the server. Dead, gone, nothing left of him but his voice and his music. I felt a bit sick.

"That's the way it goes, lady, that's the way it goes. . . ."

The CD stopped. Silence. Dead air. Nothing at all.

"Where's the rest of it?" Mac, who hadn't known Vinny, had no reason to be affected by his voice; he was concentrating on the music. "Nice little ballad he had going on, but hell, it's not even half a song. That can't possibly be all of it, can it?"

"Damn." Kris was shaking his head. "Oh, man. Problem. This was one of Vinny's, one he wrote, music and words. We hadn't touched it yet. I don't even know if a full solo version of it exists. Damon?"

"I don't know either." Damon sounded as worried as Kris. "I know he was planning on hitting Freelon for some late-night solo work—he wasn't satisfied with this one, especially the vocal. I showed him how to make sure the Korg downloaded, a couple of weeks before. Anyway, if there's more, it's on the server."

"Shit." Tony blew air out, a noise of pure frustration. "JP, dude. Any chance in hell we can sweet-talk your pal at Homicide into letting us back in to get this off the server? Who would we have to bribe, or blow? Because we're seriously fucked without it, unless someone wants to come up with a replacement song in a hurry."

Mac took a long pull at his spring water. "Can't you do a cover? An old standard? Maybe a nice bit of classic rock and roll, Fats Domino, or something basic, like Robert Johnson? I'm always up for singing a classic or some good blues."

"Man, don't I wish. But the contract says ten original songs." Billy was looking glum. "Right now, the label is pissed off enough at us over the delay to not want to cut us any slack. They're really being dickheads at this point. And anyway, damn it, how the hell long are the cops planning on locking us out of our own studio? They've had nearly two weeks. Hell, they've time to fingerprint the fingerprints by now—hi?"

The studio door squeaked open, and Bree stuck her head in, looking apologetic.

"Hey, guys. Sorry to interrupt—John, it's Patrick Ormand on the phone for you."

"Damned good timing. I need to ask him something. Let's take a break, guys, all right?"

I headed up the stairs, Bree right behind me. It occurred to me that if we did end up getting our hands on a usable CD and covering this one, I had Vinny's PRS downstairs, even if how the hell it had got to where we'd found it was still a mystery.

"Hey, JP." Patrick actually sounded apologetic. "Bree said you were working in the studio—I'm sorry to get you out of that, but this wouldn't wait."

"No problem." Bree had slid into a kitchen chair. I perched on the table beside her. "I'm actually glad you rang, because I need to ask you something. What's going on?"

"I was wondering if I might come by today. I've got what I think is a photo of the missing Zemaitis, and I suspect you're my best shot at confirming that."

"Hell, yeah. We've been in the studio all morning, but we've hit a fallen tree in our path, so we can't really get anything else done on the song we were working on until we can get back into Freelon Street and get some work in progress off the server there. So yeah, come on over and bring your photo and I'll offer you a cup of coffee—I can make coffee reasonably well, especially since we got one of those pod things. They seem to be designed so that some poor sod like me, who can't make toast without burning it, can use it without fucking up. Um—hang on half a mo, okay?"

Bree had opened her mouth, but I put one hand over the phone and shook my head at her. I knew what was coming. "No," I told her. "Don't even bother making the offer, lady. You are not offering to cook the bloke lunch, Bree. Matter of fact, you aren't offering to cook anyone lunch, and no arguing, either. You're supposed to be resting. He'll have a cup of coffee and that's all. If he wants lunch, he can go off somewhere and eat doughnuts, or whatever policemen eat."

I was becoming quite good at bullying her for her own good, I think—either that or she recognised I was right, because she didn't argue. She stuck her tongue out at me, but she stayed quiet, no arguments. It made quite a change, that, considering we'd spent the past quarter-century doing exactly the opposite.

"Sounds good." Now that he'd got his way, Patrick had stopped sounding apologetic. He sounded the way I'd have expected him to sound: a cop on the hunt. "Can I come by now?"

"Hell yeah. The sooner the better."

Patrick turned up twenty minutes later with a brown manila envelope in one hand. If he'd been at his desk when he rang up, he must have set the phone down and hit the ground running, or had a car waiting and warm out in front of the cop shop. I let him in; back in the kitchen, Bree was setting a few cups out for coffee and tea.

"Thanks for helping me with this." He followed me down the hall. Out in the garden, my mates were all having a good stretch. I had a moment of wishing I was out there as well. "Thor the Destroyer—you know, the self-appointed Zemaitis watchdog from the Internet—sent me this picture, express mail. Apparently, the photo has some value of its own—it's from his private collection and I basically had to promise not to let it out of my sight. There's a handwritten note on the back. I'm hoping you can help me make sense of it, and also confirm the guitar in the photo as the one that's missing. Well—the pearl-top, anyway. The other one seems to be a red one. And what's really odd is that both guitars seem to have names. Is that common? Guitarists naming their instruments?"

"Yeah, pretty common. I don't name mine, but that's not to say I wouldn't, if a guitar basically sat in my lap and told me its name. As for helping you sort this out, well, do my best, mate. Here's Patrick Ormand, Bree. Here, have a seat and a coffee—black, three sugars, yeah?"

We sat at the kitchen table, the three of us. Patrick took a sip of his coffee, set the cup aside, and carefully slid the photo out of the envelope.

"I really appreciate this," he told me. "Any help you can give us would be very useful."

I reached out and picked up the photo.

I don't know what I was expecting, really; maybe just a shot of the instruments themselves, laid out in their cases or on stands. But this—it shook me.

I didn't just recognise the pearl-top. I recognised the red guitar, as well. It was a bass, one I knew. And I recognised the man holding it.

"Is that the missing instrument?"

"Yeah." Something in my voice must have changed, gone wrong somehow; Bree jerked her head up, looked at the photo, and looked back at the photo, and then at me. I swallowed, hard. Getting words out was going to be dodgy. This was like a kick over the heart.

"Yeah, that's Vinny's pearl-top. I recognise both guitars, as a matter of fact. I don't know who's holding the pearl-top, though."

Oh, Christ. That bass, the man holding it . . . My throat wanted to clog up. I turned the picture over.

TIM HOLDING BIG MAMA PEARL, JACK WITH RED DEVIL.

I turned it back over. My hands were shaking.

"Is something wrong?" Patrick was staring at me. So was Bree. She didn't need to ask, though; she knew damned well something was wrong.

"Just a bad memory. A sad one." Heartbreaking might be a better word, but he didn't need to know that. "The other guitar, the red bass, double cutaway, brass inlays. I've actually played it—last time I saw it, I was picking it up and demonstrating just what a crap bassist I would have made. Seeing the picture—damn. Hurts, that's all. Wonderful bloke, old friend called Jack Featherstone. Red Devil was his bass."

Next to me, Bree sucked in her breath. She'd got there, of course. Jack's name said it all.

"I'm very sorry." Patrick reached a hand out and slid the picture away. He was having one of his rare moments of genuine kindness. "I wasn't trying to harrow you—I didn't know I was bringing up a bad memory. All I really need is identification of the pearl-top. I gather your friend is no longer alive? What did he die of?"

I heard Bree, swallowing hard. She'd got it now; I saw her hands weave together tight. I couldn't see her face, didn't want to meet her eyes, because there was a good chance that, if I did, we'd both start sobbing like children. Fucking memory. Why does the past always seem to hurt so much?

"Yeah," I told Patrick. "Jack's dead. He was one of my oldest friends—we'd played together first when I was about twenty. Last time I saw him was back in 1985, a few days before he died—I was in London, and we got some friends together, all of us went over to hang out with him, try to cheer him up, play him some music. He couldn't play himself anymore by that time—he was in a wheelchair and his hands were basically dead. Same thing that killed him. Complications from multiple sclerosis."

After Patrick had gone, I stayed in the kitchen for a while, just sitting there. I'd got hold of Bree's hand; neither of us were talking, and I had the feeling we'd both gone for a wander down memory lane. Thing is, I didn't see how we could have gone down the same road, at least for part of it. I was following a line I really could have done without, because it hurt, every step of it.

Jack Featherstone had been one of my earliest big-name friends on the London scene, back when I'd just turned twenty, and was starting to try and prove to people—people who could give me a leg up and get me into sessions and then into live gigging, people who mattered—that I could play. He was a few years older than me, a big burly bloke from the West Midlands. He was already established at that point, starting out as a session bassist in the mid-sixties, a sideman in high demand by anyone who was anyone who needed a fresh, distinctive approach to bass on their new record. That was where my head was at, from very early on. If anyone had told me in 1970 that I'd end up as a guitar player for a stadium band, I'd have thought they were off their nut.

Jack first turned up at a gig I did at the old Speakeasy Club, in London. I'd been asked to sit in with a few local blokes, and Jack had come along to watch, as he often did. After the gig, he'd come over and introduced himself. I'd immediately got the impression of tremendous energy, good nature, and something really rare, especially among musicians: a genuine interest in the details of the world he moved in. We can be a very self-absorbed lot, you know? But Jack noticed the world around him, and what's more, he cared. I liked him enormously.

We got to be good friends, and stayed that way all through most of the seventies. I sat in on several sessions he was playing; it was mostly due to Jack that I came to the notice of most of the bands I played with. He actually knew a lot about guitars, as well as basses, and I've got warm memories of a few times we'd wandered out of the studio after someone's all-night session, looking for a café and a quick meal, because booze wasn't on the cards at five in the morning, talking about politics, jazz trumpet, city planning, women, Elvis, anything and everything.

We lost a lot of the closeness after I moved to the States, and there was a long gap, between 1980 and his last days in 1985, when I didn't see him at all. He'd been diagnosed with progressive MS, the nastiest kind, in 1979. Of course, that was right in the middle of the biggest upheaval of my life, leaving my wife, moving to America, getting off drugs, stopping drinking. I'd rung him up when I heard, of course, but he wasn't inclined to do a lot of talking at that point, especially not over a crackling phone line with the Atlantic Ocean in between. And I was pretty rocky at the time, myself—bourbon was much harder to let go of than heroin or coke had ever been.

The last time I saw him alive was during my third absence from San Francisco and Bree. Cilla had rung me up, saying she was ill again, and could I come to London and help? Turned out there'd been nothing wrong with her; she'd just wanted to see if she could get me away from Bree, and she'd managed that. Looking back, though, I can't be sorry I went. For one thing, that was the trip I finally got it across to Cilla that she and I were done. The main thing, though, that was Jack.

I'd been gone only a couple of weeks. I sussed out early on that Cilla was playing some sort of game, and I'd decided by then that I'd had enough of it, I wasn't going to let her jerk me around anymore. But during that two-week absence, I'd checked around to see if I could hook up with Jack. The first person I'd rung up had been a drummer, an Irish mate of ours.

That was when I'd found out Jack was dying. A bunch of old mates were popping round to Jack's place down the Highbury Road that night, to be with him, play some music, cheer him up as best they could. It would be brilliant if I wanted to come along, because Jack didn't know I was in London. . . .

Of course I went—nothing could have kept me away. But it was hard, an acting job from a lousy actor. I hadn't expected him to be so far gone. I can still see him in that wheelchair, the big strong frame gone to seed, mostly paralysed, barely able to talk. It horrified me, made me want to break down and sob like a damned baby, what time does to us, what life does to us.

And Jack didn't deserve this, not any of it. He was a good bloke. When you stop to consider some of the evil shits running around, who spend their time fucking over other people and never seem to know a moment of pain or regret or loss, it can make you ask yourself some scary questions.

Of course, I couldn't show any of that. The whole idea was to give him one nice thing to take with him, a sweet memory that would be there in his head when the light went out for the last time. This was his set closer.

There were ten of us there, all musicians, and we threw ourselves into it. We played and talked, we laughed and told rude stories from years of memories, shared histories.

Sometime near sunrise, one of the blokes, a bassist, muffed a riff from a song Jack had written a good twenty years earlier. It was a riff I knew quite well on guitar, and I played it, not stopping to think. I had my Deluxe with me on that trip, since I never go anywhere without at least one guitar.

"Good job." It was Jack, managing to talk, trying to grin. We all swivelled round. "JP—try it on bass?"

He managed to jerk his head, and I watched the tendons in his neck trying to move, to somehow connect the gesture to the man. The bass had been Red Devil, the Zemaitis he'd had built for him right after I'd first got to know him. It was sitting right there on its stand the entire time. No one had wanted to touch it.

I picked it up and plugged it in. It was late, and we had the volume down low; I noodled the riff, just once, and even though

I knew it perfectly, I found my fingers wanting to clench round the neck, as if maybe by holding on to it, I could keep Jack with us just a little bit longer.

"Come off it, Jack, you know I'm a lousy bass player." I set Red Devil carefully back in the stand. "I'll stick with six strings. Anyway, I'm happier with my Pauls. But thanks for the vote of confidence. Cheers, mate!"

I'd left for San Francisco two days after that last get-together. Three days after that, he'd died in his sleep.

That had been a bad few days. I couldn't wrap my head around the memory of the man I'd known all those years, and the most recent sight of him, unable to play, nearly unable to talk, the huge body gone soft. I'd had a couple of hours when I'd nearly gone off into a crying jag. Bree, who'd been cool and distant since I got back, sussed out something was seriously wrong; she held on to me and made me tell her.

So Bree couldn't have followed me down the first half of that road, because she hadn't been there. The rest of the road I'd gone down, I was pretty sure Bree was right there with me. I was remembering a day in September of 1997, when the two of us had sat there side by side in my neurologist's office, looking at the results of the MRI I'd had taken two weeks before.

I don't want to draw it out. The full story is really dull, and anyway, why pile on the agony? Bottom line was that I'd woken up in early July, a few days after Bree's birthday party, and my right foot and leg were both numb. After a while, the numbness became this sort of stabbing and tingling, and then it was numb again. Putting the foot to the ground hurt. Putting shoes on was no fun at all. After a day or two, my right knee had joined the party, and didn't seem to remember that it was connecting two parts of the same leg.

Bree had been freaked; I thought I'd done something to my back, maybe pinched off a nerve or something. It wasn't pleasant, but it wasn't really worrying me, either. Still, Bree'd been worried enough for both of us, and I wasn't having that. So I'd rung up my doctor, who'd listened, asked me some interesting questions about symptoms that seemed to have nothing to do with what was happening now, and then sent me off for some neurological tests.

I remember that I'd been calm, or at least I thought I was calm. That was probably because Bree wasn't. Something about the symptoms had left her completely freaked, on the edge of disintegrating. I'd never seen her this way, and I couldn't deal at all. I'd had an instinct, even back then, that on those rare occasions when she was going to need the space to fall apart, I had to pick up the slack, you know? Only way to do it was staying calm.

Those questions, about whether I'd had certain symptoms when I was much younger? I know what he was after. I didn't then, but I do now. The thing with my leg and foot, that was classic MS. He was trying to suss out whether I might have had MS for a long time, and not known. The disease works that way, sometimes. It can sit dormant, not showing any symptoms, while it's damaging you in total silence, invisible, stripping the myelin off the nerves that keep you going.

I don't know whether I'd had those other symptoms or not, but it's possible. I remember odd stabbing back spasms, and my jaw going numb around the same time, back in 1980. And there'd been a hospital stay that coincided with the month when Viv Hedley had deteriorated and died of end stage ovarian cancer. Nothing short of being flat on my back in hospital could have kept me from being there for Luke, but I was so sick, Bree didn't even tell me what was happening with Viv. She was afraid it would break me, not being able to be there, and sick as I was, not being able to do a damned thing, would have made me nuts.

She knew that, and she carried that weight until I was out of hospital.

That first MRI—I'm still amazed at how much I hated it. The indignity of the procedure, the shot full of something designed to turn my insides into a blackboard for them to read, the claustrophobia of the machine itself, I just bloody hated every minute of it. I made the mistake of letting that show to Bree; she'd melted down completely, crying, flipping her shit, demanding that the techs find a way to make it easier for me. And of course, there wasn't any easier way.

Two weeks of waiting, while they processed the results and got it all back to my neuro. It was amazing how much worse things could get in the space of two weeks. The other foot went numb, the jaw began to lose feeling, my digestion—always a bit dodgy—started being completely uncooperative. No one had used the term *multiple sclerosis* yet, and I must have been deep into some serious denial, you know? Because I never even thought back to Jack, in his wheelchair. Not once.

It never leaves my memory, that diagnosis. I can see it all sharp and clear, no matter what: The visit to the neurologist, with Bree at my side. Dr. Dahlberg, putting the films up on the backlit screen. My own brain, right up there, visible.

I remember I had hold of Bree's hand. For some reason, all I could really see in my head was her face on a particular day, long ago. I kept seeing the white, bleak look she'd had, hopeless and desolate. I kept hearing the way she'd pleaded with me not to go, that first time I'd gone back to London in 1980, left her here, to go take care of Cilla. All I could remember was how miserable that had been. I suppose I was clinging to the idea that that day in 1980 was the worst thing, the most unfair thing, life could possibly throw my way. "Okay. So, what is it I'm supposed to be looking at, exactly?"

"These." She touched the screen with one forefinger: one small white spot, another, two more. "These white spots are lesions. They're typical of the lesions we expect to see with multiple sclerosis."

Silence. I had no words, nothing to say. I closed my hand hard over Bree's, and not entirely for my own sake; she'd begun to shake.

"They match your symptoms, correspondence to areas of lost myelin, the covering on your nerves."

Dahlberg was really calm as she stood there, damning me. Not fair to blame her for that. I suppose she had to be casual. If a doctor couldn't stay calm and uninvolved when they have to dish out this sort of bad news four times a week and twice on Tuesdays, she wouldn't last long. "I think we can safely make the diagnosis, here. Of course, if you'd like another opinion, I'd be happy to refer you to a colleague—I'm not infallible, and confirmation is never a bad idea in any case."

Bree had collapsed, and to this day, I'm grateful for that. I had no time or space to flip out, myself—I had to focus on her, and bloody lucky, too. She was on her knees, incoherent, sobbing hysterically, Bree who never cries about anything. She couldn't get a sentence out, and she was hyperventilating.

"I'm so sorry. Can I get you anything? A glass of water?"

Maybe Dahlberg was human, after all. I shook my head at her and gathered Bree in, and pulled her off the floor and safe up against me. Somehow, remembering how I'd had to leave her all those years ago? Even the diagnosis I'd just been handed didn't quite measure up.

I remember that I looked at Dahlberg over Bree's head, Bree sobbing against my chest and babbling, her fingers clutching my shirt, and heard my own voice, completely calm. "Right. So, how we do treat it?"

And here we were, eight years later: eight years of weekly

interferon shots, of daily medications for spasms, for pain, for digestion, for everything the disease seemed able to throw at me. Eight years down the road, with relapsing-remitting MS, not the progressive monster that had caught and killed Jack, years before anyone knew what to do about it.

I took in a long deep breath and looked at Bree, leaning hard up against me, and realised that, oh yeah, she'd gone right down that second memory road with me, just the way she'd always done. And she'd done it right there at my side every step along the way, just the way she always was, and had always been.

CHAPTER THIRTEEN

I found out the police were letting the Bombardiers back into the Freelon Street studio at the same time I found out that Bruno Baines was being held for questioning.

Just for a change, I got to the phone first. As usual, my cell phone rang too early and as usual, Bree tried to grab it before it could disturb me. This time, though, I woke at the first ring and got to it myself. She was supposed to be resting, damn it.

"JP? It's Tony." He sounded very energised for that early in the day. "Did I wake you? I just got a call from your pal at Homicide. He says we can head back into Freelon tomorrow. So I've been thinking. Did you want to take a day off, and we can start back at Freelon in the morning? I mean, shit, Mac's been here working his ass off. Considering how much he's done for us, I'm feeling kind of guilty."

"Yeah, sounds lovely. Hang on, will you?" Bree was glaring

at me. "I'm awake," I told her. "It's okay. We're getting a day off, so you can just stop giving me the evil eye, lady."

She gave me one more glare for good measure and headed off into the loo. I took my hand off the mouthpiece.

"Right. Ring me up later, okay? We can sort out when you want to get started tomorrow."

"Will do. Oh, by the way—did you hear about Bruno getting arrested?"

"What, Bruno? Arrested for what?" *Shit*. Bad timing; Bree had just come back in, and she'd heard that.

"Murder, I guess. Or maybe it's not an official arrest—Ormand said Bruno was being detained for questioning. Don't know why, but it seems pretty stupid to me. I mean, come on, the guy spent months building that guitar. We're talking blood, sweat, tears and time. I'm not saying he wouldn't have gone up-side Vinny's head—hell, there were days I wanted to go upside Vinny's head myself—but no way in hell he'd risk even a chip in the finish of that thing. That studio is crammed with stuff he could have smacked Vinny with, but that guitar? Not one of them. Ormand just doesn't get it, does he? Hard to believe he could be that dumb, but, well, that's dumb."

"No, I agree. Ormand's got no clue. Has Bruno got a law-yer? If not, I can call Blacklight's people and get a local rec."

Bree had frozen in place. She'd swapped the pyjama bot-toms she'd be sleeping in until she stopped the post-op bleeding for a pair of knickers. She stood there, naked except for those, hands on her hips, mouth slightly open. She looked furious.

"Not sure he can afford a lawyer," Tony told me. "After all, the cops wouldn't let him cash that cheque Vinny gave him. If they think he killed them, he can't profit from his crime, or something. It all sounds pretty bogus to me."

"Yeah, it's complete bullshit." I swung myself upright. "Okay, right, look. Give me ten minutes to brush my teeth and have some coffee, and I'll ring up Ormand and see what's going on, all right? If Bruno needs a lawyer, we'll get him one. Keep your cell handy. Cheers, mate."

"What the *fuck*?" Bree's hands had balled up into fists, and her cheeks had a scarlet wash over the pale. "Is Patrick Ormand out of his tiny little mind? What's going on?"

"Bree, love, you were standing right here. Did you just hear me tell Tony I'd call Ormand and find out? Bloody hell, can I have a piss first? Maybe a shower, and a cup of coffee, take my morning meds? Can you give me a few minutes to wake up and get my head together, before I beard the big bad homicide detective, please?"

"Sorry." *Fuck.* All the colour had ebbed out of her face, and she'd gone even paler. Bree's odd that way—she gets red with rage, but she can't seem to blush. Upset her, embarrass her, hurt her feelings, and she goes all ivory. "I didn't mean—I wasn't trying to—"

"No, don't apologise, love. I'm the one who's sorry. I didn't mean to snap at you. I need to wake up a bit, that's all." I looked her up and down. "Love that outfit, by the way. My favourite of yours, except for that bit at the bottom. You can lose that."

She grinned at me. Good, back to normal. "Three weeks to go, and then at least I can ditch the pyjamas—I know, total passion-killers. If I really wanted to be a bitch, I'd put on some Jimmy Choos and dance for you. Little reminder you've got three weeks before you get any."

"What, no seven veils?" I headed for the loo, stopping to pat her on the bottom. "That's a lovely bum you've got there. The upper half's quite nice, as well. Seriously, love, I have no clue what's going on. Let me wake up and I'll ring Ormand, okay? I'm more impressive when I've had some caffeine. Anyway, I want to get this taken care of so we can find out what Mac wants to do with his day off."

It was actually closer to half an hour before I got downstairs and rang Ormand. Mornings are never the best point of the day for the MS, but this morning seemed a bit worse than it had been recently. There was no way I was telling Bree that; I just hoped she wouldn't suss out that the needles and pains were why I'd snapped at her.

It was a nice clear morning, the fog nowhere in sight. Mac and Dom were both out in the garden, settled in and relaxing at the glass-topped bistro table, Mac with his Earl Grey tea and Dom with her bitter drinking chocolate. There were biscuits as well, and fresh fruit; Bree had shown them where everything was kept the first morning they'd been here, basically given them an all-access pass to her kitchen. I settled into a chair and explained the situation to Mac.

". . . so, bottom line is, we're horrible wretched hosts who've taken shameless advantage of your good nature and kept you working like a navvy, and now we've seen the error of our ways. Seriously, mate, you've been stellar, and Dom's been incredibly patient, and here's to a nice bit of holiday, even if it turns out being just one day. Anything we can do?"

"Working us?" He snorted. "Yeah, I fancy I see Dom, here, as Little Nell, all Dickens orphanage rubbish. Johnny, mate, I came here to work, remember?"

Mac stretched his legs out. Something caught my eye, a kind of glint in our uphill neighbour's bedroom window. Bloody hell, was that a pair of binoculars? "I don't think we need to drag you and Bree all over town—there's bound to be a hire car firm around here. Any way of finding out what's on at the various museums? I've had a major jones to stare at some world-class paintings, after seeing what Paul Morgenstern was doing at his place the other night, rearranging his collection like that."

"Yeah, that should be easy enough. Hang on, though. I

promised Bree I'd call Patrick Ormand and see what the hell's going on with Bruno Baines. They've apparently pulled him in—detained for questioning, whatever that actually means—and he might need a lawyer. I thought I'd call Carla and have her get local recs from our people in New York."

I turned to Bree. "You've got Patrick's direct number programmed into your phone, love, yeah? Can I use it, please?"

"This is Ormand." He'd picked it up on the first ring, and he sounded quite cordial. I wondered if Bree's name on his caller ID had anything to do with that. I mean, right, I might know rationally that Bree has zero interest in Patrick Ormand as a man, but that didn't mean Ormand shared the lack of interest. In fact, I was pretty sure he fancied my old lady. Since I got the impression that he liked me, as well, the balancing act he must be doing when one of us rang his phone had to be as good as anything a circus trapeze artist could pull off.

"Morning, Patrick. This is JP Kinkaid." Bree picked up my cup, made a pouring gesture, and lifted her brows: I nodded, mouthed my thanks, and she headed off towards the kitchen, Dom on her heels. "I was hoping to get some gen about Bruno Baines. Tony Mancuso told me you'd arrested him. Is that true? And does he have a lawyer? Because if not, we'll get him one. Blacklight has the New York firm on retainer, and I'm sure they can get us hooked up with someone out here."

"Really." He didn't sound enthusiastic, and suddenly I remembered how we'd sparred and circled, back in New York, when he'd been sniffing round Bree, thinking she'd smashed Perry Dillon's throat. I'd come off the winner in every one of those matches. I don't think he'd forgotten that fact, or forgiven it, either, and frankly, I didn't give a toss. "Well. Yes, we've detained him. It turns out he filled his van at a gas station right around the corner from the 707 warehouse the night Rosco

Galliano was killed. And it was well within the time frame established as the time of death by the ME. He has no alibi for either death, he admits he was actually at Freelon Street when Fabiano was killed, and he was right in the vicinity when Galliano was killed. He's also the only person with no alibi for either death. Under the circumstances . . ."

His voice trailed off. He didn't say that the DA and the media had glommed on and were getting on him to nail someone, but then, he didn't have to. We'd seen the papers the past few days. It was front-page stuff, and he was nowhere near an arrest. Not a good start for the newcomer's first big case.

I snorted. It was a rude little snort, but really, I couldn't help it. He had it coming.

"Look," I told him, as kindly as I could. "I'm going to ring off in a minute and find him a lawyer, but first off, let me tell you something, okay? My old lady's already pointed it out to you, but you don't seem to have got it. That guitar, the one that was trashed on Vinny's skull? It represents eight solid weeks of loving, painstaking, detailed work. It's beyond a labour of love—it's more like a piece of the bloke's soul."

"What's your point?" He sounded completely unyielding.

"Oh, for fuck's sake, Patrick, use your head! There are road cases at Freelon Street, stacked up and handy. There's a Korg board, nice and heavy. Hell, Kris always leaves one of his basses on the stand—it's probably sitting there right now. You could cave in someone's head quite nicely with that. The point is, if Bruno was going to bash Vinny, you know the one thing he *wouldn't* have used? Come on, mate. Take a wild guess."

Silence. I grinned at Bree, who'd come back out with a tray: buttered toast, coffee, a pot of jam. Wonderful woman. I took a mouthful of coffee and went back to the phone.

"There's also that whole motive deal, you know? Right,

okay, so Vinny Fabiano was an obnoxious berk. A lot of people are obnoxious berks—you need something a bit stronger than that to fetch up taking a custom guitar across the head. Hang on a moment, would you?"

I set the phone down, spread some jam on my toast, and had a bite. Bree had taken the fourth chair and was watching and listening, her chin propped in her hands; I took my sweet time, chewing, getting it down. Hell, I enjoyed the food almost as much as I was enjoying making Patrick wait.

"Sorry. I needed a mouthful of food, to settle the morning meds. Okay—where was I? Right, motive. Maybe you're thinking Bruno'd be narked that Vinny'd been dodging paying him. But that won't fly either, because he'd got paid, hadn't he? Unless you think Vinny wrote him a cheque for nine thousand dollars and told him to wait two days to deposit it *after* Bruno bashed him? You can't have it both ways, Patrick."

"Wait a minute." His voice sharpened up. "What's that about Baines being asked to wait two days to deposit it?"

"That's what Bruno told us, about a week ago. He didn't tell you that? I'm willing to sign something, a statement or an affidavit or whatever the hell those things are, if you need something in writing. Because he told us—what, last Friday. We were all having lunch, talking about it, and that's what he said. That's why it wasn't already in the bank when you took the cheque away from him. What, don't you even know what you grabbed up as evidence? I don't know if the cheque was postdated. That would show he was telling the truth, yeah?"

"I don't think that was in his statement. We knew about the cheque, of course—we have it. I don't know whether it's postdated, but that's not relevant; banks don't honour postdating anymore." He took a breath. "All right. Did you say you'd provide him with a lawyer? I'll make sure he knows that. If you want to give the lawyer my direct number, that would be fine."

I rang off and handed the phone back to Bree. "Right," I told her. "That's shaken him up."

I sounded so smug, I surprised myself. I was starting to think I took far too much pleasure in coming off the winner against Patrick Ormand.

I wasn't sure how hard walking into Freelon Street was going to hit any of the Bombardiers. I wasn't really expecting it to upset me too much; after all, I was just the session bloke, and this wasn't my patch. And I hadn't been mad about Vinny anyway.

I was wrong about that. For one thing, the construction across the alley had been going on the entire time we'd been locked out, and construction can move really quickly. So the bare scaffolding had somehow got itself transformed into the outer walls of the condo lofts that were going up, and you could even see what the colour scheme was going to be.

And if we're talking about colour, there was a nasty smear of it on the floor, right near the Korg. The Bombardiers had done the sensible thing when they'd bought the place: laid down carpeting over the industrial flooring already in place, and then put a raised stage in for rehearsals. The Korg was sitting on carpet, and the stain on the carpet was reddish black, and there was the remnant of powder around it, probably the stuff the police use to make bloodstains show up.

I set my Deluxe case down, keeping it well away from the Korg. My stomach wanted to do a flip-flop.

"Oh, shit." I heard Billy gulp. He'd changed colour himself. "We're going to need to replace that. I'll call the carpet place tomorrow. Shit, shit, shit."

It was bizarre. There were shreds of yellow tape lying about, and that stain on the carpet. Kris's P Bass was on its stand, where he'd left it. Everything looked normal, until you looked down at the floor, and after that, normal wasn't in it.

I caught a flash, a little sparkle on the rug, out of the corner of my eye, a good three feet away from the Korg's stand. I reached out and picked up a fragment of gold wire.

It took me a second to realise it had probably come off Bruno's guitar—it looked like the Homicide forensics team had missed it. I suddenly had a picture in my head, of how hard the damned thing must have connected to make that gold wire land where I'd found it, that far from the stain on the carpet.

"Jesus." Tony looked spooked. "Man, this is so damned weird. Ghosts. You know?"

"Yeah. But we've got work to do, and this is where we do it." Damon was at the server, scrolling down the screen. "Give me a minute—let me see if there's anything from a couple of weeks back. If he did any late-night stuff on 'If You Have to Go,' that's where the file would be. Here we go; let's try it."

He did something with the mouse—I've never really got the computer thing down—and the playback monitors jumped to life. The studio was suddenly full of Vinny's voice, and this time, he was playing an acoustic guitar, probably his Martin.

"So you say you have to leave me, you say you have to go? Go for it if you want to, baby, who am I to tell you no. . . ."

"Man oh man." Tony sounded as if he might throw up his breakfast. "Wow."

"You say I've got no answers to the questions that you pose, babe I ain't your answer man, that's just the way it goes. . . ."

The acoustic guitar sounded superb. There was something about his playing that had a completely different touch, a more honest feel, than anything he'd ever managed to get off his outrageously pricey collection of electric guitars. It was as if, without the tempting little candy-shop display of stomp boxes and tube screamers and pedals to play with, he'd been forced to just play guitar, and really, it was a damned shame he hadn't found himself in that situation more often, because he was actually a very good guitar player.

"Why was he mucking about with an electric guitar?" Mac was hearing the same thing I was; his shoulders were swaying to it. "It's brilliant with the acoustic. The lyric just grabs."

"That's the way it goes, lady, that's the way it goes, time's the road we travel on, the river ebbs and flows. . . ."

"Tony." An idea was percolating. "Look, mate—would an acoustic version, say me and Mac, get up your record label's nose? Or do we need full band on this one? Because, you keep it simple, this could be one of the two that nails the critics. I think 'Liplock' will be the matching electric bit. But it's totally your call."

Tony was nodding, listening. "I think maybe we should do full band, but minimalist. You know what I'm talking about, right? Bass for emphasis only—I can do some keyboard stuff against it, way down low and way up high, a little tiara stuff. Don't know about drums. But dude, I'm with you. Keep it clean, stripped-down, stark. Mac?"

"Not my call, Tony. But if you want an opinion, I'd say yes, as stark as we can, let the lyric carry it, by way of the vocal. Why the hell he wanted to tart it up in the first place is beyond me. Johnny, you don't happen to have an acoustic guitar here, do you?"

"No, but I can get one. I hate to drag Bree cross-town twice—Tony, can you drive me?"

"You told me when we started you had some things to do; I never asked for details, just sat back and trusted you. . . ."

"Sure. But let's hear the whole song first, okay? Damn, this one's a beauty."

Tony had powered up his rig. He ran his right hand down the high end of the Roland, counterpointing the vocal and the single guitar with a gorgeous little trill, a faint regretful sparkle of the treble keys. I saw Billy's mouth twist up a bit. Bloody hell, the damned thing was so effective, even the band was feeling it.

"I don't know why you're leaving, I only know it hurts, but not for me to stop you, girl, I haven't got the words. . . ."

"Right." I plugged in the Deluxe, setting everything really clean. No effects, no overamping; Tony was right, the song wanted minimalism. I played a few short runs, light, a bit distant, not too emphatic, and lifted an eyebrow at Kris. The P Bass spoke back, a deep little rumble, call-and-response to me, and to Tony. The drums were silent; Billy hadn't done anything at all. He was just listening.

"I can't say a word, lady, if you have to go, there is nothing I can do, I can't tell you no, got no answers, got no hope—if you have to go."

A lovely cascade of finger-picking, middle D, down the scale to a tuned-down E string, and the song was over. And then Vinny's voice, satisfied, alone in the studio, talking to no one but himself: "That's more like it."

We were all quiet. Damon broke the silence, trying for a note of normalcy, not quite pulling it off.

"Okay, guys—are we taking a break, to get JP an acoustic? Because if you want to do that, I can burn this one and see what else is on here. I've got the list of the other five we need to work on, and I keep a log of the approximate dates we did them. It shouldn't take too long. JP? You good with that?"

"Yeah, that works for me. I like the idea of doing this on acoustic, and I can always fill in any electric parts later on."

I turned my amp off, and set the Deluxe down. "I'm curious, Damon—I thought you downloaded every night?"

"The Korg downloads every night," he corrected me. "It's an automatic thing—I've got a program. It dumps everything it's recorded onto the server, as part of the nightly download. But that doesn't mean I listen to every file every day, JP, and I don't burn every version of every rehearsal onto CD. If I did that, I wouldn't have time to do anything else. I just burn off multiple CDs of the stuff the band says it wants. We've been doing nearly everything for these sessions, because the stuff was all new and everyone had to learn it, plus you were sitting in. Now Mac's here, too, I think I'd better plan on checking everything and then burning it off."

He reached out and patted his multiple CD burner. "And man, is it easy with this setup. No offence, I like your studio, but this is my playhouse. Good to be home."

Once we'd got a couple of my acoustics—the Martin and a beautiful twelve-string Santa Cruz—the song went perfectly. I don't know, really, but I think a lot of Mac's ease with the material came from his familiarity with what I was likely to do on guitar. When you've played together as long as we have, you learn each other's musical vocabulary at a bone-deep level. It's why I know just where he'd be likely to pause, take a breath, push, hold back an emphasis point in the vocals. We feed off each other's patterns, the same way the Bombardiers do with each other. It was really a trip, meshing our style with theirs, feeling how well it worked.

We finished up "If You Have to Go" right round five o'clock. The song had taken exactly three tries, me changing from the Martin to the Santa Cruz for a touch of lushness, to get it so close to perfect, it was audience-ready. We could have walked out onstage at the Oakland Arena and brought down the house with it. That's a damned good feeling, especially when it's a band you haven't recorded with much.

"Man, we're really on a roll. What a beautiful fuckin' buzz." Tony cracked his knuckles. "Hey, how would you guys feel about getting a start on the next one? No need to make a late night out of it, but maybe a dinner break and another couple of hours? JP, are you okay with that, or do you need to be home doing stuff for Bree?"

"I'm fine with that, if JP is." Mac raised his brows at me. "I'd have thought Bree would be delighted to have us out of her basement after the last couple of weeks, but you know the girl better than anyone. Would she mind? Are you up for it?"

"Let me ring home, yeah? I'll tell you in a minute."

She was fine with it herself, once I promised to take my meds and convinced her we'd get something decent for dinner, and not just make do with pizza or a lot of starchy junk food. Just before I rang off, she stopped me. She sounded really pleased.

"I almost forgot. Bruno Baines is out of jail—he called about an hour ago, to let us know. He said to tell you, thanks for the lawyer."

"Cool." I was distracted, one ear on the usual argument about what to order out for going on behind me. "I wonder how much bail money it cost us?"

"Probably about an hour's worth of time, because it turned out he didn't need the lawyer. He's not out on bail, John. He's just out, period. Patrick Ormand told the lawyer that he was looking at some new evidence, and he just shooed them out of the building, as if he couldn't get rid of them fast enough. Bruno was out in the waiting room, and he said Patrick's office was full of strange guys in suits. The lawyer told him that as soon as he walked in, they all clammed up, went totally silent. He thinks there's something major about to hit the fan."

CHAPTER FOURTEEN

"On four—take two, 'Move on Out,' JP leads it in. One—two—three—"

It was nearly midnight, and the couple of extra hours we'd thought we'd be spending at Freelon Street seemed to have settled into something that might turn into an all-nighter. That's what happens when a session gets into a groove, a nice even place where everyone synchs up and the band starts eating up the hours, getting it together, getting it done. That can get costly when you're on rented studio time; hell, you get a band or a producer who wants to micromanage every aspect of every song, a CD can run up half a million dollars just in recording time before you stop to add it up. Good job this was the Bombardiers' own studio.

I'd kept my promise to Bree about not eating a crap meal, and we'd sent out for a very good dinner from a famous steak house across town. Then Damon, who was spending every minute of every break hunting through the server downloads of every session since rehearsals for the CD had started, punched another song we hadn't touched yet up on the monitors, something Kris and Tony had written together. It was a nice hard-edged rock number, very old-school, if the school you'd gone to happened to be Led Zeppelin Comprehensive or Who Polytechnic: nice raunchy lyrics, and an almost bitchy guitar sound. And the Zemaitis wasn't needed for this one. It was an absolute beggar for my Les Paul Deluxe. We'd tried it, and Mac nailed it on the first go.

Bloody hell. I'd done eleven Blacklight albums, and I knew how slick and professional he was in the studio, but this was ridiculous, well above even his usual average. At this rate, the Bombardiers were going to chain him to a road case and refuse to let him leave.

When we finished up with that one, Damon had decreed a twenty-minute break for a CD burn and another hunt through the download files. Mac reached out and nudged me.

"Not that I'm your nanny or anything," he remarked. "But you know, it's gone nine. You might want to ring home and reassure Bree. Let the poor girl know you haven't been seduced into a night on the tiles with all your rowdy rocker mates. You know, boozing, whores, loud music . . ."

He dodged back, laughing, at my mock backhand. "Bree knows what sessions are like," I told him, but I was grinning; he was absolutely right. He'd sussed that if I left it too late, I'd feel guilty about it later. "But yeah, I'll ring her. Where are Dom and Doug, by the way? Or is that a rude question, and none of my damned business anyway?"

Mac got up and jogged in place, stretching, limbering up. He does a lot of yoga, which gave him something to discuss with Bree; she's done yoga for years. "What, Dom and little Dougie? Who knows? Probably in a cheap motel room. That is, if they've got any sense. I gave her the day off, told her I'd be locked up safe in the studio, and shooed her off to play. I'm supposed to beep her when we're done—she'll come straight here, no matter what time we finish up. Right now, though? My guess is, in bed with Doug."

"Crikey, Mac, I was joking! Are you serious?"

Mac looked surprised. "Of course I'm serious. He definitely fancies her, and since she hasn't said anything about snapping his head off his neck, or about hurting him in any way he's not begging for, I'm guessing they've gone off for a nice rowdy slap and tickle somewhere. If they show up together, and he's wall-eyed and limping and incoherent and possibly drooling and a bit off, we'll know. I adore the girl, but she's definitely scary. Why do you think I pay her so much?"

I went outdoors, shaking my head, and rang Bree. As I'd suspected, she had no problem with me working late.

"Just check in periodically, if you can, please, John. I don't care what time it is. Okay?"

"Okay." I knew what she meant. Back in the eighties, there had been a couple of sessions that had gone until four in the morning. I'd decided to be a nice considerate gent and not wake her up. This was well before cell phones, or even pagers, and when I'd got home, she'd been frantic and furious, either imagining my mangled body in a Dumpster, or else imagining me having a mad romp in a hotel bedroom somewhere with a bunch of nubile little starfuckers. I was never really certain which scenario was running through her head, but after the second time, when she didn't speak to me for three solid days, I finally got it through my head: She'd rather be woken up and told it was going to be an all-nighter than not hear from me. As she pointed out, it wasn't as if she was going to sleep well, anyway.

We went back to work, down to only four songs left to do.

217

One of the earliest ones, another ballad, was given a good listen and was unanimously shelved for last—it had several very complex changes, a few too many I thought, and was obviously going to require either a lot of work or a bit of rewriting. Either way, it wasn't going to happen tonight. We were going to want a whole new day for that one.

Another break. Billy broke out the coffeemaker in the kitchen at the back of the studio and made a pot of good dark roast. Damon checked off the downloads, made some very pleased noises because the files on the server were finally thinning out, and punched up "Move on Out." That took us through until ten minutes of midnight; I actually did some string-bending, which hadn't occurred to me before. It sounded brilliant.

We broke again. While I wasn't going to take any meds that might put me to sleep, I did want my antispasmodics. The MS was very far off in the background tonight. If this was going to go on for a few more hours, I wanted to go on that way.

Tony and Kris, both nice and pumped, volunteered to do a run to the all-night convenience store to get some nosh for later on. Not being babies at recording sessions either, they knew just how badly we were all likely to want some good pointless crunchy carbohydrates as the session went longer. Mac rang up Dom and told her he'd probably be here until the small hours, and to get some sleep, if she felt like sleeping. I checked in with Bree again and gave her a progress report.

Around half past twelve, we settled down with a few bags of salty potato crisps and pretzels and some cheese. Damon, sitting at the server with his headphones, suddenly spoke up.

"Huh." He sounded puzzled. "This is weird."

"What is?" Billy had a handful of snack food and was preparing to munch. "Here, have some pretzels."

"None for me, thanks. There's a second file here—from

Thursday, the night Vinny was killed, I mean. It's a big one, too. He must have turned the Korg back on that night, when he came back. I turned it off before we left, remember?"

"Another file?" Tony tilted his head. "What's the time stamp on it?"

"Four twenty in the morning, on the Friday." Damon looked up at us, bewildered. "What the hell?"

No one was eating, suddenly, or drinking, or making any noise at all. We were all too busy staring at Damon.

He moved, just one hand, and suddenly the monitors came to life, and there was a familiar voice flooding the room.

"Yo, Vinny, I'm heading on out. You need anything else before I go?"

The voice was Rosie's. He sounded normal, himself, the way he'd always seemed to sound. And he was answered immediately.

"Actually, yeah, I do—I'm not going to need the PRS anymore tonight. Bruno Baines is coming by with my new axe, like, in about five minutes. Do me a favour, and drop the PRS off at the warehouse on your way home, okay? Wait a minute, let me get you my key. Don't forget to lock the place when you split."

I opened my mouth, and closed it again. So, Rosario had taken the PRS up—that was one question that had been driving me nuts, finally answered. But why had he lied to Tony about not having a key? All he'd had to do was tell us he had Vinny's. There was nothing at all dodgy about Vinny letting Rosario use the key—Rosario had handled Vinny's gear all the time.

But he hadn't. Instead, he'd said we'd need to get hold of Paul, and get him to let us in. It didn't make any sense, and I couldn't come up with one decent reason for him to have lied about it.

The sound of footsteps, ghostly and distant through the monitors. The rattle and snap of the front door closing. Quiet, as the Korg recorded the ambient noise in the studio. Vinny, humming to himself; I recognised "If You Have to Go."

We sat there and listened. No one said a word; if we weren't holding our breath, every damned one of us, we were really close to it.

The muted echo of footsteps. The sound of the front door opening yet again.

"Bruno! Hey, man, glad you got here. Oh, cool, you brought it with you. Listen, I've got a cheque for you, the full nine thousand. I bet you thought you'd never get paid, huh? But do me a favour, and wait until Monday to deposit that? I need to hit the bank tomorrow morning myself, and it'll need a couple of days to clear."

Right. So, Bruno had told us, and Ormand, the plain truth: Vinny had handed him a cheque and asked him to wait. Patrick Ormand was apparently going to have to find himself another suspect. This looked likely to clear Bruno, definitively enough even for Patrick, and I was really quite pleased about that.

Some conversation, trivial technical stuff. Explanation of the electronics. Vinny sounded appreciative but also impatient; it was obvious, to me at least, that Vinny was edging the luthier towards the door, and I found myself getting it, feeling a bit of that impatience. Hell, if that had been my shiny brand-new toy, I'd want to be alone to play with it as well.

"Cool—thanks, Bruno. Remember, give me a day or two to get the funds in my own account clear, okay? Drive safe, man. I'll talk to you next week."

The slam of the studio door closing behind Bruno. Quick footsteps. Then, unexpected and absolutely gorgeous, a flood of power chords pouring out of the monitors and washing over us. Vinny had plugged in his new toy, cranked it up, taken it for a test run. . . .

The banging on the door this time was so loud and unexpected that we all jumped; for a moment, I thought it was actually someone outside kicking the door, here and now, wanting in. I wasn't the only one, either. Kris jerked his head around, realised it was on the monitors and not in real time, muttered something under his breath, and blew air out, hard.

"*Dude! Come on in, man, you've got to hear this thing. It's totally hot. Bruno dropped it off and picked up his cheque. I told him to wait a couple of days—what?*"

A new voice, distorted with rage. I knew the voice, but I'd never heard it sound this way before.

"*You miserable son of a bitch! You're asking me, what? I'll tell you what, you asshole! I just spent an hour on the phone with my delightful ex, that's what. Turns out you not only can't keep your fly shut, you can't keep your mouth shut, either!*"

"Jesus!" Billy's jaw had dropped. "Who—? Is that—?"

"*What the fuck were you thinking? You were nobody, Vinny, no one out here knew squat about you. So I bring you out here, I give you a shot, I hook you up with a really good established band, I cut you in on some of the perks from my side business, and this is how you say thanks? You screw that bitch and then give her some weapons to screw me with? You told her about the warehouse! You told her about the trailer! Well, guess what, Vinny—you just screwed all three of us, you fucking moron! You happy now?*"

"That's Paul." Damon was staring at the monitors. "Isn't that Paul?"

"Oh, yes. That's Paul Morgenstern." Mac sounded completely unsurprised, if a bit regretful. I twisted my head and blinked at him. He nodded towards the monitors. "Listen."

"*Paul, no, hey, wait—you got it wrong, man.*" Vinny was almost stammering. "*I'm not putting the stones to Angie—I dumped her. Man, I don't blame you, either. That chick is seriously hard. And I didn't tell her anything, not really, I just let it slip that you maybe had something going on the side, out of the warehouse. Dude, how could I have told her? I don't even know what you're dealing out of there.*"

Damon was chewing on his lip. He looked sick. "Guys, should we stop this right here, maybe? Get that cop in?"

"No. Play it out." Tony was really shaken, but he was really grim as well. "If we're offering him something, let's make sure we know what it is we're offering. Sorry if I'm being rude about your pal, JP, but the truth is, I don't trust him. Jesus, this is ugly. This is just so ugly."

"You told her enough, you stupid piece of shit! So she takes me for over a million bucks when we split up, and now she calls me up, she knows I've got a moneymaker on the side, and she knows I'm running it out of the warehouse. She wants a piece. And if she doesn't get it, she goes to the cops. And how does she know there's anything to get? Because you told her! You don't have the brains to not tell the greediest bitch west of Chicago her ex has a sideline? Why the fuck couldn't you keep your fly zipped up and your mouth shut?"

It was completely surreal. I mean, right, it was Paul, but what was coming out of the monitors, the rage in his voice, the twist, the hate? That simply didn't sound like the nice, urbane producer who donated his time for PSA sessions and gave new musicians a leg up. I just couldn't wrap my head around it.

"Paul—"

A slight hiss, a slight hum: Vinny, powering down Bruno's masterpiece, unplugging it. The faint rattle of a guitar, being set on its stand.

"Forget it, Vinny. The gravy train is officially derailed. Angie wants a hundred grand, and she wants it by the end of next week, in her account, no questions, no arguments, no ifs, ands, or buts, or she goes to the cops. You know what? This is your goddamned fault. I don't have a hundred grand to give her. And you know why? Because it went to buy you that pearl-top you were drooling over. It went to buy you that PRS Private Stock you wanted so bad. Well, you can kiss the Zemaitis bye-bye, Vinny. I've already told her it's hers, and I've already told her what it's worth. She wants to sell it, maybe she can get

back the sixty grand it cost me. The PRS, I'll sell myself—I've already got a few bites on that one. She gets the cash from that, too. Here's a word of advice: Next time someone hands you a shitload of bribes to keep your mouth shut, keep it shut."

"Bribes? What the fuck?" There was a new note in Vinny's voice; I'd heard it a few times, mostly when his own incompetence with his gear had left him swearing, angry, lashing out, losing his temper. *"Those guitars are mine, Paul. You can't just take them and sell them out from under me. That's bullshit. They're mine, and I'm keeping them. Just tell Angie to fuck off—it's what I did. It's not like she can prove anything anyway."*

Silence, both from the monitors and in the room. It felt, really, as if even the walls of the Freelon Street studio were waiting to see what would happen next.

"You really are dumb, Vinny, you know that? You are, like, the Lord High Archduke of Dumb, or something. I said bribe, I meant bribe. You think I was so quick to get you eighty grand worth of guitars because you have a pretty singing voice? Because you're such a nice guy? Because you earned them?"

It was incredible, how contemptuous he sounded. I was glad I hadn't seen his face while he was spitting out this much venom. *"You really don't seem to get it. You got those axes because you were in the wrong place at the wrong time. If you hadn't been hiding out behind the damned Bambi when Mr. Hiroshi and I did our little deal, you'd be playing a fucking Silvertone right now. They were bribes, Vinny. Look it up in a dictionary: B-r-i-b-e-s. And you were so busy playing Italian stallion with my ex-wife that you had to share the wealth. I'll tell you what, Vinny—share this."*

A moment of quiet, and then a really unpleasant noise. Unmistakeable, you know? It's hard to miss the sound of someone gobbing at another person. From the way the conversation had gone up to that point, I had the feeling that the gobbing had been done straight into Vinny's face.

"You motherfucker!" Vinny was screaming with rage. *"You spit on me! I'm—"*

Confusion, noise, voices. There was nothing to take apart, nothing to separate. But we all heard the crunch, the sound of wood splintering. It might have been bone, not wood. Either way, the noise wasn't something I want near my dreams at night.

A soft, nasty thud as something heavy hit the carpeted floor. Whimpering ragged breathing. I was fairly close to puking up the excellent dinner and my evening meds along with it at that point, and I really didn't think anything likely to come out of those damned monitors could come close to the ugliness of what we'd just heard—after all, how often do you sit and listen to a taped murder, in real time?

But, in a way, the sounds that followed after were actually worse: soft, suggestive, and stealthy. I shut my eyes, and there it was, the picture of Paul Morgenstern, thanking his luck that the guitar had only punched in Vinny's skull instead of spattering them both with blood, wiping all the gob off Vinny's ruined face because the police can get DNA from spittle, wiping down the neck of the guitar, wiping down anything at all he might have touched. Another damned image I don't need near my dreams at night. Unfortunately, the circumstances didn't give me a choice about that.

Footsteps, quick ones, not quite running. The door opening and closing. And after that, the Korg recording nothing at all until it clicked, time-stamped the file, and shut itself down at 4:20 the next morning, just Vinny's body lying in the pool of blood that had begun a slow steady seepage out of the hole in his head, cooling as the night went on.

Maybe it was because I'd already had some recent exposure to sudden violent death, but I was actually the first one to get my wits back. I stood up, a bit shaky. It was very late.

"Right. Okay. Here's the thing—we've officially got evidence in a murder investigation. And that means we'd better wake up Ormand and let him know that he needs to get his hands on Paul Morgenstern."

I reached for my cell phone. Mac laid a hand on my wrist.

"I think you'll find he's already done that, Johnny." Mac had that odd regretful note in his voice again. He sounded—I don't know, like a hanging judge or something. "See, I had the hire car driver stop off at Ormand's office yesterday, after I'd gone museum-hopping."

"What?" We were all looking at him as if he'd just dropped in from Mars or something. He sounded so calm. "Mac, you don't mind me asking, what in hell are you on about?"

"The Sundown Gallery." He got up and stretched. "You know, down at the Wharf? They've got a Goya exhibit on at the moment: the Age of Reason series. So I had a few things I wanted to share with your copper chum, about Paul Morgenstern's art collection."

The next night, Bree had everyone over to our place for dinner, including Patrick Ormand.

Of course, I raised some hell about that—she was supposed to be resting, recovering from surgery. What with studio sessions in the basement and people getting thumped over the head with guitars and whatnot, not to mention me being out half the night talking to the cops, she really hadn't got much rest. I announced there was no way I was allowing her to stress out and cook for a mob. She stuck her tongue out at me.

"Too late, John. I already invited everyone. And anyway?" She suddenly shot me a grin. "You are not the boss of me."

"The hell I'm not. Don't lay money against that one, lady." I pulled her down next to me, on the sofa. "Seriously, Bree. Why in hell do you want to end up knackered cooking for—wait a minute. How many people are coming to this little do, exactly?"

"John, it's a big bowl of salad and a pot of pasta. That's not cooking. And it's just for twelve people, including you and me. The Bombardiers, Katia, Sandra, Mac and Dom, Damon and Doug."

I lifted an eyebrow. "I can do basic sums, you know? That's eleven, not twelve. And why the guilty look?"

"I invited Patrick Ormand, too." She looked at me out of the corner of her eyes. "Well, I want to hear the whole story, damn it! I want to hear about Paul's art stuff—and can you look me in the eye and say you aren't dying to know what happened at the warehouse? Because Paul didn't kill Rosario, or Rosco, or whatever his name was. Did he? Didn't Patrick say he had an alibi for that?"

I shook my head at her. "You're a cat, you know that? Right down to the curiosity. Yeah, okay, I'm curious. But why do you have to cook? Why can't we just send out for Chinese takeaway or something?"

"Because that won't make the house smell wonderful."

Of course, everyone showed up. We'd finished up everything on the CD that needed the Zemaitis that morning, and Magnus had gone back to Santa Barbara, taking his gorgeous guitar with him, so he wasn't at dinner. Neither was Bruno Baines, who'd rung up to say thanks for the invite, but he'd lost a few days of work time, what with fixing the Zemaitis and then being detained by the SFPD, and he needed to stay in his Mendocino workshop and try to recoup some of his deadlines. That sounded as if he'd got some work, and I didn't blame him for staying home and doing it. After all, he was going to be out nine thousand dollars, now that Vinny was dead.

I'd actually helped tidy up the house, taken the Dyson to the floors, and even run a wipe over the furniture. Bree caught me at it and tried to shoo me away, but I told her she wasn't the only one who could ignore her own health issues and act like a nutter, and I was hoovering the floors whether she liked it or not. So the house was reasonably tidy and free of cat hair when our guests arrived.

The conversation over dinner started off being about the Bombardiers sessions, where they'd be taking it for mixing and mastering and whatnot, but of course, the main thing on everyone's mind was Paul's arrest, and what had come out of that. No one was really bothering to try to hide it, and Patrick was in a particularly mellow mood. I really wished I could shake the feeling I always got from him, that there was something about grabbing someone and locking them up that had the sort of effect on him good sex had on me, but there it was, and I wasn't likely to shake it any time soon. And besides, he seemed willing to answer questions. Might as well take advantage of the moment, you know?

"Yes, we pulled Paul Morgenstern in yesterday. Nice, easy, painless bust—he didn't give us any trouble at all. Of course, he wasn't expecting the guys from Interpol I brought along with me. That might have taken some wind out of his sails."

"Interpol?" Kris glanced at Tony. "Why?"

"Because there were fourteen pieces of original art on the walls of his Sausalito house, and eleven of them were stolen." Patrick raised his glass towards Mac in something that might have been a toast. "Mr. Sharpe gave us the information we needed to get things started, the information about the Goya. Of course, we'd have figured it out once we heard the download from Freelon Street—that reference to Mr. Hiroshi is damning—but the early tip got us there before he had time to move any of those pieces."

"So—what? Paul was subsidising his income from the music business with stolen art?" Sandra reached for the champagne. "Tony, pass the raspberries, please. You're saying that Paul was an art thief, right?"

"Not a thief, just a broker. He was the go-between in a few major deals, and we think possibly quite a few smaller ones. He made a mistake, a really bad slip, when he admitted to Mr. Sharpe that the Goya was an original. If he'd said it was a reproduction, Mr. Sharpe might not have been suspicious that early on." He shook his head and forked up a mouthful of salad. "Thanks for having me over, by the way—the food is great."

Bree had put me at the head of the table and snagged the chair at my right. She dropped a few berries into her champagne flute and poured herself bubbly. "You're welcome. What is all this about the Goya? You keep talking about it."

"It was stolen." Mac was dipping bread into olive oil. "Genuine, and stolen. When I stopped in at Patrick's office—and by the way, Patrick, no one calls me Mr. Sharpe, unless I'm being served with a bogus paternity suit—I brought one of the gallery's exhibit brochures with me. It has every plate in the Age of Reason series, including the one on Paul's wall. I read the blurb for that one, and it was listed on the Art Loss Register. It turned out to have been stolen about six months ago. It's worth a small fortune—I recognised it straight off. Then there was all the rearranging he'd done, between the first time I was there and the memorial."

"What's so weird about rearranging artwork?" Katia asked. "I do it all the time. I get bored, the lighting changes with the seasons, we decide the paint on the walls needs changing, we get new slipcovers, I move things around. That's not criminal."

Mac grinned at her, full wattage, and she turned the colour of one of the champagne-soaked raspberries. "Yeah, love, but I'm fairly sure you don't take down a bunch of obviously mass-produced posters and replace them with a genuine Manet, or a genuine Chagall, or a genuine Cassat. He did, all at once, and of course I noticed. It's been a long time since university, but I keep up with art."

"So he should have said no, that Goya's not genuine, ha-ha,

don't be ridiculous, I wish I could afford the real thing, of course it's a reproduction?" Kris was looking thoughtful. "Would you have believed him?"

"For a bit, yeah. There was no reason not to, and I wasn't taking a hard look at the piece. Not for long, though."

"Where he really screwed up was taking down trash and putting up the stuff from his warehouse, the stolen stuff he was brokering that was waiting to be picked up." Patrick sighed. "He told us, in his statement, that he thought the best place to hide a bunch of trees was in a forest, so he put it up in plain sight. It was his bad luck that Mr.—that Mac, here, knows his art. Paul had been storing everything in the warehouse, in his trailer—the Bambi. According to his statement, he cleaned that trailer out completely as soon as he got home, the night he killed Vinny, brought everything back down to Sausalito, and had the entire pile in his bedroom closet. But after Rosco got killed at the warehouse, he got nervous."

"Okay. Clear something up for us, yeah?" I was drinking cold water; good thing champagne had never appealed to me anyway. "You said there was no way Paul could have killed Rosario, that he was recording at the Plant with other people at the time. Right. If he didn't, who did?"

"Ah, yes. Rosco Galliano and what happened at the warehouse last Monday night. No, Morgenstern didn't kill him." We were all watching him. "That would be Vinny's erstwhile girlfriend. A nice lady by the name of Angie Morgenstern."

"What!" Katia shrieked. "No fucking way!"

"Wow." Sandra whistled. "Were Paul and Angie in collusion, or whatever it's called? I mean, did they plan this together? Because they ought to get Oscars for the acting job they've been doing. The entire Bay Area music scene was buzzing over their divorce. It was really messy, and really expensive, and oh, yeah, really, really loud."

"Working together? No, just the opposite." Patrick was putting on a show, pausing for maximum effect, making sure everyone was watching him, including my old lady. Bastard.

I slipped my right hand under the table and ran the tip of one finger down Bree's thigh. That got her attention away from Patrick and back to me, where it damned well belonged.

"Paul rolled on her, once he knew we had him on the grand larceny charges." Patrick kept talking, and Bree slipped her hand under the table, up between my thighs; she found what she was after, cupped with her fingers, and gave me a good hard squeeze. I made a small noise, turned it into about the most unconvincing throat-clearing imaginable, and glared at her.

"Go on," I told Patrick. "Why did he roll on her?"

"Because he's not an idiot. He's got no reason to like the lady—he seems to think that if she wasn't so rapacious, he wouldn't be in this mess in the first place. Plus, he's hoping to cut himself a deal, and he's going to need everything he can get his hands on if he wants one, because we've got him nailed for smacking Vinny Fabiano. I'm thinking his lawyers are going to use the Freelon evidence to prove that he spit on Vinny, that Vinny lost his temper and went for him, and that Paul grabbed the nearest thing and swung instinctively, in self-defence. That's what Morgenstern says happened, anyway. And you know, I think that's probably the truth. From what Ms. Godwin told me about her confrontation with Vinny Fabiano, it sounds like something he'd do."

"Right. It is, was, I mean." Bree'd let go of my nuts, and I was speaking normally again—or nearly normally. She still had her hand on my thigh, high up. If she wanted me to be aware that she could grab anytime she wanted, she was doing a brilliant job of it. She had an innocent little smile on her face. "Okay. If Paul and his former missus weren't working together on the whole art-brokering thing, then what in hell was she up to? And why was she up at the warehouse in the first place? And how did she get in? And why'd she cosh Rosario?"

"Maybe I should just tell it." Patrick sounded very dry, a bit too amused. He glanced over at the space between my right elbow and Bree's left elbow. I suddenly thought, *Oh hell, he knows damned well Bree and I are being naughty under the table. Well, sod him if he doesn't approve—it's our house, after all.*

I slid my hand up, got it under the elastic on her knickers, and let it just sit there. Next to me, she bit her lip, and I grinned.

"Right," I told Patrick. "You tell it."

"Sure. Vinny had given Rosco his key to the warehouse; Vinny had a legitimate reason to have a key, because he stored his guitars and equipment there. That's how he'd come to be rooting around at two in the morning, the night he overheard Morgenstern give his scary Japanese money guy a Jasper Johns sketch that had been stolen from a private collection in Amsterdam, in exchange for a suitcase with eighty thousand dollars in it."

"Jasper Johns?" Mac whistled, long and low. "I remember that robbery—it was all over the news."

"I'm not surprised. The money guy, by the way, is known to Interpol and his customers as Mr. Hiroshi; his full name is Hiroshi Takemitsu, and he's at the top of the list of people Interpol wants to talk to about underground traffic in stolen art. I tipped off an old friend of mine in Marseilles—art theft isn't his thing, but he had the right personnel on it before we hung up. We got our hands on Takemitsu in Tokyo, and his passport shows a dozen visits to the Bay Area in the last fourteen months." Patrick sounded grim, but also very pleased. "He's also wanted in connection with the death of a museum guard in Lisbon. Then there's the matter of the money trail, some of the funds from the stolen paintings being used to finance some key terrorist organisations. He's got some serious explaining to do."

"So, Vinny blackmailed Paul?" Billy sounded sad. "Dude.

That's so damned dumb. I mean, if someone's doing shit like handing scary strangers paintings and taking lots of money from them, blackmail sounds like the worst idea since invading Iraq."

"Morgenstern doesn't think Vinny was trying to blackmail him, or at least he thinks Vinny wasn't thinking of it as blackmail. Morgenstern seems to have had a rep for being willing to give musicians a break, for a very long time. He'd always been nice to Vinny, and that was genuine—no ulterior motive. He'd let him play the 707, fronted him equipment, hooked him up with the Bombardiers—Morgenstern has done that for a lot of people, with apparently no ulterior motive. Vinny, in Morgenstern's view, was self-deluded enough to think that saying, 'Hey, I want that fifty thousand dollar guitar,' and having Morgenstern buy it for him was just a continuation. The guy sounds like the poster child for self-entitlement."

"The Zemaitis!" I sat up straight suddenly; Bree gave me a pinch and let her fingers spider-walk up the inside of my thigh, stopping just short of the various bits and pieces she was aiming for. I got my own hand free of her knickers and slapped her hand lightly. "What's the word on the pearl-top?"

"Don't worry, JP, it's safe." Patrick smiled at me. "We have it. We found it at Angie Morgenstern's place—she was the one who'd tried selling it to the Japanese collector. Problem is, she asked him for seventy-five grand, and it turns out that particular collector was the same guy who'd sold it to her ex-husband for sixty grand in the first place, not even a month earlier. Not unnaturally, he was annoyed, and he alerted the Zemaitis people on the Net. Thor the Destroyer let me know—but you know about that part."

"Thor the *Destroyer?*" Domitra spoke up for the first time. "Who the hell is that?"

"Turns out to be a guy in his midtwenties, who owns a couple of Zemaitis guitars—they belonged to his father."

"Oh." She shrugged. "Can we take a breather? I want dessert and some hot chocolate. I saw a cake plate in the kitchen. Bree, you want me to bring it out? Looks like your hands are busy doing other things, at least one hand is."

Bree turned pale and got her left hand out on the table with the other one, a bit too quickly. I caught Mac's eye. He was grinning as well.

Over dessert, Patrick picked up where he'd left off. "Basically, Angie Morgenstern had been really stung by the divorce. They'd been calling each other a lot of ugly names, it was all over the county, and she decided that a good way to get back at her ex would be to have an affair with his protégé. She sat up and paid attention when Vinny, who had no money of his own, suddenly started showing her his new toys: the Zemaitis, the blue waterfall PRS, a few other things. When he let it drop that Paul was going to pay twelve grand for a guitar from Bruno Baines, she dug in hard and he spilled it, at least what he knew, which wasn't much—just that Paul had some kind of side thing, maybe drugs, that he was running out of the warehouse. Vinny didn't know it was art; he just knew it was lucrative, and probably illegal. Keep in mind, Vinny hadn't told anyone about it, except Rosco. And he followed up that piece of stupidity by dumping her immediately after. So you can imagine how pissed off she was."

I helped myself to a slice of the chocolate cherry torte Bree had baked. The story was nasty, it was unpleasant, but the hell of it was, it wasn't unfamiliar—for me, it was basically a "been there, done that" moment. Christ, at least one reason I'd used to justify staying married to Cilla all those years was not wanting to deal with all the legal and financial fallout a divorce would have caused. . . .

"So, the morning Vinny died, Angie called her ex to tell him that she'd been shacking up with his friend Vinny, that Vinny had told her about the warehouse dealing, and that she wanted a piece of the take, and she wanted it now. That nailed both guys. She could squeeze Paul on one hand, and make sure he didn't have anything to spare for Vinny on the other."

"Yep." Katia sounded almost sad. "That sounds like Angie, all right. One of the original hard-edged Gimme Girls."

"Just how lucrative was this brokering, anyway?" Bree wanted to know. "I mean, people who broker legitimate stuff, real estate and stocks and whatnot, they don't make humongous amounts. They just get a commission. How does it work with stolen stuff?"

Patrick nodded approvingly at her, and I thought about smacking him. "It was pretty much the same story. He'd do a few of these deals every couple of months, most of them smaller-scale stuff; he might see three thousand on a painting worth a hundred thousand. The point for him was, staying small-scale meant he could fly under the radar and keep it going. He was getting a nice chunk of change off the eleven stolen paintings he had on his walls, because that was a single theft, one big job out of Madrid. He knew the payoff was coming, which is why he felt he could afford the Zemaitis and the PRS out of the funds he already had. But it wasn't nearly enough to satisfy Angie and keep Vinny quiet. So he came up with the idea of repossessing Peter to pay Paul, basically."

"'Repossessing Peter'—that's brilliant." I was sorting it out in my head. "What did he do, tell Angie she could have the Zemaitis and the PRS waterfall to sell? That's what I remember it sounding like, from what we heard at Freelon."

"Yep—he figured it would even up, financially, and get his ex off his case. But that night he killed Vinny, and he told her to lay low for a few days, we'd be watching the warehouse and that's where the Zemaitis was. Once we'd closed up and moved on, she could have it. She agreed to it, right up until she got a phone call from Rosco Galliano, two Sundays ago."

"Rosie called Angie—what the fuck?" Tony was blinking. "Why would he call her?"

"He called her because he'd done some thinking. He'd decided that only two people in the world could have conked his cousin on the head. And in his worldview, the scorned woman was a likelier culprit than Paul, especially since Paul had always been nice to Vinny."

"Sexist," Sandra remarked drily. "Typical."

Patrick ignored that. "He ran into a problem on that one; Angie has an alibi, no holes at all, for Vinny's death, and she proved it to Rosie. Which left Rosie out for revenge on Paul, and he had a bright idea: He had Vinny's key, the Bambi was—according to Vinny—full of valuable stuff, probably a lot more valuable than the guitars. She arranged to meet him at the warehouse just after Tony called him."

"So the idea was that she'd leave the guitars and take the art?" Bree was following this mess with ease. I was quite proud of her; myself, I was just short of being completely lost. "And that we'd take the guitars? Leaving Paul with nothing at all? Damn, that's mean. Really torturous. It sounds like something out of the Borgias or the de Medicis."

"That's right. She got there, he let them both in, he pointed her towards the Bambi. She came out seething and snarling and calling him names, because of course, Morgenstern had emptied the trailer by then and hung the contents all over his living room." Patrick paused. "The tendency to swing at women who called them names must have run in the family, because he socked her. It must have been a serious left hook, because she's still got a major bruise on her jaw. She's very strong, very fit: yoga, Pilates, kickboxing, all the usual stuff. Well—she swung back. Unfortunately, she swung with her right hand, which happened to be holding a Halliburton attaché case. Do you guys know what I'm talking about? It's a bulletproof Kevlar thing."

"Damn!" Katia blinked. "Is that what that thing is? I remember the first time I saw it, she let me hold it—it hardly weighs anything. She killed him with that? How could she get enough force to do that, with something so lightweight?"

"Yes, she did. She always carries it, apparently. Says she doesn't like purses. As to the weight of the thing, she got lucky—or unlucky, depending on your point of view. She put the full force of her arm behind it, and the corner of it caught him in just the right spot—he was off guard and off balance. It snapped his head around too far, just far enough to snap three vertebrae in his neck. Super-whiplash, and game over. She had enough presence of mind to find the Zemaitis and take it with her. But like everyone else involved in that little ménage, she got greedy, trying to sell it for too much. Once we pulled her in, we got a few details, until her lawyer shut her up."

We were all quiet for a minute. Two people were dead, and two more, at least two more, were probably going to prison for a good long time. I reached out and took Bree's hand, suddenly wanting a moment of basic human touch.

"I think that pretty much covers the basics." Patrick stood up. "That was a great dinner. I need to head out, and get home—not much sleep the last few days, and tomorrow's going to be just as busy. Thanks for having me over."

CHAPTER FIFTEEN

We finished up the rehearsals a few days later, and the band headed off to the Plant in Sausalito for a couple of weeks of mastering and mixing the new Bombardiers CD.

I didn't really have much to do with that. If they needed me, I was available for overdubs, for input, for additional guitar parts as needed, but the sessions had been so close to perfect that I felt they'd have what they wanted without a lot of extras.

I was quite pleased about that, actually. It had been a genuinely bizarre month, and the house had seemed full of people for too long a time. I mean, I love Mac, you know? He's a very good bloke, and he'd turned out to be a very considerate guest. So had Dom.

But it couldn't have been easy for Bree. She'd been trying to plan a wedding on her own—our wedding, no less—and I'd been no use at all. It wasn't me being a lazy sod, not this time;

I'd offered, and she'd told me not to worry. It was just now coming clear to me that she'd always say that, tell me not to worry, to save me any additional grief. At least this time I'd copped to it early on. Not to mention she'd been damned near as fragile physically as I usually am, and I'd been the one who'd been constantly nagging at her to rest. So, yeah, I was feeling guilty.

I waited until the house was empty, Mac and Dom off in Sausalito with the Bombardiers, playing with the mixdown. I picked a nice sunny afternoon when I had her all to myself, and asked her how the wedding planning was going, and could I help?

I don't know what I was expecting: maybe the usual smile, the vague reassurance, the usual rubbish. But not this time. Things were certainly changing.

"Oh, *God*." Her lip started to quiver; her eyes filled up. "Oh, God, oh damn."

"Bree?" What the hell? "Baby, what is it? What's wrong?"

"I'm so tired of this. I'm just—John, I'm sorry. I can't do it. I've called everywhere. I've had phone interviews with nine separate venues. Nine! In the City, in Marin, in Berkeley, on the Peninsula. And the only thing they all want to do is drive me crazy."

"Bree, wait a minute, hang on—"

"They're all sweet and cute and cloying and hearts and flowers." She sounded damned near panic-stricken. "They keep asking me these insane questions: Do I have the exact date? Do I want a live band? How many bridesmaids? What kind of flowers do I want?"

She swallowed, and got control of herself—her voice went really nasty, sort of fake sugar and spice, mimicking them. " 'Do you want a cake, dear? Of course you do, *all* brides want a nice cake. How many tiers? You mean you haven't thought about tiers? Now, about the cake toppers, have you thought much about what you want as cake toppers? Do you want pink table-cloths? Have you decided whether you want the invitations completely engraved, return envelopes or just the exterior envelopes? Or would you prefer them embossed? Oh, not just the reception, the ceremony as well, how sweet, are you Catholic, or Jewish? What about the officiant? Will you be having a priest, or a rabbi?' "

Oh, bloody hell. I knew fuck-all about planning events; I'd never planned one in my life. When Cilla and I had got married, we'd gone round the Clapham council registry office with my mum, who was still alive back then, and some friend of hers. We'd signed things, swapped rings, said vows, and that had been the end of it, bob's your uncle, you know? I opened my mouth, realised that telling Bree about that particular piece of history was probably not on at the moment, and closed my mouth again.

"I hate this. I just loathe it." Her eyes filled up again, and her voice shook. "I feel like a hamster on a wheel in the middle of somebody's dirty joke. A priest and a rabbi walk into a wedding planner's. Why do I have to do this? Why is this all so *fussy*? I don't care about a stupid cake or how many pink table-cloths they can rent me—I just want to get married. And don't you dare even think about telling me I'm a caterer and I ought to be able to ace this. I can't and I don't want to. I'm screwing it up, and this is my *own damned wedding*!"

She started to cry, serious tears this time. How the hell had I not noticed how stressed out she'd got, coping with this?

"Bree, stop. Okay? It's okay. You don't have to do a damned thing. Just—stop." I pushed her into my rocking chair. "Here, sit. Gordon bleedin' *Bennett*, I had no idea about any of this. Look, love, I'm with you, yeah? I just want to get married as well. Sod this rubbish—the only reason I give a damn about the actual wedding is because I thought you did. If you don't, that's brilliant, end of problem, you know? Fuck the wedding. Let's just go get married, okay? We can have a nice catered party after, if you want."

"You mean, elope?" She'd stopped crying, and she had the big wet green headlamps straight at me. "Okay. Where?"

I'm not sure why I said it, or where the idea came from. But all of a sudden, out of nowhere, there it was.

"Right. Listen, Bree. I've got an idea. . . ."

I spelled it out for her. It was really amazing—the whole thing, the organisation, everything, just came out as if I'd been thinking about it from the moment I picked out the stone for her ring. Who knows, maybe I had been.

She listened, and her eyes opened all the way, and then they crinkled up, the network of laugh lines around the corners bunching because she was grinning like a maniac.

"Oh, yeah. Oh, hell yeah. Oh, wow." She got up and kissed me, a real kiss, tongue tip to tongue tip. I counted back in my head. We had eight days of post-surgical celibacy left, and her appointment was on the next-to-last day. "When?"

I snaked a hand round the back and rubbed her bottom. Might as well get a bit of my own back, you know? "What's today, Friday? Two weeks from tomorrow? Your post-op visit's on that Friday. If everything looks okay . . ." I stopped. "No. Sod that. Not if, when. After that, we can build up a head of steam for a couple of days, head out, have our nice wedding, and then I can pin you to the bed and cripple you. Sound good?"

"Yes, please. But I think three weeks is actually a better idea—I doubt two floors of a hotel are going to be open at this short a notice, even with Carla handling it." She pulled her head back a bit. "And you're really going to make sure all the work gets handled? You're really okay with that?"

"Absolutely. All I want from you is to do what Carla tells you, okay? Let her deal with it."

It turned out that all Carla needed from Bree was a list of e-mail addresses. She listened to my idea, and got into it so fast, I began to realise I'd actually done something brilliant.

"No problem, JP. Mac and Domitra are already there, and I've got almost everyone's e-mail address. Two floors of the hotel, suite, flowers, chapel, limos. I'll let everyone know—and I'll RSVP right now. I wouldn't miss it. Hell, last time I saw Dom, I told her she needed to get down to L.A. so I could take her shopping on Melrose. Fluevog has a store there, and I bet she'd like those. Just have Bree e-mail me with that list, okay?"

It was as simple as that. I put her on the phone with Bree and went off to put new strings on my Martin. Our wedding plans were officially in the most competent hands I knew. If Carla couldn't pull it off, no one could.

And of course, she could, and did. We told Mac and Dom when they got back from Sausalito that night, and Miranda and the Bombardiers by phone; everyone else got the official e-mail two days later.

If you're reading this, it's because you're invited to watch John P. Kinkaid and Bree Godwin finally make it official. The groom says to tell you all he's very sorry for the short notice, but he only just came up with the idea, and he and the bride both hope you can make it.

The reception will be held at the Bellagio Hotel, Center Strip, Las Vegas, Nevada, with the ceremony at the Love Me Tender Chapel, North Las Vegas Boulevard, on Saturday, 29 October 2005, at 6:00 pm. Officiating will be the Right Honourable Elvis Presley. Accommodations will be provided, as will great food and music, of course. Bring a guitar or whatever you usually play. RSVP to

And, well, there we were. In three weeks, we were off to Vegas to get married.

I couldn't remember the last time I'd felt this good.

"Ladies and gentlemen, boys and girls . . ."

It was a gorgeous night in Las Vegas. Usually, I can't deal with the place—it's so hot and dry, it always reminds me I'm a Brit, that I come from a chilly damp climate. Still, it wasn't as if I'd actually been out of doors for longer than a few minutes. I'd left my suite at the Bellagio, been ushered into a limo containing me, Tony, Luke Hedley, Kris and Mac, and driven off to an interesting chapel on the North Strip.

I hadn't seen Bree since early afternoon; apparently, there's something about the groom not getting a look at the bride's gown ahead of the ceremony, some sort of superstition, and she'd been secretive about what she was planning to wear. So she'd been down in her mum's room all day, getting done up. She was coming in a separate limo, along with her own friends, as well as Dom. Mac had shooed Dom off to keep the bridal party company, because Solange Hedley was with them. As Mac pointed out, a girl as young and tasty as his goddaughter on the loose in Sin City needed a bodyguard a lot more than he did.

"My name is Elvis Presley. Some of y'all might know me as Elvis the Pelvis, and it fills my love-me-tender heart with joy to be able to help a fellow rocker escape the confines of Lonely Street, down at the Heartbreak Hotel. . . ."

The place was packed. I hadn't checked with Carla, but if there were no-shows, I couldn't put a name to them. We'd booked two solid floors of the Bellagio, plus the high rollers

242

suite for the party. Every room had a guest or two in it, and we'd ended up apparently needing a few overflow rooms as well. The Bellagio is a brilliant hotel, luckily, with world-class concierges, and they never get it wrong. If the demands Carla made put them out, we never knew it. Everything was perfectly done, and the gears were silent and invisible.

I've got to admit, I was beginning to understand the whole idea behind separating the bride and groom before the wedding. Knowing that Bree was sleeping in her own suite down the hall, that I couldn't just get up and go knock on the door and be let in, added a definite *Just you wait, lady!* edge to the whole thing.

"*. . . ladies and gentlemen, the bride. . . .*"

The houselights were already down, and suddenly there was a simple spot, and here came Bree.

Since she'd been so mysterious about her wedding dress, I hadn't devoted much thought to what she was planning on wearing. I've got a tux, very dark grey, made on me by an Italian designer; I was wearing that, black silk shirt, and dark grey tie. Really, it was just a slightly more tarted-up edition of my stage gear.

Maybe I could have guessed what Bree's choice was going to be, had I thought about it. But when the light hit her, my heart did a stutter-step. I knew the dress, blue velvet, vintage, buttons down the back. The last time I'd seen it, she'd been just shy of her eighteenth birthday, at the Miyako Hotel. There was something making a lot of noise under my rib cage.

Right about then, I stopped being aware of what was going on, basically. Back when I'd seen that dress for the first time, the same thing had happened: I'd looked up, backstage at Candlestick Park during Blacklight's 1980 tour, and seen her standing there, responding to the invitation to her I'd broadcast over a local radio station during an interview, and everyone and everything else had just sort of melted into a blurry backdrop. She was the only thing I'd been able to see that night.

So while I'd like to be able to tell you about the wedding, I honestly don't remember much about it. I don't remember much of anything other than Bree. I watched her come up, Miranda at her elbow, peeling off and leaving Bree to step up on her own.

I do remember that the place was completely quiet, which when you think about it is ridiculous. We're a bunch of rock and roll musicians, and the officiant was an Elvis Presley imperson-ator who also happened to be an ordained minister, so the place should have been roaring with noise, but it wasn't. We stood there, side by side, and we listened to Elvis, who was actually a charming and very dedicated bloke called Ron, reading off a prepared list of stuff.

Bree was watching me, and I was watching her. We must have nodded when we were told to nod, or responded when he asked for something, but honestly, if you asked me, I'd have to say I remember fuck-all about it, at least until we got to the end and he said something that jerked both our heads around.

". . . this is a little unusual." He was still using his Elvis voice. "Before the ceremony, I got identical separate requests for this from both the bride and the groom. I guess that just goes to show how well-matched they really are. . . ."

Oh, bloody hell. Perfect. I felt a grin coming on. Not sure if you're supposed to be grinning at your own wedding, but I was, and so was she. And we listened to Elvis up there, and he read out one line, added to the vows.

"Do you promise to always leave the light on? To always keep it burning?"

If I'd thought the place was quiet before, I'd been mistaken. I couldn't even hear anyone breathing, but that's probably just me, where my head was. I looked up at Elvis, and he was looking at me, and I opened my mouth. I think I was planning to just say yes, you know? But that's not what came out.

"Always," I told him, her, whoever might be listening, and then I got this feeling that I ought to say it again, louder, so I did. And he looked at Bree, and asked the same question, and she said something so damned perfect. . . .

"Keeper of the flame," she told him, very calm, very clear. "It never goes out." I started hearing a bit of noise from our guests, finally, some sniffling out there in the dark.

It went nice and quick after that. Miranda was our ring-bearer, I think that's what it's called, and the rings fit perfectly, those simple gold bands Bree had held out to me when she proposed, backstage at Oakland. When he asked for the vows, do you take this woman, I damned near yelled it: *"Oh* hell *yeah!"* And Bree was laughing, I think, but she got her *"I thought you'd never ask"* out.

And then he pronounced, or whatever it is they do, and a huge rowdy cheer went up and so did the houselights, and there we were, twenty-five years and three murders, one suicide, sickness and health and addiction and withdrawal, all this time later, so much behind, and maybe even more to come.

If I remember the wedding itself as really just a series of vignettes starring me and Bree, the reception afterward, in an incredibly posh top-floor suite at the Bellagio, was a different story entirely.

We'd stuck around the wedding chapel for the obligatory newlyweds' dance. Since I don't dance, it was actually me standing in place and holding on to Bree and both of us swaying in the sort of stylised fake-sex thing people who don't dance always seem to end up doing. The song playing on the overheads was "Love Me Tender"; I saw Ron, our officiant, in conversation in one corner with Mac. I found out later they'd been discussing the vocal breathing tricks and techniques each of them used when doing an Elvis cover.

We didn't talk, me and Bree; we just swayed in place. She had her left hand round my neck, and even as used to it being there as I was, I found myself thinking, *Right, there are rings on it now, that she won't take off, not now, not ever.* I'd stopped wearing my own wedding ring, the one Cilla'd had the mate to, the day I found Cilla's works and dope stash in our London house in Camden Town, back in 1979. Now I had another one, and this one was staying right where it was, no matter what. I know there are blokes out there who find the idea claustrophobic, but I'm not one of them.

After a while, we headed out to our limo and back to the hotel. We were among the last people leaving the chapel—most of our guests had already gone, even Miranda. A nice quick, quiet ride back to the Bellagio. Riding the lift to the party suite, with its killer views of the city and desert.

The first thing we saw when we walked in was Mac and three of our other guests, world-class singers and members of some of the biggest bands in the world, all of them, standing and waiting in the middle of the suite.

We stopped where we were, just inside. Everyone went quiet.

"Right," Mac said. "On three. One—two—"

Four singers, four good long deep breaths, and they started singing, a capella, perfect harmonies:

"I knew the bride when she used to rock 'n' roll. . . ."

Bree was grinning like an idiot. I ran the rest of the lyrics over in my mind, nice and fast, but before I could get them completely sorted out, I realised the lads had just gone for specific lyrics, leaving out the ones that might not work. Good job, too. I wouldn't have wanted to upset Miranda.

"Well, I can see her now with her Walkman on / Jumping up and

down to her favourite song / I still remember when she used to want to make a lot of noise / Hopping and a-bopping with the street corner boys. . . ."

I caught Mac's eye. He grinned at me and raised his voice.

"Take a look at the bridegroom, smilin' pleased as pie / Shakin' hands all around with a glassy look in his eye / He got a real good job and his shirt and tie is nice / But I remember a time when she never would have looked at him twice. . . ."

"That's what he thinks," Bree said under her breath.

"I can see her now, drinkin' with the boys / Breaking their hearts like they were toys / She used to do the pony, she used to do the stroll / Oh, I knew the bride when she used to rock 'n' roll / I knew the bride when she used to ROCK 'N' ROLL!"

They stopped. Mac, who'd been holding a glass of something bubbly while he sang, raised it on high.

"Cheers, Johnny, you jammy sod. Here's to you both!"

After that opening, of course, the tone of the rest of the party was pretty much set. There was champagne in ice buckets, and bottled water for those of us who don't drink alcohol at all, and of course, the Bellagio had provided a fantastic spread of food, crab legs the size of drumsticks. Even Bree was satisfied with it. They'd also provided a few pretty girls in fishnet tights to circulate with trays and champagne. I suspected the bed in Mac's suite would be getting a workout later on.

People ate, laughed, toasted us and each other. I circulated, and so did Bree; between us, I think we managed to talk to every single guest. We'd propped the suite's doors open, and Carla and Dom went out in the corridor to have a nice gloat over their shoes; apparently, Dom had gone shopping with Carla in Los Angeles and got herself a pair of something called Fluevogs. Bree, of course, was in a brand-new pair of heels. There's actually a couple of Jimmy Choo shops in Vegas, next door at Caesars, and over at the Venetian. She'd been extremely pleased about that. A few guests—Patrick Ormand, Bruno Baines, some other people—joined them out in the hall.

Quite a few of our guests, being musicians of various flavours, had done what Carla's e-mail suggested. They'd brought their instruments with them, and one corner of the suite had been set up with stands and amplifiers. Good job the high rollers' usual hangout was so damned big. The Bellagio, at my request, had supplied a small upright piano for the suite so that Tony could play. A nice little impromptu jam session had started up, and Kris waved me over.

I shook my head at him. "Sorry, mate, I'm in the audience tonight. I haven't got an axe with me."

"Well, actually . . ." It was Bree. "You do."

She had the strangest look on her face: amused, guilty, other stuff. While I was staring at her, Mac came over, and they exchanged looks, a nice clear signal. What the hell?

"Right," he said, and tapped his champagne glass with someone's tuning fork. "No time like the present. Oi! Ladies and gents! Lend us your eyes and ears for a minute, if you please. Time for the presentation of gifts to the groom."

Oh, bloody hell. My stomach took a dive. The what? No one had mentioned anything about presents. Mac had said gifts, as in, more than one. If any of these were from Bree, I was hosed. I hadn't got her a damned thing.

Bree must have caught sight of the panic on my face. I probably looked like a stuffed fish or something, glassy-eyed, because she leaned over and whispered, "Nothing to worry about, honestly, it's okay."

Yeah, right. Nothing to worry about. Just two hundred guests and I was being given presents, and hadn't bought anyone anything, including my brand-new wife. Shit, shit, *shit*. Why in hell hadn't anyone told me I was supposed to buy gifts?

Mac had headed off to the bedroom no one was using. When he came back out, he was holding a guitar case. Oh fuck, oh hell, oh damn.

"Bree says we should do the band's prezzie first." Mac was pitching his voice to carry, and he was aiming it straight at me, because I seemed to be rooted in place. "Johnny! Get your arse over here, mate."

Like I said, I wasn't moving. So he put the case down in front of me, faceup, ready to open. It was a custom case, a bit old, a bit battered. I saw the Zemaitis signature logo, and my throat went dry.

"Come on, JP, get on with it! It won't bite—open the bleedin' thing, so we can cut the cake and make some music!" It was Stu Corrigan, Blacklight's drummer, obviously in on the whole thing. There were hoots, cheers, catcalls.

My hands were damp. But I knelt and got the latches undone, one after the other, and finally got the lid up.

The guitar, christened Big Mama Pearl by the brilliant luthier who'd built it, sat there in its case, blinking up at me. It was gaudy, shiny, staggering. It was fucking absurd.

I looked up at Mac—I didn't need to ask the question, which was a damned good thing, because I didn't have any breath to ask questions with. But he answered it anyway. He had a gleam in his eye.

"Virtue, own reward, all that. And a lesson to Solange, over there, to stay in school. See, it turns out five separate insurance companies had rewards posted for information leading to the recovery of the stolen works. It's a cumulative fee: flat ten percent of the appraised value, and they recovered nineteen pieces. So this little lot, what the Zemaitis cost, won't even make a dent. I bought Luke the PRS blue waterfall for his birthday—that's next month. I'm splitting the rest of the dosh between a few of my favourite charities, and there's going to be a nice 'going off to university' prezzie for my goddaughter as well, assuming she ever chooses one."

I ought to have thanked him, you know? Problem is, I had no words. Between the reality of the guitar and the quick sum I'd just done in my head, I'd been left speechless. That reward for information he was talking about—that was probably close to a million dollars on its own. No wonder he looked so pleased.

"Be warned, that damned thing weighs a metric fuckload." Mac still looked pleased with himself. "I nearly put my own back out, carrying it around. I figured it might live down in your basement studio, to play with, trot it out on tour when you've got extra roadies to help."

I was still speechless. Mac craned his head and caught sight of Patrick, watching and looking amused by the piano.

"Patrick, over there, deserves a toast, as well. He got both axes released in time for me to get them here. So, cheers, mate, and here's to you! Lucky for us, Paul had all the paperwork. Turns out Vinny was slightly confused about whose instruments they actually were—he didn't legally own either of them, not on paper. Paul did. And I think the poor sod'll be able to use the money from the two guitar sales towards his legal fees." He grinned suddenly. "Not to mention the Picasso horse I just bought off him. Lovely thing."

"Bloody hell." I finally got my voice back, closed the top, and latched it. I got to my feet, shaking the needles out of my legs, and realised Bree had slipped away. "Where—?"

"Right here." She'd gone into the bedroom while I was mooning over the Zemaitis and gawking at Mac. She had a guitar case in her left hand.

Okay, right. This was clearly an acid trip flashback thing, or would be, if I'd ever messed about with acid. Thing is, I hadn't, so I was obviously seeing what I thought I was. *Another* guitar? What in hell was going on?

Bree stretched out her neck and kissed me. Mac had already slid the Zemaitis case out of the way, making room for the plain case Bree was holding. "Bruno? Where's Bruno? He needs to be here for this."

At that point, the penny dropped, with a big hideous clanging noise. Another guitar. Right.

"Here, I'm here, right here!" He'd been out in the hall, and came hurrying back in. "Is it time? God, I'm nervous."

"From the bride, to the groom. Go on, John, open it." She sounded indecently pleased with herself, watching me pop the latches. "With a little help from our friends. And now you can't claim you don't have any guitars with you, right?"

First look, I swear I thought she'd somehow talked Magnus Mattson out of the red maple Zemaitis. Same electronics package, same red maple top—but then I took a look at the peghead, and saw the double-*B* logo, inlaid in fine gold wire. If the pearltop was gaudy and gorgeous, this one was elegant, sleek, just bloody stunning. It had a soft dull gleam to the wood, to the brass, to the neck.

"Try it out." Bree still wasn't looking nervous. "Really. Anyway, you need to look at the back. And then I need to thank Bruno for getting it done at warp speed. And also Patrick, for not being dumb enough to keep Bruno in jail and prevent him from working on your wedding present." She looked around and spotted Patrick. "Because if that had happened? You'd be investigating your own murder, Lieutenant. Anyway, here's to our friends, for being our friends. John? Check it out, please. Do you like it?"

I reached in, expecting it to weigh a ton. After all, maple top, masses of electronics—the Zemaitis I'd fallen in lust with had been at least ten pounds.

So I got a lovely shock when I picked it up. Bruno had done me up a virtual clone for the Zemaitis, with one exception: The bloody thing was light as a feather. If it weighed six pounds, I'd be surprised. He'd either completely chambered the interior, routed out most of the wood inside, or else it was basically hollow, just a top, back and sides over one small block of wood. If it played as good as it felt, this was about to become my number-one road guitar.

Big Mama Pearl was likely to be a studio guitar, primarily, just as Mac had suggested; she was far too heavy to drag out on the road, and far too valuable. You don't take a seventy-thousand-dollar axe out on the road with you—that was how Ron Wood had lost his Zemaitis, if I remembered the story properly. Hell, I was planning on talking to Gibson about having copies made of my two Pauls. But this . . .

"Gordon *Bennett*!" I turned it over. There was a brass plate on the back, etched out with my name: *JP KINKAID.* Under that, inlaid lightly in dull brass wire, two words: *LITTLE QUEENIE.*

"Little Queenie. Go, go, go!" I lifted it in one hand, towards Bruno. "Someone plug me in, yeah?"

The damned thing was beautiful. It was light, it sounded incredible, the neck was exactly right for the body. It sang under my fingers. There was nothing about this guitar that didn't work for me.

"When did you get this bright idea?" I asked Bree. Next to me, Luke was plugging in the PRS; he was actually crooning to it under his breath. "So that's why Bruno couldn't make it to dinner that night—he had a commission, did he? And yeah, by the way, I'm completely in love. The pearl-top is incredible, but Mac's right, I wouldn't take it out on tour: too heavy, and too much a target for thieves. This one, though—crikey, it's stone perfect. Bruno! Brilliant job. Cheers, mate."

Unlike Bree, Bruno was a blushing type; he turned bright

252

pink. I wondered what colour he'd turn when the orders came in from some of the superstar blokes now wandering in and out of the suite. Most of them would be checking out both my new axes during the course of the party. Bruno was going to be working late hours for months to come.

"I got the idea back in Angelino's parking lot, the night I kicked Vinny." Bree reached out a hand and touched the guitar. "When we were waiting for the valet to bring the car around. I originally asked for a chambered Paul, but then there was the murder, and you'd seen the Zemaitis, so I sat down with Bruno, and we called Luke in England, and talked to Magnus Matts-son, and then to some of the collectors on the Zemaitis boards. And we confabbed, and came up with the design. And, well, there you go. Happy wedding, John. Little Queenie—she just seemed to name herself. Isn't she a pretty thing? Light her up, okay? I want to dance."

Bree was swaying in place. I played a few runs with the switches straight up, listening to the guitar. She had a brilliant voice, singing clean and clear on the high end, solid midrange, a bottom end with as much punch as either of my Pauls. I began getting into the electronics package, the five dual-ganged knobs, the six toggle switches.

Behind me, people were picking up their own axes. Tony vamped evil Delta blues run on the upright piano, and I dirtied up the sound on Little Queenie, matching it. I recognised the song; Mac, who'd been singing it a lot recently, gave an exuber-ant little hoot and grabbed his wireless mic. He was eyeing one of the waitresses, and damned if she wasn't eyeing him right back.

"Mama, pretty mama, honey lock your lips on me, slide 'em down lower, I'll be yellin' like a banshee. . . ."

People were dancing, eating, partying. I flipped a toggle and there was that growl, that bite, that Bree had called groiny.

Brilliant word, yeah? Stone fucking perfect, especially tonight, all things considered. She knew, and I knew, that the music wasn't the only thing getting groiny tonight.

"Lock 'em on me low, there's a fire down below, lock me down, honey, take it deep, take it slow. . . ."

Bree's hair was flying, and so was the hem of the blue velvet dress. Her legs, from her high heels to mid-thigh, showed with every hard move, every twist of her hips, every jerk of her shoulders.

"Just a little nibble, honey, just a little touch, don't bother sayin' that I want it too much. . . ."

Bree looked really hot, all curves and high heels and long legs moving to the music. I was glad she was digging the dance; she didn't know it yet, but one dance was all she was getting tonight, at least up here.

"Lock it up, lock it down, you got me in a liplock!"

I flipped the amp to standby mode, set the guitar down, and grabbed my wife around the waist.

"G'night, all. We're off." Catcalls, whistles. "Bedtime. Groom's privilege. Keep it going, and have a lovely party."

Downstairs, to our suite. I was dragging her, basically, one hand clamped round her arm, and she was laughing. She'd kicked off her pricey shoes and was keeping up with me nicely. Between the posh hotel, the blue velvet dress with the buttons down the back, and my own lack of anything resembling sex for the last five weeks, the entire thing was a definite déjà vu moment, back to that glorious first time together, when she'd been not quite eighteen and I hadn't known. . . .

In through the suite doors. I remembered to put the DO NOT DISTURB notice up on the door. I also put the privacy latch on. It's amazing that I was so together, you know? Considering how little blood was available to my brain at the moment?

I turned. She was standing there, her hands together, looking nice and pale, not quite meeting my eyes. I thought I caught a bit of a smile, but it was all very *Mona Lisa*, so I wasn't sure.

"Now, then." I got my hands on her shoulders and turned her to face away from me. There were those damned buttons, just as I'd remembered. That first time, at the Miyako, she'd been so nervous she'd let me undo every last button before she'd remembered the zipper down the left side. "I think I said something about crippling you, yeah? Let's get this off. Lift your arm, lady, will you?"

"Okay."

Her voice had gone trembly, but she lifted her left arm. She had her head down, and her shoulders were shaking. A moment later, I realised why. She was trying not to laugh.

"What in hell?" There was nothing there but a smooth seam. "Where's the damned zipper? This dress had a zipper!"

She turned her head, looking at me over her shoulder; her face was bright with laughter, but her eyes were clear shining green, her sexual *on* signal. "Oh, honey, I'm a few pounds heavier than I was the first time I let you ravish me. The original is in my closet, at home—it didn't fit nearly as well as it did when I was seventeen. So I had an exact copy of the dress made—well, okay, not quite exact."

I was already busy with the buttons, and they were taking forever. When I got the damned thing undone and off her, my wife wasn't going to be able to walk properly, or sit or anything else, not if I had anything to say about it.

A dozen buttons, fifteen, eighteen. She didn't seem to be wearing anything underneath. . . .

"Come on, John, show me you mean it." Big deep green eyes. She was holding her hair out of the way of my fingers. "If you can get me out of this thing, you're welcome to do anything you want to the contents."

CHAPTER SIXTEEN

"Good evening, ladies and gentlemen, and welcome to the 707 Club!"

The dressing room was a bit too warm, but it was almost showtime. I had Little Queenie in my lap and was busy giving her a final tune-up. Mac was drinking room-temperature spring water to clear his throat; the Bombardiers, except for Kris, had done their sound check early on. Doug and Mike were doing their last-minute tweaks out on stage—I hoped they'd remembered my stool. Damon was hanging out at the soundboard, keeping the house sound tech company. Bree, with Sandra and Katia, had gone out to commandeer a table near the stage. Dom, as usual, was outside the backstage door, keeping her eyes open, looking for trouble.

"Nice and loud out there." Mac shot an approving look in

the general direction of the audience, took another mouthful of water, gargled, and swallowed. "Full house, I'm betting."

"I wouldn't take the bet, mate." According to Carla, who'd handled the arrangements for this benefit show, all thirteen hundred tickets had gone within two hours of going up on sale. At fifty dollars a head, we were going to raise a decent pile of money to ensure the 707 stayed open for business while the American legal system tried to figure out just how long Paul Morgenstern was likely to be sitting in jail. According to the permit on the wall near the front doors, the club was rated for just over a thousand people seated, thirteen hundred and change standing. The place was packed to capacity.

"I'm Jeff Kintera, and in case anyone out there didn't know this, tonight's show is a fund-raiser for Keep the Music Going. KtMG is a great organisation, dedicated to keeping small venues for live music in Northern California open and available to fans like you. Over the last thirty years, the Bay Area's seen too many places close down: the Lion's Share, the Keystone, the Shady Grove, the Green Earth, the Sleeping Lady. In addition to what we raised tonight with ticket sales, both the Bombardiers and Blacklight have contributed matching amounts. So give us a round of applause to say thanks to everyone involved tonight, starting with Guitar Wizard *magazine, for sponsoring the show."*

Thunderous applause, and some serious foot-stomping. "Natives are getting restless," Mac laughed. "Let 'em build up to a good rowdy fever pitch, and then we're on. Nice of the people at *Guitar Wizard* to kick in on this, wasn't it?"

"Total piece of luck." Billy, playing with a pair of drumsticks, was beating a light, regular rhythm on the scarred old dressing room table. "But we owe you and JP, big-time. The new guys wouldn't have learned the material in time, even if both of them had been available to do it. Plus—no reason to be naive about it—you guys are a huge draw. I'm sorry it was such short notice, but there wasn't any sane way to say no. This is the best way I can think of to premiere the new CD."

"The money raised tonight will go a long way to make sure that the doors here stay open, with the local acts you love and some good new talent, too. So give yourself a round of applause, because you all rock!"

More applause, louder stomping. "So, you've got the new guys coming in when? Next week, was it?"

"Yep. They've got advance burns of the new CD—Tom Johansson, that's the guitarist, said his eyes nearly bugged out of his head when he heard 'Liplock,' the work JP did on it. He was almost reverent." Tony was grinning. "He said something about getting up the nerve to ask you to show him how you did it. I had to break the bad news to him that if he wanted that particular sound, he was going to need a Zemaitis with custom electronics up the wazoo. Broke his heart. And Pete says he's been working on vocal variations for 'If You Have to Go.'"

"But that's enough of me talking—time to give you what you came for. Ladies and gentlemen, put your hands together and give it up for the Bombardiers, with special guests JP Kinkaid and Malcolm Sharpe!"

"Right—we're on." The walls were shaking. I got up and headed for the dressing room door. With Mac and the Bombardiers at my heels, I pushed it open, went down the short tunnel from the band room to the front of house, and stepped out onstage to a huge surge of cheering, clapping, stamping.

The gig went brilliantly. No surprise, really—after all, we'd been playing the entire CD for what seemed like months, now. We'd also got Mac to sing "Walking the Dog," since he could do it so much better than I could. I'd done it a couple of times with our pickup band, the Fog City Geezers, and it had become a sort of private gesture, from me to Bree. I wanted to see my wife's face when she watched Mac perform it, the full sex-on-a-stick thing, hips and all. I found myself hoping she'd be up close and visible. Yeah, right, I know, fucking pathetic. I was such a damned newlywed, and at my age, no less.

The audience was loving every minute of it. I think Mac had forgotten just how different the small-venue thing was, that energy. Blacklight had been a stadium band for a good long time, all through the seventies and up to nearly the nineties. Then we'd opted for smaller indoor arenas, between ten and twenty thousand capacity, doing two nights at the smaller place instead of a series of one-night shows at the enormous outdoor venues. Now, with all of us well into middle age and me with this damned disease to consider, we'd scaled back to the indoor arenas, mostly single shows.

But a thousand-seat gig is a different deal entirely. There's no barricades, nothing between you and the crowd; the energy is there, right there, just a few feet away. It pushes you up, washes you down, feeds you while you're playing, and if you're faking it, phoning it in, they know right off and you're in deep shit. It's like the difference between live theatre and filming a movie: You'd best do it right because you need the audience with you for every word, every movement, every line, and you don't get fifty takes. It's all about the intimacy. If you're bringing it, really bringing it, every single person in that crowd goes home thinking they've made eye contact with the band, some kind of connection. And of course, in a way, that's just what they've done.

I found Bree's table right off, and caught her eye. We'd been back from Vegas only a few days when Billy rang up to say that *Guitar Wizard* magazine wanted to do a fund-raiser for the 707, to fund it for the house staff, since Paul was now out of the picture. Mac had postponed his flight back to London, and here we were. And I was damned glad to be here.

We wrapped the show, played our encores, and headed out,

back into the City with Dom up front next to Bree, and me in the back with Mac. There was something we needed to discuss, and we'd decided to leave it until after tonight's gig.

"Excellent show. So, anyway." Mac had snagged a few bottles of water from the backstage cooler and passed me one. "Should we be talking about this film thing? About what we want to do about it?"

He was keeping his voice low, too low to be heard up front. The film in question, *Playing in the Dark*, had been a sort of white elephant in the Blacklight management's front room since its eccentric fiftyish director, Cedric Parmeley, had shown a rough cut to the musicians involved, at a private screening in London in 1982.

The idea had sounded reasonable enough when he'd first run it past Blacklight. What he'd done was, he'd taken a film crew and followed three bands, big-name acts in their day, into the studio while they worked on their albums. Then he'd followed the bands out on the road, touring to promote the albums in question.

It sounds simple, doesn't it? But I remembered that screening very well. So did the rest of our band, and the noise we'd made was actually quieter than the other two bands. The film was awful.

For one thing, the rough cut was a complete nightmare. It jumped from band to band, people were shown saying half a sentence that either had no context or was actually connected to something he wasn't bothering to show, and the studio footage of two of the three bands' recording sessions made them look completely stoned. Of course, they probably were stoned, but that didn't mean they wanted that shown on a thousand screens across the States or Europe. And to top it off, the sound quality was beyond crap and into actual garbage.

It was a mess, and nothing like what we'd let him follow us

about to accomplish. The entire project reeked of directorial ego; Parmeley had refused to allow anyone to edit a single frame of his so-called masterpiece. In the middle of all that, some idiot in a dusty office decided to give Parmeley a theatrical knighthood, and of course, that made him even more stubborn and swollen-headed. Nothing like an OBE or whatever it is to give a bloke the idea that they're God's Gift to the rest of the world.

But the film was total rubbish, and of course, we'd refused our permission to release it. So had the other two bands involved. There'd been a nasty little battle, all played out in the press and in the courts, because if there was one thing you couldn't say about Cedric Parmeley, it was that he had any subtlety. It had fizzled out after a while, when it finally dawned on Parmeley—who was a conceited prat with an enormous ego and a reasonable amount of talent—that none of us were going to back down, knighthood or no knighthood.

So the rough cut of *Playing in the Dark* had sat in the basement of Parmeley's villa near Nice, while Parmeley sat and sulked over it and refused to let anyone near it. That had pretty much been the status of the whole mess for the past quarter century. Personally, I'd forgotten about it.

Just a couple of days ago, though, we'd got a call from our London management. It seemed that Parmeley, who was now in his eighties, had got a sudden urge. He'd taken the film out of the can, run it, blinked, and decided that everything we'd said was wrong about it in the first place was actually wrong.

So he'd done about a month's worth of intense editing, adding back some of the good solid recording and concert footage he'd originally taken out and replaced with bad jump cuts and crappy pointless backstage shots. He'd then sent it along to the management of everyone concerned. And according to our people, the film had been drastically improved, to the point where they felt allowing its release would be a brilliant move, especially since it would be premiering in time for inclusion at the next Cannes Film Festival.

But of course, our management weren't giving an okay until every member of the band had seen it. Blacklight's got this very sort of Three Musketeers thing, not only musically but as a financial entity as well: Everyone in the band has to approve of something before management makes it happen. I don't know whether the surviving members of the other two bands do that, and I don't give a toss. What matters is, Blacklight does. And what our management wanted to know was whether I personally needed to see it to give my approval, or if I could trust the rest of the band and just sign off on whatever they had to say.

Basically, that was a no-brainer. Of course I trusted them, as far as it went. Where it got tricky was, Parmeley had done most of the Blacklight footage from the *Pick Up the Slack* sessions, and the tour that followed the release of the album. That meant there was a very good chance that Cilla would be in too damned many of those shots. The entire thing sounded like a land mine just waiting to explode under my feet and, more to the point, under Bree's feet. And I wasn't having that.

So here was Mac, asking me what I wanted to do about it. I'd had a quiet word with him—he knew there was no way I'd discuss it within earshot of Bree. But he was leaving for London the day after tomorrow, and I needed to get it sorted out. He needed to know what to tell our corporate office back in London, once he got there.

"Why don't you ring me up when you've seen it, yeah? Let me know how bad it is. If it's not bad, I'm all for it; otherwise, no damned way. I trust your take, okay?"

Bree was talking to Dom; they seemed to be discussing shoes. Mac lifted an eyebrow, and mouthed *Cilla?* and I nodded. Smart bloke, Mac. He never used to have anything in the way of inhibitions, but these days, he seemed to be developing some-thing he might reasonably call sensitivity. Either that, or he had it all along, and I'd just started noticing. Either way, Mac had been surprising me since he'd got here, one way and another, and that included musically.

"Right. We'll do that, then." He changed the subject. "I was thinking we might hit your basement for a while tomorrow, get those songs we wrote together worked out. Four songs are a nice beginning to the next studio CD, and I want to have them in hand, play them for the band when I get home. . . ."

The songs he was talking about, we'd written them during breaks in the mixdown sessions at the Plant. Back at the house, we got the songs down and burned CDs for Luke, Stu, and Cal; listening to them, I was surprised how powerful they were, how well they flowed, especially since Mac's writing partner since university days had been Luke, pretty much exclusively. Mac's lyrics this time were still sexy. But they were also wistful, and a bit regretful, and one of them was straight-up political. He'd pulled off quite a feat, managing to keep any hint of self-indulgence out of them. They'd pulled a response from me, matching the mood and the sense of maturity. After all these years, we seemed to be growing up.

These were adult lyrics from Mac, with strong music from me behind them. If this was the core of the next studio CD, Blacklight might have a major seller in the works.

So there was that, taken care of. And then we took them to the airport, and waved them off towards London, and finally, for the first time since we'd got married, we had the car and the house to ourselves.

The next day, the postman rang our bell with a small certi-fied package, which required a signature. I was just handing him back his pen when Bree wandered into the hall.

"What's that?"

"No idea, love. It wanted signing for, though." It was a bubble bag, one of those padded things. I looked at the sender's name, and something went down my back, I wasn't sure why. "What in hell? It's from the New York police department."

I heard Bree suck in her breath and saw her hands weave together. That gesture—she'd done it so many times, so many attempts to ward off hurt over the past twenty-five years, that I suppose I'd got so used to seeing it, it had become invisible. But I was noticing it these days. I seemed to be noticing all sorts of things these days that I hadn't before.

I tore the bubble bag open and pulled out a letter, and a smaller envelope, paper this time. It was heavy; there was something in there, something that wasn't paper.

I unfolded the letter. It was a typed list: *Contents of evidence locker*, and a number. *Belongings of Mrs. Priscilla Kinkaid, cremated July 25, death by heroin overdose certified by NYC Medical Examiner.*

I felt my hands close around the paper envelope, still sealed. *25 July.* Cilla, or what was left of the underweight, drug-ravaged woman so different from the woman I'd loved enough to marry, had gone to the flames while we'd been sleeping in after Blacklight's Dallas show. It had been a good show, that one, the last calm one before the news about what had actually happened to Perry Dillon backstage at Madison Square Garden had hit the media.

I looked up at Bree. Her hands were still tight, still together. She wasn't meeting my eyes.

"Hey." I loosened my grip on the envelope and the note, and tilted her chin down towards me. "Oi! It's okay, Bree. Really. Whatever this is? It's history. It's done with."

She said nothing, but one hand got loose from the other and came up to touch her cheekbone. It was instinctive, that gesture; there was nothing there, not now.

But there had been. She'd had a spectacular bruise there, courtesy of Cilla's thrashing as Bree had tried to keep her from damaging herself, way deep and cold into heroin withdrawal.

There'd been a livid mark in the centre of that bruise, a small hard knot of discoloured flesh, where something hard had met bone. And suddenly, I knew what had to be in the envelope, and I knew Bree had already guessed.

I tore the envelope open and tipped the contents out into my palm.

The ring was bright gold, ornate, and heavily chased. I'd worn its larger-sized twin once, but those days were long gone; these days, I had a simple elegant dull gold band in its place.

I looked up and met Bree's eyes.

She'd sat there, imprisoned at Cilla's bedside by her own belief that my love for Cilla obliged Bree to take care of her. She'd sat there, at the McKinley Residential Hotel in Manhattan, for the better part of a week. It's really weird, you know? I'd never had much in the way of imagination, all that seems to go into music for me, but maybe I was developing some of the same thing I'd seen Mac developing.

Because I could suddenly picture it, Bree sitting there, hour after endless bloody hour, staring at Cilla's wedding ring, remembering that the first couple of times she'd seen me, I'd worn one just like it. She'd have sat there, hating the damned ring, hating Cilla, probably hating me along with the rest. And, Bree being Bree, she'd have been hating herself, as well. Joan of Arc, always inches from the flames. It was ridiculous.

I'd be willing to bet that bruise had come from a glancing blow off Cilla's wedding ring. And they'd sent the ring to me because there'd been no one else to send it to.

I found myself hoping, wishing really hard and with everything I could put behind it, that this would be the last damage Cilla could inflict on Bree. Somehow, though, I didn't believe it.

It might be history, past tense, but there was a lot of it. There were still land mines lying about, just under the surface, waiting to be stepped on.

For right now, though, I was holding this one, with some control over it. And wonder of wonders, for once, I knew how to defuse the damned thing.

"Right." I held it out to Bree. "What do you think we should do with this? Any ideas, love? Because I haven't got a clue. And you know, this ring? It really is just a piece of jewellery. We can throw it in the rubbish bin if you'd like. Don't look so harrowed."

She held my eye, steady and unblinking, for a few seconds. I saw her face relax a bit.

"She wouldn't like it to be here, that's for sure." Her voice was under control, no shakes. I hoped I was reading her properly; I hoped I'd done the right thing, offering her the choice, giving her the power to deal with it for both of us. I'd meant what I'd said—whatever she decided we ought to do about the damned ring, I'd do. "She hated San Francisco."

She stopped. Something came into her face, something I couldn't quite put a name to. I had an instinct that I ought to just shut up and let her process, and I was right; she reached out and took the ring from me.

"I think we should take it to London with us, when we go. I think it ought to be buried in London. Because she wasn't—her ashes are back in New York. So this—this would be something, some way to get her back to where she belonged." Her voice was quiet. "To get her home. It's where she ought to be, John. I think—I think it would have mattered to her."

I nodded. "You're right, it would. That's a brilliant idea, love. Have you got Bruno's number around anywhere?"

"Programmed into my phone—it's in the kitchen." She must have thought I was changing the subject. "Why?"

I smiled at her, not saying anything, and headed for the kitchen, Bree following slowly. I scrolled down through her directory until I found Bruno's number.

"Hello? Bruno? Yeah, this is JP Kinkaid—right, no, nothing's wrong at all, Little Queenie's just as glorious as ever. Nothing to do with guitars, not this time. I want to commission you to make me something else—no, not an instrument. I need a box, a really beautiful box, that can hold a piece of jewellery inside it. Thing is, I want to be able to seal it so that it can't be opened, at least not easily or visibly, and it's going to need some sort of finish on it, to make it last a good long time, even if it's buried, maybe in a garden somewhere. . . ."

Bree had left the room. For a minute, I thought she'd gone weepy or sentimental; it took me a moment to consciously realise that, while I was on her phone, mine had been ringing, and she'd gone to get it. She came back in, holding her hand over the mouthpiece.

"Right, good, I'll ring you up with the specs. It might be a bit of a rush job—we'll want to take it to London with us, and we were thinking of going just after Thanksgiving. Right. Ta, Bruno. Cheers, mate."

I rang off and reached for my own phone. Bree still had her hand over the front. I started to say something cheerful, but I took another look at her face, and any desire to be amusing withered and died.

"Bree? What?"

"It's your neurologist," she told me. "She says—she says she has your MRI results in."

EPILOGUE

I'm not sure what Bree was thinking about, sitting in Dr. Dahlberg's office with her hand hanging on to mine for dear life. Me, I was remembering Jack Featherstone.

There are times I wish doctors would just fucking say what they want to say, you know? Instead of all the assing about, dancing and dodging and being mysterious, and tactfully avoiding the subject they claim to want to talk to you about in the first place. Maybe it's some kind of power game for them, all that *I know a secret* rubbish. What's really infuriating is that, half the time, they haven't actually got anything to say. Of course, when they do, it's usually serious stuff, stuff I really don't want to hear. So I'm sort of careful about what I wish for, on the off chance I get it.

When I took the phone from Bree, my neurologist—who makes a habit of being mysterious on the phone when she's got nothing to be mysterious about, and laconic when she's about to drop a bomb on her patients—was doing just what she always did. I wasn't really worried. Besides, it sounded pretty casual.

"John Kinkaid here."

"Hello, John—it's Dr. Dahlberg. We got the results of your latest MRI in a few weeks ago. I was surprised you hadn't called in to check the results."

"Yeah, well, it's been nuts. Besides, I thought that if there was anything to tell me, you'd ring me. You usually do."

"Well, I'm ringing you up now. Are things less busy for you right now? When would you like to come in?"

So a week later, there we were, sitting in her office. She was in surgery that morning, and her receptionist told us she'd be a few minutes late, and did we want to wait in the inner sanctum?

On my own, I'd probably have said no. To be honest, her office gives me the creeps, with its charts of the human brain and all the things that can possibly go wrong with the damned thing, and a hideous plastic brain that looks like a bad prop out of a horror flick. But I wasn't on my own, and Bree was nervous. Plus, there were a few other patients in the waiting room, and a couple of them were giving us looks, as if they thought I might be someone they ought to recognise. So I said, yeah, that would be good, and here we were.

Dahlberg came in, not really late at all, just a few minutes. By doctors' standards, that's nothing. She had the big cardboard portfolio under one arm, the same one I've seen every year from the MRI people. It has the scans in it.

We exchanged the usual pleasantries, and she got down to business.

"Well." She was pulling the four oversized films out, and sorting them. "I've had a good look at these, and I wanted to ask you about something. Have you noticed any difference in the

269

relapses or exacerbations over the last few months? Any changes in the frequency, or severity?"

I glanced over at Bree; she had her teeth sunk into her lower lip. Oh, bloody hell—I'd never got round to telling her about the nightmare exacerbation that had hit me in Central Park, the morning after Perry Dillon's murder. This wasn't exactly a good time or place to mention it, either; it wasn't what you'd call an *oh, by the way* subject. I'd messed up by not telling her about it, and right royally, too. I was going to have to dish, later on, and she was going to flip her shit. "Well—yeah. I had a huge flare-up in Boston, just before I had my little heart attack. But I always do get jumps like that when I'm touring. Stress seems to bring them on, and so do time zone changes. Why?"

"I was curious, because there are some changes from your last MRI. Have a look at this, will you?"

She slipped two of the films up into the lightboards, side by side. "This one, on the left—this was last year's. There were six verifiable visual lesions—the demyelinated areas are here."

Her fingertip snaked out, touching each one. Bree was barely breathing.

"Right." I sounded nice and calm; strange how Bree at the edge of panic always managed to turn me into a damned yogi, a Zen master or something. "And this is the most recent one? So what's the bad news?"

"It's not bad news, strictly speaking. It's not good news, either. It's an oddity. You seem to have lost one of the lesions entirely—the big irregular one, the one that worried me last year, on the lower edge of the parietal lobe. But here?" She reached out again, touching a spot on the more recent MRI. "This one—it wasn't here last year. So you've lost one, which is good, but replaced it with another one. What's worrying me is the location of this new one. It's on the corpus callosum."

"What—?" Bree cleared her throat. Dahlberg must have

forgot that Bree is a doctor's daughter, because she thought she knew what Bree was trying to ask.

"That's the brain section that lets the two hemispheres of the brain communicate with each other. It's particularly vulnerable to demyelinisation. And this is also the first lesion John's had there, after what, nine years. So I wondered if he was experiencing any notable or consistent differences. That could be an indicator."

I wondered as well. I remembered the ataxia in New York, the complete shutdown of the jaw the night we'd found Rosario dead on the floor of the 707 warehouse, the myokymia that had hit as I stood in a posh New York hotel, demanding the truth from Bree, getting it, walking out, leaving her there. And my mind went back to Jack, unable to talk, his hands permanent curls, everything gone soft, caught, gone. . . .

"It did get pretty noisy, the MS did, on that last tour." I managed a good smile for Bree, who wasn't smiling back. "And I had a bad relapse a few weeks ago, but that was a quickie, gone the next morning, and I'm pretty sure it was brought on by stress—we'd just found a dead body, a murdered friend. I've actually been fine for the past couple of weeks. The hands have been great, perfectly functional, and the usual tingles in the feet have been way down, even first thing in the morning, and that's usually the worst time of day for me. The past couple of weeks, I've felt better than I have in a couple of years."

"That's good to know. I do want to keep an eye on this for a while—and did you say you'd had a heart attack? Care to tell me why no one saw fit to tell me about that?"

I filled her in on that and got back a terse little rant about the damned medical privacy regulations that kept doctors from talking to each other, and endangered their patients, and the rest of it. I finally managed to steer her back to the topic at hand.

"Okay. Look. Let's get down to it. You're worried about this new lesion, and yeah, I agree, it wants watching. I need to have a talk with my cardiologist as well." And damn, he was going to be furious with me; I'd had a heart attack two months ago, and so much had been going on, I'd never bothered to ring him up and tell him. "Can you tell me what the bottom line is? What am I supposed to be doing about this? Do we need to change my meds? Change dosages?"

"No, not yet. But I want you to go in for another MRI—what's the date on this one?" She glanced at the portfolio. "Let's get you in there mid-December. Full court, extra views, gadolinium. I want to see if anything's spread. Nothing to really worry about just yet—as you say, you've had a stressful few months—but I want to keep an eye on it for the next little while, myself."

"But we were heading off to Europe for a couple of months, right after Thanksgiving!" Damn the woman and her casual commands. "It's our honeymoon! Besides, I just had one of the damned things. Can't the MRI wait?"

"No." Bree and Dahlberg had spoken together. Brilliant, I thought bitterly. Now they were ganging up on me.

Bree leaned over suddenly and rubbed her cheek against mine. "It's okay. Europe's not going anywhere, is it?"

"Nicer in the spring, anyway. Try Florence, and Paris. And oh, by the way? Congratulations on the wedding." Dahlberg turned the overheads on. "I'll get the MRI scheduled, and you give your cardiologist a call. And for heaven's sake, John, call me if you start relapsing. We'll take another look at your meds."

"I will." I got up and stretched. Both feet felt as if they'd never had a problem. "Florence, and Paris? Good call, that. Bree's never been out of the States. We're definitely going to London, there's business that needs taking care of, but Paris and Italy—yeah. Bree needs to see Europe."

"Then you really should take good care of yourself, so that you're well enough to take her, shouldn't you? Now that you've got a wife to stay around for?"

She said it casually, her usual *nothing gets to me* thing, but it hit me right between the eyes.

She was dead right.

I'd been somehow separating how I dealt with the disease from how Bree dealt with it. The only time I'd let it connect in my head was when her panic had dragged me into a kind of calm.

But day in and day out, for eight years, I'd done to Bree exactly what I'd busted her for doing to me: I'd built up a nice protective wall and never stopped to think that maybe I was keeping her out, as well.

Multiple sclerosis is a damned tricky thing. It's completely unpredictable. It could go silent for years. It could ebb and flow. It could suddenly explode, the way it did with Jack, shifting phases and going progressive, becoming something that couldn't be stopped.

I didn't have the first clue what it was likely to do. Neither did anyone else. What I did have, now, was a reason to watch what it did.

And that being the case, there wasn't a single reason to sit and brood over it. Besides, I was damned if I wanted to brood. What I *did* want to do was walk home—it was a nice sunny day, no fog anywhere—and take Bree upstairs. I wanted to get her out of her clothes, take her places, watch her ripple, watch her eyes go distant and come back again, until she'd gone salty and sweet and sweaty. And after that, I was going to suggest sending out for takeaway, and let her try to talk me out of it. By the time we shut down for the night, the cats would be curled up in their usual spots, and the fog would come rolling into the City, under the Golden Gate Bridge.

I reached out and got hold of Bree's hand, pulling her to her feet.

"Yeah," I told my neurologist as we walked out into the waiting room, heading for the sun, and for home. "You're dead right. I've got a wife to stay around for now."